THE RANGER AND THE HURRICANE

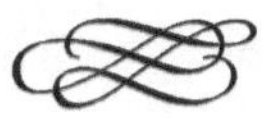

VANESSA GRAY BARTAL

DRY CREEK PRESS

PROLOGUE

Rodrigo Gomez was in the zone. He had been driving the same route for five years now. He could do it in his sleep, and some days he almost did. Pick up the cargo from Corpus Christi, haul it ten hours to El Paso, eat, sleep, repeat. Day after day after day, it had been his life so often it could only be distinguished by which audiobooks and podcasts he chose to listen to. When the day was new and he was fresh and energetic, he preferred westerns, something to make him appreciate the iconic surroundings of the vast Texas flatlands. When he felt cynical or world weary, he played spy thrillers or true crime. And when he was exhausted, he blasted heavy metal. Right now Metallica blared through his speakers, bearing witness to the heaviness of his lids. Three more hours. He could make it three more hours.

As far as trucking went, it was a pretty cozy setup. Staying solely in Texas meant the picky federal rules didn't apply. But, being Texas, it was large enough to afford him ten solid hours of driving a day. And really, ten hours was nothing. Not to a seasoned teamster like Rodrigo.

But lately he had begun to wonder if he was too seasoned. Sometimes, like now, his mind began to wander, his eyes began to droop.

With effort, he turned up Metallica and dragged his mind back to the road. *Focus, moron.* At times like these, all he had to do was picture the possible headline to wake himself up. *Trucker Falls Asleep At Wheel, Takes Out Family of Five in Minivan.* Not that there was a minivan nearby. Not that there was anyone nearby. The beauty, and curse, of Texas was that parts of it were virtually deserted. He was in one of those parts now, a two-lane highway so flat it seemed one dimensional, like a cartoon rendering of a road.

Until suddenly it wasn't deserted. A car emerged in his blind spot and darted in front of him, so fast it was like seeing one of the ubiquitous jackrabbits that lined the roadway.

"Ease up, buddy, it's all yours," Rodrigo muttered. The car, like so many fast little sports cars that dotted the roadway, seemed to have something to prove. Little car syndrome, as Rodrigo laughingly labeled it. They were the Chihuahuas of the highway, eager to take on the big dogs and prove their toughness by being faster and more aggressive. Rodrigo's response was to let them. To him, they were as a fly to a cow—annoying but nothing to get worked up over. He was the biggest and baddest thing on the roadway, hands down, no contest. With one tap of his foot, he could flatten the little car. He knew it so deep in his bones he felt no need to prove it. When other drivers were aggressive or threw up a challenge, he backed off and conceded. He might occasionally say things under his breath his Mama would be ashamed to hear, but he never retaliated, never played their game, never engaged in the driving version of chicken. It wasn't worth it, not worth the loss of his job or the loss of someone else's life. Because that was what would happen; Rodrigo wouldn't be the one who would be injured. The person sitting on eighteen wheels was rarely ever the one who paid with his life.

The little car didn't speed up, though. Once it had achieved first place in front of Rodrigo, it tapped its brakes, causing Rodrigo to do the same, albeit not without a muttered curse. What game was this guy playing? Did he not realize how long it would take the truck to come to a complete stop? It amazed him how many people discounted the basic laws of physics while driving. An object in motion stayed in motion, especially an object as large as Rodrigo's semi. Though it might have been a woman in the driver's seat. From this distance, Rodrigo couldn't tell. He hadn't glimpsed the person, merely the car's taillights as it hovered an impossibly short distance ahead.

Rodrigo sped up as if to pass. The car sped up and moved to the center of the two lanes before slowing down again. *What game are you playing?* Did the car's driver have a death wish? Hate truckers? Not realize what it was doing? What?

Before Rodrigo could decide, the little car sped up and zoomed out of sight. *Weird,* Rodrigo thought, and then forgot the little car completely in his quest to stay awake. *At least you had twenty minutes of alertness while you tried to figure out what it was up to.*

Wearily, he finally arrived at his destination. He wanted a steak, a shave, and a nap, in that order.

"Problems?" Sheila, the distribution company's team leader, always greeted him the same way.

"You have a suspicious mind," Rodrigo said, the same rejoinder as always. It was their little routine. If she'd been a bit cuter, he might have thought she was flirting with him. As it was, she was ten years his senior and looked like more of a trucker than he did.

"That's why they pay me the big bucks," Sheila said, cackling at her own joke before turning away to spit a stream of tobacco.

"You kiss your husband with that mouth?"' Rodrigo asked, making no effort to hide his grimace.

"Not since he ran off with my cousin ten years ago," Sheila said, spitting again. She tapped the back door of the truck, Rodrigo's signal to open it up for her inspection. She made the inspection at every arrival, signing off on it before it could be unloaded. With so much riding on each shipment, the added layer of security was a matter of course. And of course they couldn't *require* Rodrigo not to make any stops, but it was the unspoken rule, one he gladly followed. The sooner he dropped his load, the sooner he could reclaim his time. His bladder didn't thank him for ten hours without a break, but his wallet did.

He opened the door and stepped back, checking his phone as Sheila leaned forward to make her inspection.

"This some kind of joke?" Her sandpaper voice was suddenly taut. Rodrigo's head rose lazily, glancing behind him. Was she talking to one of her coworkers? But, no, she was talking to him.

"What?" he asked, focusing on her instead of his truck.

She motioned there, angry. "Think you forgot something, dummy."

"What are you talking about?" he asked, genuinely confused.

"Where's the load?" she demanded.

Rodrigo poked his head into the trailer. He forgot his bladder, his exhaustion, his hunger. He forgot everything in light of the sight that greeted him—a trailer so empty it glistened. "What…" he stammered.

"What happened?" Sheila demanded. She forced concern into a tone that would otherwise be panicked or angry. "Trailer swap? Did you forget to load up? It happens, the nights get long and…" she trailed off, unable to be convincing with the care and concern any longer. "What happened?"

Rodrigo swallowed, but it did nothing to relieve the parched feeling in his throat. "I saw them load it."

"Where'd you stop?" Sheila demanded.

"Nowhere! I swear I didn't stop for anything. I never do, you know that."

"Then how do you explain this…" she waved a hand at the blank trailer, using her other one to grip the door and hold herself aloft. Five hundred thousand dollars in cargo. Gone without a trace.

"I can't. I saw them load it. I *saw* it. I came straight here. Nothing unusual happened. Noth…" He broke off, remembering the little car that cut him off. But surely that couldn't have anything to do with this. He had been doing eighty at the time. Until the car cut him off and slowed his pace to sixty. Rodrigo thought they had been challenging him, but what if they'd done something worse?

"Call the Rangers," Rodrigo said, his voice sounding reedy and thin and full of shock. "I think I've been robbed."

CHAPTER 1

Ranger Sully Langford did one final patrol of the town before calling it a night. He didn't have to; he wasn't on duty. In fact he had spent the better part of the evening at a wedding, but it was his habit to do one final check before ending his day. He was a few months shy of thirty, and he could feel himself settling into habits and routines that would soon become entrenched. Someday he would be one of those old codgers who had a regular table at the diner, along with a standard meal order. Who was he kidding? He was already that guy.

His mother had been not so subtly hinting that it was time to settle down and get married. Sully didn't disagree, and tonight's wedding between two of his friends, Calhoun Ridge and Bailey Dunbar, had done nothing to lessen his desire. The problem was that he could never find a woman who stuck. Every time he thought he might have found the one, his feelings for her soon faded into the realm of friendship. He had a lot of female friends now. Some men he knew were afraid of commitment. Not so Sully. He was ready and willing to spend his life with one person. But he also wanted a bit of enchantment, perhaps some kind of sign from heaven telling him he'd found the one. So far that hadn't happened, and his prospects were looking dim. He would soon reach the point where he had to decide if he was willing to settle for some nice, ordinary girl or continue to hold out for some as yet unknown spark of wonder.

He didn't expect to see much going on in town. It was a sleepy burg, far away from the big city. Occasionally they had some drunken fighting, a few domestics, and always drugs to contend with. But not much in the way of hard, violent crime, and that was how Sully liked it. Even though it was probably thanks more to the strong morality of people in the town, Sully liked to believe it was because of him, because he was doing such a stellar job no one wanted to commit crime in his territory, and certainly not his tiny hometown.

He was about to call it a night when he saw someone sitting in the gazebo. No one actually used the gazebo, save for the occasional teenage couple looking for a quiet spot to push the limits of the town's aforementioned morality. By all rights, more than a few babies should be named "Gazebo" in honor of their conception. To make sure it wasn't one of their local addicts shooting up, Sully parked his car and headed to check.

What he found instead was a girl, one he recognized as one of Bailey's younger sisters. Which one, he had no idea. She had two, and somehow he had gone the whole evening without meeting either one. He felt a bit bad about that. It hadn't been a large wedding, and his avoidance of them had been halfway intentional. It was just that, as a Texas Ranger, he was sometimes mythical in women's minds, and they tended to react to him a certain way. He hadn't wanted to spend the night fighting off advances, especially not those of his friend's younger siblings. One of them had a serious boyfriend. He hoped it was the one now sitting before him.

"Evening," he said, tipping his hat to her.

"Evening," she replied, smiling at him in an amused sort of way, two dimples so deep he could see them even in the dim moonlight. She was a cute kid, adorable really, but a kid nonetheless. She looked like the quintessential little sister—fun, ornery, and loveable. He relaxed slightly and sat on the step beside her. She was too young for him, much, much too young, and therefore safe.

"Everything okay?" he asked.

"Out for an evening stroll," she said.

"It's kind of late," he replied.

"I'm on New York time," she informed him.

He checked his watch. "It's two in the morning in New York."

"And just getting started," she said. She leaned back on her hands, staring out at the muggy, starless night. "Is it ever not hot here?"

"We have about two weeks in winter where it settles down to about sixty degrees or so."

"Brr," she said, feigning a chill.

"Hypothermia's a real danger for our older folk," he added, and she laughed. She had a nice laugh, infectious and sparkling. "Which sister are you?"

"What do you mean?" she asked.

"Are you the anthropologist or the baker?" Sully asked.

She huffed a little sigh of displeasure. "Leave it to Bailey to describe us that way."

"Not accurate?" Sully surmised.

"Not comprehensive. I'm passionate about dance and music and art. I live and work in one of the largest most vital cities in the world. I'm a friend, a daughter, a student of life."

He waited her out, staring blankly through her impassioned speech.

She tilted toward him, leaning on one arm. "I'm the baker. And who might you be?"

"I'm a Texas Ranger," he replied, also tilting toward her. He was flirting with her, but what was the harm? She was a pretty kid.

"You play baseball?" she asked, sounding impressed.

At first he thought she was joking, and then he realized she wasn't. "No, I'm a Ranger."

"Like a park ranger?" she clarified. "Which park?"

He let out a breath. "Are you joking?"

She shook her head. "I feel I've somehow offended you, but I'm not sure how."

"Texas Rangers are…we're iconic."

She sputtered a little laugh and quickly pressed her hand over her mouth. "I'm sorry. It's just that I've never heard a man describe himself as iconic before." Another little giggle escaped and she fought hard to push it back in.

"Your sister knew what a Ranger was without being told," he said.

"Of course she did. My sisters know everything. Between them they have all the combined knowledge of the entire world. They're also skinny with freakishly high metabolism. I mean, not Bailey. She probably has normal metabolism but has trained it to do her bidding by sheer force of will. But Jane, that girl can eat and eat and never seems to gain weight. In fact I'm beginning to think every time she eats, I'm the one who somehow gains the weight." She drew her knees to her chest and wrapped her arms around them.

"Or, and I'm just spitballing here, it could have something to do with the fact that you're a baker."

She turned and grinned at him. "Well, there is that. You have to know those people who say being skinny tastes better than anything have never tried a warm brownie with ice cream and hot fudge."

"Stop it, you're making me hungry."

"I make a mean brownie, Mr. Park Ranger," she replied.

"I'm not a…never mind," he said, sighing. "You should probably get wherever you're going."

She giggled.

"What now?" he asked.

"You said 'git.'"

"I did not."

"You most assuredly did. You said I should probably 'git' wherever I'm goin'."

"And so you should. We don't have a lot of crime here, but it's best not to tempt fate," he said.

"You're awfully concerned with crime, for a park ranger," she noted.

"Child, for the last time, I am not a park ranger."

"Oh, that's right. You're *iconic*," she said the last word with forced breathlessness, and he laughed.

"I get the feeling you could drive a sober man to drink," he said.

"I drive men to do lots of things, namely run away screaming," she said, resting her chin on her knees.

"I highly doubt that."

"No, it's true. I'm what's known in park ranger vernacular as a natural disaster," she said, sighing.

"Why would you say such a thing?" he asked.

"How well do you know Bailey?" she asked.

"Well," he replied.

She tilted her head at him. "Are you in love with her?"

His face scrunched. "Ew, no. She's married to my good friend. And *she's* my good friend. She's like a sister to me."

"Easy there, just asking. Coincidentally she's like a sister to me, too, but men tend to fall for Bailey, and fall hard. Not that she's ever paid them any notice, save for one Calhoun Ridge. Anyway, if you know Bailey, then you'll understand what I mean when I say I'm her opposite in every possible way. My life is a train wreck of poor decision making and impulsive behavior."

"How old are you?" he asked.

"Twenty four."

She was older than he thought. He would have guessed eighteen. Apparently he was now getting to that age where everyone younger looked pubescent. "Darlin', when I was twenty four, I was the same. Absolutely no one has their life together when they're twenty four."

"Both my sisters did. Bailey was already an officer in the marines. Jane already had her doctorate and got a job at the Smithsonian."

"You can't compare yourself to your sisters," he noted.

"Why not? Everyone else does. And who else am I supposed to compare myself to? There are a lot of junkies in New York, and I'm doing better than they are, but I don't think that counts."

"You should only compare yourself to yourself. You should be the yardstick against which you judge your growth as a person," he said.

"Either way, I'm still failing," she said, sighing. They sat in silence for a minute. "How old are you, Yoda?"

"Twenty nine."

"And how is your life progressing?" she asked with a shocking amount of sincerity. She tipped her face toward him, actually awaiting an answer.

"Can't complain," he said.

"Sure you can, I'll teach you," she said.

He laughed and shook his head. "I have the dream job I always wanted."

"You always wanted to be a park ranger? You must really love nature."

"I'm not a…never mind." He sighed, exasperated.

"What about a girl?" she asked.

"What about one?" he countered.

"Do you have one?" she asked.

"No, ma'am, I do not," he said.

She smiled. "How does a boy who looks like you, who talks like you, who dances like you, arrive at the ripe age of twenty nine still unattached?"

"I guess I haven't found what I'm looking for," he said.

"And what are you looking for?" she asked.

He faced her, took in her pretty smile and sparkling, amused eyes. "Magic."

"Uh-oh," she said, the smile slipping.

"Uh-oh what?" he asked.

"My heart's doing the thing," she said.

He sat up, slightly alarmed. "What thing?" Did she have a heart problem? If so, he had an AED in his truck.

"The thing where it stops listening to reason and begins running instead on impulse," she said.

He blinked at her, processing. So she wasn't dying then. "I'm not sure I understand."

"I think, park ranger, you are about to become another bad decision," she warned.

"What…" he began but stopped talking when she leaned forward and pressed her lips to his, kissing him. Sully was so shocked he sat stock still and let it happen, not responding, not doing anything but staring at her with wide open eyes as she kissed him.

She broke off the kiss and leaned back. "Sorry. But at least I got it out of my system. Maybe I should take your advice and..."

Now it was her turn to stop talking because he reached for her and kissed her. Unlike him, she responded, easing her fingers into his hair as his slid onto her waist and cinched her against him. The kiss took off, skyrocketing to unearthly levels before Sully broke away, practically gasping for air and sanity.

"Sorry," he wheezed. "I don't...I don't usually do..." he blew out a breath.

They sat in heavy silence a moment, each of them trying to reorient their brains and grasp for some shred of self-control. "I should go," she said. "But can I say one thing first?"

He gave her a questioning glance.

"I'm a stranger, and after this night we will likely never see each other again."

Sully had no idea why that was the catalyst that made him reach for her again, to turn off his brain completely, but it was. And when she walked away and finally went inside for the night, he realized he still didn't know her name.

CHAPTER 2

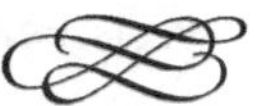

Three weeks later, Sully started to let go of the guilt. Bailey had been on her honeymoon for eight of those days, allowing his conscience a reprieve. When he faced her again, he had to fight the urge to confess as if she were a priest. It would do nothing to make the situation better, might complicate the relationship between the two sisters, and would likely end in his death. If Bailey found out what Sully had done with her baby sister, she would kill him, literally end his life. He would be her twelfth kill, and she would likely not feel a whit of remorse about it, and neither should she. How could he have had such a horrible lapse in judgment? He was monogamous and disciplined, the kind of man who took relationships seriously. And yet he'd had a one-night stand, his first ever, with his close friend's little sister. Worse, he still didn't know her name. And there was no good way to ask. If he brought it up now, Bailey would be suspicious.

His only hope was that the mystery sister would let it go and move on, as he was trying hard to do. If she went crazy and started stalking him, he was sunk. Three weeks in, he began to relax. He hadn't glimpsed her again before she left town, and he hadn't heard from her. Of course she didn't have his number, but if she really wanted it, she could find it.

Just as he began to let down his guard and move on, he received a text from an unknown number. He was about to delete it when the name caught his attention.

This is Poppy Dunbar, Bailey's sister. From the gazebo. I was going to call, but I figured you wouldn't answer an unknown number.

His heart sank. She wasn't going to let it go. She was reaching out, and propriety forced him to respond, much as he wanted to let it go and forget everything, mostly his glaring lapse in judgment and self-control.

Hi, how have you been? He hit send and waited anxiously. Maybe she was feeling as guilty as he was. Maybe they could hash it out and both move on. The realty was he had no idea because he didn't know her at all, though now he knew her name. Poppy. It fit somehow, and he smiled slightly at the memory of her smile, pushing away all the other memories of her that tried to intrude. The phone buzzed, and he held it aloft, reading.

I'm pregnant.

He stared at the words, unable to comprehend them. With shaking fingers, he managed to type a single word:

What?

Don't make me retype it. You seem like the kind of guy who would like to know, so this is me, letting you know. Otherwise I'm fine. No involvement from you necessary, unless you'd prefer it that way. Cheers.

Cheers? *Cheers??* Who ends a text that way? Who texts that sort of information in the first place? He called her, and it went to voicemail, her sparkling voice inviting him to skip the message and "text like normal people instead." He didn't leave a message, but neither did he text a reply. He couldn't possibly. What could he say to that? There was nothing, no reply he'd be able to conjure that would match what she wrote.

He contemplated going to Cal and Bailey, laying it on the line, and asking for advice. After all, they knew her. Maybe they would have some insight into her character, would give him some understanding of what type of person she was. Was she actually a serial one-nighter? Did she routinely trick and trap men into fatherhood? Then he imagined asking Bailey those questions about her little sister and realized how it would sound. What it came down to, no matter what, was that he was a man and he had gotten a woman pregnant. His mother had given him several lectures on the subject throughout his teenage years, but back then there'd been no need. And now, at the ripe age of nearly thirty, he had turned into a monumental screwup. And it was time to take charge and fix it.

He picked up his phone again and made a call to his boss, cashing in a few days of unused personal time. Next he booked a flight. After that he did call Cal because he had no idea how to find Poppy.

"Hey, Sul, what's up?" Cal asked, and Sully's chest knifed with renewed guilt.

Not much, got your sister-in-law pregnant. What's new with you? "I'm heading to New York for a few days of vacation. I remember Bailey said her sister works there in a restaurant, and I thought it would be fun to try it." He held his breath. Did that sound like a reasonable explanation, or would Cal be able to hear the anxiety in his tone?

"It's a fancy place," Cal said.

"I've been known to shower and put on a tie," Sully replied dryly.

Cal laughed. "I believe it. It's called *Burton's*. If you go, give us a report and say hello to Poppy for us."

"Will do," Sully promised.

"Word of warning, that gal is ornery. Hold on to your hat," Cal said.

"Will do," Sully repeated. "Thanks." He disconnected before the call could devolve or spiral out of control. And then sat still in his truck, his mind playing six words on repeat. *I'm going to be a dad.* Regardless of the shock, the shame, the guilt, it wasn't an unhappy thought.

P*oppy's* stomach rolled and tossed, the smell of butter almost her undoing. The nausea had started two days ago, adding to the litany of symptoms now assaulting her. She knew immediately she was pregnant. Almost as soon as she left Texas, the exhaustion hit like a sledgehammer. A few days later she developed a metallic taste in her mouth, as if she'd been sucking on pennies. A few days after that, she took a test. It was positive. Yesterday she went to the free clinic for another test and an ultrasound. Both things confirmed what she already knew—she was growing a human.

The first difficult step was over. She told the baby daddy, whose name she now knew was Sully. She could only imagine what he must think of her, especially based on her actions and the things she'd said. She'd been having a bad night after her sister's wedding, a few moments of self-pity in an otherwise good day. And he'd gotten the blast end of it, the blast end of her pathetically tossing herself at him and laying out for him her absolute ineptness as a human being. The thing was, she wasn't *that* inept. True, she was occasionally impulsive and made some bad decisions, including some poor dating choices. But she had never tumbled into bed with a stranger before. Ever. Worse, there hadn't even been a bed. There had been a gazebo, a very public gazebo that likely violated several Texas laws. As a park ranger, Sully should probably have known that. Not that he seemed at all in control of himself, either.

Both of them had messed up, monumentally. And now she was left with the lasting effect of yet another poor choice. All those warnings she read in the subway really were true—it only took a moment to live with a lifetime of regret. Not that a baby could ever be a regret. She would love it the best she knew how, as would everyone in her family when she eventually told them. But at some point she would have to make a decision about her career and her future, and she felt sick about that. The stats on single mothers weren't good. In fact, they were abysmal. Was she prepared to spend the next two decades of her life in poverty or, worse, on welfare? She shuddered, imagining all the times she would now have to swallow her pride for the sake of her child.

And she could forget having a social or dating life after this. It was hard enough to find nice guys to date when she wasn't knocked up or toting a kid. From now on she would have to put it out of her head completely. She was doomed to roam the earth alone, as penance for her night of passion. It was likely the guy in question, Sully, would go on to fall in love, get married, and have an intact family of his own while she, Poppy, remained a pariah for eternity. As a culture, they hadn't come all that far from *The Scarlet Letter.* The weight of everything was on the woman—of pregnancy, of birth, of childrearing. She would be the one to give up her career, not him. She would be the one to bear the weight of judgment, not him. It was likely no one would ever even know about his part in things. She would certainly never tell. Bailey would kill her and then probably kill him.

Still, she wasn't remotely tempted to "get rid of it," as some euphemistically termed it. She had done the crime, so to speak. Now it was up to her to do the time. The upside was that Poppy loved babies. Soon she would have one of her own, even if she had no earthly idea how she would take care of it.

There was always adoption, but Poppy wasn't sure she had the internal fortitude and selflessness necessary for such an act. On the plus side, she had a lot of time to think about it. Nine months, in fact. Surely in that time her brain could find some kind of resolution and make a plan, even though planning had never been her strong suit before.

"Poppy."

An unknown voice said her name. She turned with a smile that quickly faded. The park ranger stood in the tiny basement kitchen of her work, filling the space with his broad shoulders and white cowboy hat. Poppy stumbled back a step, bumping the counter.

"You," she breathed, momentarily forgetting his name.

"Sully," he reminded her.

"I know," she said, though she was thankful for the reminder. "What are you doing here?"

"We need to talk."

"I'm working."

"We *need* to talk," he reiterated.

"I'm *working.*"

"Give me a time, or so help me I'll carry you out of here," he said.

"I get off at ten." She flicked her fingers at him, shooing him away.

He stared around the tiny kitchen, undaunted. "I thought this would be bigger."

"It's New York. Nothing is big," she said.

"Hmm," he said and slowly ambled away.

With effort, Poppy pulled her mind back to her work. Baking was the only thing that had ever held her interest for more than a flicker, the only thing she could lose herself in entirely. She did it now, and never had she been more thankful for the ability.

Promptly at ten, Sully waited outside the door. She exited with her coworkers, laughing. Every one of them stopped short, staring at the tall cowboy by the door. It was a testament to how arresting he was that hardened New Yorkers did a double take.

"See you, guys. This one's here for me," Poppy said, pausing beside Sully while the rest of her group trudged away, a few of them darting questioning glances in her direction.

"Are you hungry?" he asked.

"Very much no," she said, grimacing as she pressed a hand to her abdomen.

"It doesn't start that soon, does it? The sickness?" he asked.

"I could throw up on your shoes, if you like. To prove it does."

He shook his head, but he still looked troubled. Poppy sighed. "It's yours, okay? Believe me, there is absolutely, positively, Immaculate Conception level of no doubt. I'd be happy to have a DNA test, after it's born, if you'd like."

"I didn't doubt it was mine. I felt bad that you're already sick," he assured her, but he did feel better. Maybe there had been a tiny spot of unacknowledged doubt in his mind. After all, he knew less than nothing about her.

"Where would you like to go?" he asked.

"Do you have a hotel room?" she asked.

Taken aback, he was unable to hide his shocked reaction. She rolled her eyes. "I was not inviting myself over for a retake. But my apartment isn't exactly conducive to conversation. I thought the lobby of your hotel might be better."

He shrugged. "I figured I would find a place after we spoke." In truth, he was so panicked he hadn't given much thought to anything beyond arriving and tracking her down. He didn't even have his luggage. He had left it in a locker at the airport, not realizing how far the airport was from the city.

"Oh, honey, this is New York. You will positively not find a hotel at this time of night. Come on, we'll have to make the best of it at my place." She took a few steps away, and he easily caught up with her.

"We could go somewhere. For coffee or something," he suggested.

"No offense, but I'm exhausted and I've been on my feet the last ten hours. I want to go home and lie down."

"Do you always walk?" he asked.

"Yes."

"Why? Why not take a taxi?"

She stopped short. "Have you ever been to New York before?"

He shook his head.

"It would cost about fifty dollars a day to take a taxi. Walking is king here, and it's not so far."

"But it's night. That's when all the crazies come out," he said, looking around to make sure there were none in sight.

"It's New York. The crazies are always out," she rebutted. "And I usually walk a portion of the way with my coworkers." She held her hand out to him like she was the mom and he was the reluctant toddler. "Coming?"

He did a quick mental review of the pros and cons of taking her hand. Con, she might take it the wrong way. Pro, he needed the reassurance of holding on to her, of believing this was real. He clasped her hand and allowed her to tug him forward.

CHAPTER 3

Her apartment was a dump, a tiny, rundown walkup with absolutely zero security. Worse, she shared it with other people, both men and women.

"You have four roommates," he said, eyes agog at the bodies strewn hither and yon on their way to the bedroom.

"Six," she countered, opening a door and leading him inside the lone tiny bedroom. "To afford a one bedroom in this part of Manhattan, it's a necessity. And it still takes most of my paycheck."

"Where are the other two?" he asked. He had counted only four other people.

"One will be in at midnight. The other works night shift. We bed share," she explained.

"You what now?" he asked.

"I sleep in this bed at night, and he sleeps in it during the day," she said.

"He?"

"His name is George. He's very nice and very clean. And the arrangement means I have an actual bedroom instead of bunking in the living room like the others out there. It's nice, really."

"What if you're both here at the same time?" he asked.

She stopped short. "I don't know. Never happened yet. I'll let you know, if it ever comes up."

"Whose bed is that one?" he asked pointing to the bed approximately eighteen inches away.

"That's Zoe's. She'll be home in a couple of hours, so now's a good time to talk. Let me nip to the bathroom, brush my teeth, etcetera. Make yourself at home on my bed. Don't touch Zoe's stuff or she'll cut you. Not a euphemism. She's a butcher." She pushed aside Zoe's pillow to show him what appeared at first to be a machete but, on closer inspection, was merely a massive butcher knife.

He sank to Poppy's bed, his head swimming. Poppy returned in short order wearing pajamas and a clean, makeup-free face that made her look even younger than her twenty four years. Sully suddenly felt lecherous, as if he'd preyed on some teenager. The girl still had roommates, for goodness sake. Six of them. She rested her hand gently on his back.

"How are you holding up there?" she asked, her tone soft.

He released a puff of air that might have been a laugh, if his state of mind were different. "I'm supposed to ask you that."

"I'm fine," she said, shifting to cross her arms almost protectively over herself.

"Are you…" he began and then trailed off.

Her head swiveled to look at him, eyes hard. "Am I what?"

"Are you taking vitamins? I heard that's important."

She smiled, softening. "Yes, I'm taking vitamins. They're horse pills, and I don't have a lot of confidence I'm going to continue to be able to keep them down."

"What did you think I was going to say?" he asked.

She swallowed hard. "I thought you were going to ask if I was going to keep it."

"Oh. Honestly, the thought never occurred to me," he said.

"It occurred to me. In a lot of ways it would be easier, all except the one where I'd have to live with myself after," she said. "I'm not a hundred percent opposed to adoption."

"I am."

She faced him. "You're opposed to adoption?"

"Of course I'm not opposed to adoption. It's a wonderful, selfless thing. I just don't think I could do it. If you don't want it, I'll take it and raise it myself."

"I never said I didn't want it," she said, the edge creeping back into her tone. "I'm simply trying to consider all the options, to make the best choice for both of us."

"Adoption's not it. I'm comfortable. I have a house and a good job with nice benefits. My family lives in town, they're tightknit and supportive. I'm in a good place for a kid." His eyes scoured the room.

"What?" she snapped.

"You're not," he said bluntly.

She bristled. "I would make an amazing mother. I have an amazing mother, so I know what it's supposed to look like."

"I'm not saying you wouldn't be a good mother though, if we're being honest, I have no idea because I don't know you. I merely mean that this life you're currently living is completely incompatible with having a baby."

"You know nothing about my life," she said.

"I know you have six roommates," he said.

She rolled her eyes. "Obviously my living situation would have to change."

"To what?" he asked. "You said you can barely afford this place, even with all the roommates. How are you supposed to miraculously find a place close to your job with fewer people? And who is going to watch the baby when you're at work?"

"I'll hire someone. It's what people do."

"Who are you going to hire? Some random psycho? Are you going to put the baby in state-run daycare with fifty other kids and one caregiver? How are you going to afford that?"

She pressed her palms to her ears. "Stop it."

He did. They faced forward, trying to calm down. "I'm not trying to antagonize you," he said.

"You could have fooled me," she said.

"I'm pointing out that you can't do this alone in your current situation," he said.

"I have nine months to find a solution," she said.

"You'd better, or else," he said.

She faced him, and suddenly he saw the resemblance between her and her sister because the look she gave him was chilling. "Or else what?"

"I'll take sole custody," he said.

She leaned in, jutting her finger in his face. "Try and take my baby, and I'll bury myself so deep, you'll never find us. I know people all around the world, and I know how to hide."

He believed her completely. He didn't know exactly what her dad did, but he knew it was something in military intelligence, and he had no doubt the daughters had picked up a thing or two over the years. They stared at each other, an unpleasant tension pounding between them. At last she took a few deep breaths and sat back.

"Look, I want us to be amicable about this. Please believe me when I tell you that, if you want to be involved in this child's life, I want that, too. Completely. Kids need their dads, and something tells me you'll be a good one. I'm sure that, in time, we'll work out a schedule where we each get time. I can visit Bailey so the kid can see Texas, and you can spend some time up here with us. It will be okay."

He took a couple of steadying breaths, too. "I agree I want us to be amicable, but I also want to be more than a weekend dad."

"What did you have in mind?" she asked.

"I think we should get married," he said.

CHAPTER 4

"Oh, honey, no," Poppy said, shaking her head, a sad smile on her face.

"What do you mean no? You haven't heard me out," he said.

"I don't have to hear you out. The answer will always be no," she said. "I get that you're that sort of guy, the kind who wants to be honorable and make it right. And I appreciate that, I really do. My dad's like that. *I'm* like that, if we're being honest. So I can see the merits. But in reality, it wouldn't work out."

"How do you know?"

"Because we're strangers. You can't marry a stranger on a whim," she said.

"What we did three weeks ago in the gazebo, that was a whim. This I've actually put some thought into," he said. "You'd be covered under my insurance, both health and life. You'd have a safe, spacious place to live. We'd both share parenting in, wait for it, the same house."

"Those things all sound spectacular, really. But what you're offering me is only safety, and it's not enough. I need love. I need romance and spice and adventure. That's why I live here, in New York and not West Elbow, Texas or whatever the town was called. That's Bailey's life, not mine. I'm a city girl, through and through."

"But why? This place is horrible," he said. She laughed, and he smiled a little. She linked her arm with his.

"How long are you sticking around?"

"Day after tomorrow," he said.

"Good. Tomorrow's my day off. I'll show you the good parts and you'll see it's not such a bad place to raise a kid. Yes, I totally agree with you, I need to find a better place to live. But I'm not without options. I have a degree from the Culinary Institute of America. I know you know nothing about food, but that's like the Harvard of cooking schools. I can get a job pretty much anywhere in this city. Being a pastry chef doesn't pay amazing, but I can get better hours with access to better housing, or at least I'll try. And I won't stop until I do. This is important to me, the safety and wellbeing of our baby, and I'll make it a priority, I promise."

"It sounds so weird to hear you say 'our baby.'"

"I know," she agreed. "For the record, I'm not the kind of girl who..."

"And I'm not the kind of guy who..." he trailed off, mimicking her.

"I could guess that you weren't, Mr. Park Ranger."

"I am so not a park ranger," he said, slipping his arm around her and giving her a squeeze.

She rested her head on his shoulder. "Whatever you are, you should know I'm approximately thirty seconds from falling asleep right now."

"I should go," he said.

"You should stay. I told you that you'll never get a hotel," she said.

"I can't stay here," he said, motioning to the tiny, single bed.

"What's the worst that can happen? It's not like we're going to get more pregnant," she pointed out. "And Zoe will be home any minute, saving you from my further advances."

"There are further advances?" he asked.

"You've barely scratched the surface of my advances," she said, and he smiled.

"Fine. I'll use the bathroom and be right back."

"There's a blue plastic box in there that's mine. Look inside, and you'll find my toothpaste and a new toothbrush that, for the record, is not for unscheduled overnight guests such as yourself. I bought a two pack last week when I replaced my old one."

"Sounds good," he said. He left, used the bathroom, washed his face and hands, brushed his teeth, and returned. Poppy was already sound asleep. He peeled off his clothes and boots down to boxers and a t-shirt and climbed in beside her. Still unconscious, she snuggled against him. He slipped his arm around her thinking that, all in all, so far fatherhood wasn't so bad.

🗝

When he woke the next morning, Poppy draped ungracefully on his chest, her long hair half over his mouth. He stayed perfectly still, not wanting to wake her. His internal clock told him it was six Texas time, eight in New York. A movement to his side caused him to turn his head to the left where he came face to face with a bald woman with neck tattoos, staring hard at him from eighteen inches away.

"You snore," the presumed Zoe whispered before rolling onto her other side away from him.

The whisper woke Poppy who blinked at him in confusion. At least he thought it was confusion. A second later she pressed her hand to her mouth, rolled off the bed, and dashed to the bathroom.

Sully sat up, uncertain if he should follow. He had the vague notion he should try to comfort her, or at least hold her hair, but instead he remained still, waiting for her return.

She arrived a few minutes later, sat on the bed, reached for a plastic tote, and removed a sleeve of saltines, being careful to hold the crumbs over the tote while she ate one.

"No crumbs in the bed for George," she whispered. "Bad bed-sharing manners."

"I really, really don't like you sharing a bed with a man," Sully said, surprised he even had to utter such a thing. Who did that? No one in his world.

"George is safe," Poppy said, and Zoe snorted.

"George is not safe," Zoe added, still facing away from them.

"Okay, safe is the wrong word. George is clean."

"Still," Sully said.

"I told you I'll work on fixing it," Poppy said, annoyed. He remembered she probably felt miserable and clamped his lips on further protests.

"Okay if I shower?" he asked.

She nodded. "I keep an extra pair of men's underwear in my…" she broke off and rolled her eyes. "I'm joking. You really lack a sense of humor about my alleged promiscuity. Zoe, have I ever brought a boyfriend here before?"

"Try it and I'll cut you," Zoe said, holding her butcher knife aloft without turning around.

"You're welcome to a pair of my underwear, if you like," Poppy offered, grinning wickedly.

"I'll turn mine inside out, but thanks," Sully said.

"More info than I needed to know," Poppy called, and he smiled as he left the room.

As he returned to the room, he heard Poppy talking, and he smiled. Her joyful voice told him she had recovered from her earlier bout of sickness. Of course he couldn't say for certain, but she seemed like a cheerful, happy-go-lucky sort of person, and he liked that. His mother was like that, and he wanted the same for his kids. Rather, his kid. He would probably have other kids with another woman, his wife, if he ever got married. It was a depressing thought. He never imagined he would be one of those men with babies by multiple women.

He heard a man's voice and stopped short outside the door. "So, your sister moves to Texas, and you go full cowgirl on us," the man said.

"I told you it's not mine," Poppy said.

"It's nothing to be ashamed of," the male voice replied. "Lots of girls go through cowboy phases. I'll take you to one of those bars where you can ride a mechanical bull, get it out of your system before you go wild and spend a paycheck on leather boots."

"George, seriously, it's not my hat," Poppy replied.

"Then whose is it?"

Sully rounded the corner in time to see George lean in as he spoke, touching his nose to Poppy, who smiled at him in return, Sully's hat on her head. "It's mine," Sully said, and the man's eyes flew to him, shocked. Sully was equally shocked, and he got it now about why Poppy said George was safe; George was a cop. He stood, eyeing Sully with suspicion, the morning sun streaming from the nearby window glinting off his shiny NYPD badge.

"Who are you?" George demanded.

Poppy stood, put a hand to her head, and sat quickly again. "He's my sister's friend from Texas. He came to visit the city and failed to get a hotel room, so I let him stay here."

"In our bed?" George asked in the same disdainful tone Sully had used regarding the bed sharing situation.

"This is so weird," Sully said.

"So weird," Zoe echoed, the pillow now over her head.

"Yes, and he's here for one more night, so he's probably going to be here again," Poppy declared.

"You slept in the same bed with him?" George demanded. "Poppy, seriously wow."

"Nothing happened," Poppy said. "Zoe, did anything happen?"

"If it had, I would cut you," Zoe said, holding her knife aloft again.

"See?"

"Just because it hasn't doesn't mean it won't. What would your dad say?" George said, crossing his arms over his chest.

Poppy paled and forced herself to stand. She clutched George's forearms. "You can't tell my dad he was here. Please, George."

"Of course I won't," George relented, his hands settling at her waist.

Sully stepped forward. "I'm confused. Are you two together?"

From her bed, Zoe snorted.

"No," George and Poppy answered together, and then George frowned at her.

"Seriously, answer faster next time. Feels delightful," he said.

Poppy shook him off and sat down. "We answered at the same time, you goof. We're friends."

Zoe snorted again. Poppy hit her with a pillow. "Thank you for your continued input on this."

Zoe held up a thumb in salute.

Sully put his hands to his temples. "I'm getting a headache."

"Welcome to my world," Poppy said, making the same gesture.

"Are you okay?" George asked, resting his hand lightly on her shoulder. She nodded, and Sully took another step forward.

"Let's get breakfast," he suggested.

"Right, yes. Breakfast." She grimaced, shuddering against the word. "I need to grab a quick shower. She reached beneath the bed, removed a tote, sat up, pressed her hand to her mouth, and made another dash for the bathroom.

Sully and George stared at each other. "She's sick," George declared.

"I think so," Sully agreed.

George regarded the bed warily. "Wonder if I should change the sheets."

"Pretty sure you're safe," Sully said, and from her bed, Zoe snorted again.

CHAPTER 5

"Are you really a cowboy?" George asked as Poppy returned to the room.

"Forgot my clothes," she interjected with a sheepish smile.

"Poppy, are you okay?" George asked her.

"Fine, I'm fine," she assured him, rooting through her portion of their shared closet.

"I'm not a cowboy. I'm a Ranger," Sully said, answering the earlier question.

"A Ranger, huh? I've heard of you guys," George replied. His accent was native New York and heavy.

"Of course you have, George. They're *iconic*," Poppy said in a falsely awed whisper.

"Much like the NYPD," George agreed.

She turned to face him. "How are they comparable?"

"How, indeed," George said, grinning.

"Poppy thinks I'm a park ranger," Sully explained.

George laughed. "Oh, Poppy."

"What?" she asked, clueless.

"Park ranger is to Texas Ranger as Wonder bread is to brioche," George explained.

"Wow," Poppy said, staring at Sully with a slightly awed expression.

"Okay, now someone's going to have to explain the analogy in reverse to me," Sully said.

"Over breakfast," Poppy promised. "Back in a bit." She disappeared, leaving awkwardness in her wake.

"I'll wait out here," Sully said, easing from the room. But he forgot there were four other people inhabiting the living room as sleeping space. With nowhere else to go, he sat outside the bathroom, waiting for Poppy to finish with her shower. He was prepared for a long wait, but ten minutes later, the door opened so that he had to catch himself before he tumbled inside.

"Oh," Poppy said, stopping short at the sight of him.

"You're fast," he said, standing.

"House rules. With so many people waiting to get in, you can't linger. Thankfully my hair dries okay on its own. I'm fairly low maintenance, thanks to growing up in Africa." She fluffed her wet hair a couple of times and grabbed her purse.

Despite the apparent lack of effort in her appearance, she looked good—lovely and fresh in a feminine floral dress. She was a girly girl, much more than Bailey. Her figure was fuller, but pleasantly so. Sully was of the persuasion that women should look like women, with curves and soft planes. There would never be any mistaking Poppy for a man. Unfortunately for him, he knew exactly how those curves felt beneath his fingers. His face flushed, and he fought the urge to reach for her. Last night they had been too busy talking to think of much else. Now, however, it was hard not to remember and realize. He knew this woman intimately, and she was having his child. And yet she was a stranger, confusing to say the least.

"Where are you taking me?" he asked as they reached the sidewalk.

"For bagels, the quintessential New York breakfast. I have a friend from culinary school who's doing amazing things with teff and spelt." As if speaking about it increased her energy, she clasped his hand and urged him forward, hurrying him along. They arrived in a tiny, nondescript building, basically a hole in the wall, that inside smelled of fresh bread and yeast. Sully took a big breath, enjoying the homey smell. Poppy expelled a breath, grimacing, and once again pressing her hand to her abdomen.

"Will anything help?" Sully asked.

"I have no idea, but lemonade sounds amazing right now," she said. They ordered bagels and lox and coffee for him, tea with lemon for her.

"Not a coffee fan?" he asked.

She gave him a look.

"What?" he asked.

"No caffeine when you're pregnant," she said.

"Oh," he drawled. "Sorry."

"It's okay. But I'm having withdrawal and it's making me a bit cranky. Or maybe it's the hormones, I don't know. All I know is that I feel sick and tired and miserable and kind of stabby, and it's only the beginning."

"I really am sorry," he reiterated.

"We share the blame equally, I think," she said.

"Except you totally kissed me first," he said.

"Oh, no, you did not go there. I was trying to leave like a good girl when you kissed me, preventing me from escaping to safety."

"Yes, but you were the one who…"

She touched her fingers to his lips. "We should probably not." He kissed her fingers. "You stop that."

"Why? It's not like we're going to get more pregnant," he said, grinning when she picked up her napkin and began to fan herself.

"Have mercy. Definitely remembering why I kissed you to begin with," she said.

"You forgot?"

"I saw you once three weeks ago so, yes, pardon me for forgetting," she said.

"Strange, I remember you in vivid detail," he said.

"Are you flirting with me right now?"

He shrugged. "After I knocked you up, it's the least I could do."

"The very least," she said and their food arrived. To her surprised delight, she was able to eat an entire bagel with cream cheese and salmon.

"Salmon on a bagel," he said, scowling in disgust.

"And it's basically raw," she said, pausing to stare at it. "I wonder if I'm allowed to eat this."

"I'll check," he said, withdrawing his phone.

"Ungh," she said, stuffing down the last of the bagel before he could look it up.

"I take it you'd rather not know," he said.

She shook her head and swallowed the giant mouthful. "It's the first thing that's sounded appetizing in three days. I'd rather not know how many ways it could harm me or our child."

Now it was his turn to shudder.

"Because I said 'our child'?" she guessed.

He nodded. "Going to take a while to get used to hearing that. While I have my phone out, I think I should make arrangements to stay at a hotel."

"If you like," she said.

"Hmm, I kind of expected more of a protest," he said.

"It's a free country," she replied, stealing a sip of his coffee. He punched a few things in his phone and began to scroll.

"How can every space be filled?" he mused, continuing to scroll. "Wait, here we go." He leaned in close. "Five hundred dollars? Can that be right?"

"Space is at a premium. If it were that cheap and easy, *I'd* rent a room every night," she said. She rested her hand on his. "Just stay with me. It's not that big a deal."

He turned over his phone. "It would seem I don't have a choice."

"Try not to sound so thrilled."

"It's extremely unlike my life," he said. "I don't cohabitate with anyone, male or female. I haven't since I left home years ago."

"It's not unusual here. Unless you make high six figures or live in The Boroughs, you have to have roommates, usually lots of them. It's called a housing crisis, and I'm living proof of it."

"Why do you do it?"

"Where else am I going to go? This is the food capital of the country, if not the world. I could go back to Paris, but my French is lousy."

"You've lived in Paris?"

"Six months post-culinary school. Any pastry chef worth her salt needs to do a stint in Paris."

"I've never lived outside Texas."

She looked down, stirring her tea.

"What?" he prompted.

"I thought maybe you could move here. We could be roommates, raise the baby together here."

He blinked at her, trying to say what he needed to say without being offensive. "I'm a Ranger, a Texas Ranger. The Texas portion of that is rather imperative."

"But if that's like some kind of police officer, couldn't you do that here? Like George?"

"It's difficult to explain to you without you understanding what a Ranger is. It's a big deal, kind of prestigious, sort of non-transferable. I worked for years to get where I am, started as a trooper, put in tons of extra time and training. Plus there's the fact that I'm not a city boy. I'm country, through and through. I have zero, let me reiterate, zero interest in ever living here. Even visiting here didn't appeal to me. I'm only here so we could have a face-to-face discussion. Plus the same reasons you don't want to marry me are the same reasons I don't want to be your roommate."

"I guess I see your point. Rather, your multitude of points. We seem to be at an impasse," she said.

"Can I ask you a question?" he said. He picked up a straw wrapper and tied it into a knot. "I get that George is in love with you. I guess I need to know up front and right now if you're in love with him."

She blinked at him. "What are you talking about? George isn't in love with me."

"Yes, yes he is," Sully said.

She shook her head. "We're friends and quasi roommates. I see him a few minutes in the morning to handoff the bed, and that's it. Occasionally we text throughout the day or leave each other notes.

This year we exchanged Christmas presents, and I mean literally exchanged. He left one on the bed for me, and I left one for him. Otherwise, we have little to no contact with each other."

"You know the last woman I bought a Christmas present for besides my mom?" he said.

"Who?"

He said nothing for a minute then, "That's who."

"Maybe he's nicer and more generous than you are," she suggested.

"Nope. Just do me a favor and let me know if you two officially start dating. This is an awkward new world we're in, and I'd prefer there not to be any surprises."

"I guess then the same goes for you."

"I don't actually date that often anymore. It's such a hassle," he said. "The setup, the excitement, the letdown."

"Despite how much I want to make fun of you right now for sounding girlier than I do, I agree with you. I haven't dated anyone since I was in culinary school a few years ago. And my schedule is so crazy. I work six days a week, ten hour shifts, including every weekend."

"That's insane," he said. "You can't possibly keep that up."

"I know," she said, sighing. "But I love my job. It's not a huge restaurant, but it's up and coming. There's been buzz about it, about me. My boss has given me a lot of freedom and creativity. It's a dream job for me, a stepping stone to something huge. There aren't a lot of rock stars in the pastry world, hardly any that anyone outside the food world would recognize. We get looked down on a lot for not being real chefs, but baking takes just as much skill and talent as cooking."

"I believe you," he said, holding his hands up in mock surrender.

"Sorry," she said, sipping her tea. "I get a bit impassioned about it."

"It's cute," he said, touching his fingers to hers. She threaded her fingers through his and smiled. He smiled in return. The moment lasted as a hum of tension buzzed between them, confusing them both. They were each in uncharted territory with no idea how to categorize each other or their situation.

The owner of the shop arrived at their table, saving them from further action or conversation. Poppy let go of Sully and stood to hug the newcomer. "The bagels are fantastic," she gushed.

"Thank you. You still at the place?"

"Yes, and, keep it on the down low, but I'm looking for someplace with better pay, more solid hours, Katelyn."

Katelyn laughed. "Poppy, if I could find something like that, I'd take it myself." She gave Poppy another hug. "It's rough out there."

"Yes it is," Poppy agreed. They talked for another minute about spelt, whatever that was, and then Katelyn returned to her kitchen and Poppy sat down. "Is Sully short for something?"

"Sullivan."

"That's cute, I like it. Tell me, Sullivan, are you ready for the full New York experience?"

"Yes, Poppy, I am. Is Poppy short for something?"

"Poppisandra," she said.

He tried not to grimace. "Really?"

"No, it's just Poppy, like the flower. My mom loves them." She stood and led the way outside, Sully in her wake.

CHAPTER 6

Sully had to admit the day was fun. Despite a few repeated bouts of nausea for Poppy, two of which ended in sprints to the bathroom, he had to concede he enjoyed New York. But he still didn't see it as a suitable place to raise children.

"Look how nice this park is," Poppy said, leaning on the iron fence.

"It's gated," Sully said. "It's like a giant metal playpen. Kids need space to run free and explore. Here you can run ten feet before slamming into a spiked metal pole." He rested his arms beside hers, watching the children play.

"Look at that kid," Poppy said, her eyes resting on a little boy. "In a few years, that could be our kid."

"Our kid should be learning to ride a horse at that age, wearing a tiny Stetson and leather boots," Sully countered.

"Either way, the image is equally adorable and unfathomable," Poppy said.

"Yes," Sully agreed. He slipped his arm around her, and she leaned on him.

"This is so weird."

"Yes," he said again.

"It's like forced intimacy. I get now why you're not supposed to jump the gun. We're strangers of the highest order but…not."

He sighed. "Let's let go of the pretense that we're strangers. That word no longer exists for us. Instead we'll work on getting to know each other good and proper, on becoming friends, so that when the baby finally gets here we'll have a solid foundation on which to co-parent."

"I love that," Poppy said, easing her arm around his waist to give him a squeeze. "We are friends, new friends who have a pressing need to get to know each other better."

"Where do we begin?" he asked.

"With food, of course. Food is the cornerstone of community. We'll have a good supper and share stories."

"I'm going to guess you know a good place to eat," he said.

"I know *all* the good places to eat. And I have something in mind I think will make your cowpoke heart happy," she said, linking her arm with his as they resumed their walk down the street.

"Barbeque in New York," Sully said when they arrived. "Color me skeptical."

"Color me nauseated," Poppy said, looking pale and ill again.

"We don't have to go here. The smell is going to be intense," he said.

"We have to go somewhere, and I think it's going to be the same no matter what. This way at least you'll get some nourishment." He held the door for her. They put their names in. She leaned against the wall with her eyes closed while they waited to be seated.

"Poppy, is there anything I can do for you?" he asked, feeling ambiguously guilty for her misery.

"Lemonade," she whispered, pressing her lips together and swallowing hard. Sully went to the bar and ordered a lemonade for her. While there, a woman sidled up next to him and spoke.

"Are you a real cowboy?"

"Yes, ma'am," he said, tipping his hat slightly.

"Do you live here?" she asked.

"No, I live in Texas, I'm heading back tomorrow."

"Huh, do you have plans for tonight?" She rested her hand invitingly on his bicep.

"Uh," he stuttered, taken aback by her directness. The bartender set his lemonade in front of him, and Sully picked it up, glad for the easy reprieve. "Yes." He turned and walked away from her feeling... what? He almost felt as though he was on a precipice, as if he could be that guy now, the one who picked up women in bars for whatever pleasure they might bring him for an evening. He had broken a mold, had crossed a line with Poppy he thought he might never cross. It would be easy to continue on that path, and a part of him was tempted.

Then he returned to Poppy and handed her the lemonade. She was miserable, would probably continue to be miserable in one way or another until the pregnancy was over, due in no small part to him. So, no, he would not be that guy, he now resolved, wouldn't allow himself to be tempted into believing his actions had no consequences, just because he wasn't always around to see them. Feeling slightly better about himself with the resolution, he faced the restaurant again, actually looking forward to New York barbecue.

And it was good. Amazing, really. Poppy knew her food, not surprising since she was a professional. Despite her continued misery and inability to do more than nibble at her food, they talked a lot over supper. The conversation was light and casual, almost like a first date. If he could pretend there was nothing more between them, he might be able to convince himself it was a date. That thought made him tilt his head at her and take an objective look. Would he date Poppy, if he met her in the normal order of things? He had thought her adorable at Bailey's wedding, but he had also thought her too young for him and had discounted her out of hand. Now that he knew she wasn't too young, he took a second look.

She was more than adorable; she was pretty. Not beautiful like Cal's former wife, Isabel the beauty queen, but then Sully didn't actually like that untouchable level of attractiveness, if it wasn't accompanied by kindness and warmth. Poppy was girl-next-door pretty, and he liked that. More importantly, she was approachable, touchable, huggable. She oozed kindheartedness, softness, and vivacity. Whereas Bailey was tough and together, Poppy was feminine and a tad helpless. Maybe helpless was the wrong word. After all, she was gainfully employed in one of the roughest cities in the world to make a living. But she seemed vulnerable in a way that made a man want to step up and take care of her. Or maybe it was the pregnancy. Maybe when she wasn't pregnant she was fully capable and in control of every situation. Somehow he doubted it, though. She radiated sensitivity, sweetness, and gentleness. She was the kind of woman whose warmth drew people to her. Someday when she was older, she would be the motherly sort, the kind who always had fresh cookies on hand and welcomed her kids' friends as if they were her own.

"You're staring at me," she said, touching his fingers where they rested on the table.

He picked up her fingers and kissed them. "You're pretty."

"I'm green and sweaty," she countered.

"You shimmer, and green's your color," he said. "I was pondering us."

"What about us?" she asked.

"If we would be attracted to each other and date under normal circumstances," he said.

"And what conclusion did you arrive at?" she asked, tipping her head and smiling in a way that was tinged with too much orneriness for one woman to possess.

"I think yes. If I saw you somewhere like this or at a party, I would want to get your number. I'd probably ask you out, see where things went." He let go her hand to take a few bites of his food, and then it occurred to him she hadn't reciprocated the thought. "What about you?"

"What about me?"

"Would you have been attracted to me under other circumstances?" he prodded.

"Have you seen you? Good grief, you're like a real life cover of a romance novel. Just unbutton your shirt and bold type will appear over your head saying, 'The Cowboy's Last Stand,' or something."

He frowned. "That's not exactly an answer. Clearly you find me attractive."

She chuckled. "Clearly."

"But do you think we would have had a chance if we'd gone about things in the desired order?"

"I don't think so," she said.

He dropped his fork. "What?"

She looked up. "Oh, no, I've offended you, and I didn't mean to. It's not you, Sully. You're sweet and, hello, did I mention super hot. It's me. I'm a loser magnet. I always go for the wrong guy, the bad guy, the man who needs fixing. You, you're so…" she waved her hand at him. "Stable."

"Why does that sound like an insult when you say it?"

"It's an insult to me. You know what my sisters call me? Hurricane Poppy, and it's true. I have a talent for walking into a space and picking the most broken specimen of humanity available and then trying to make him whole again. I pour myself into it like a project, giving pieces of my heart and soul away until, finally, horribly, it ends. And then I swear off men until the next time I find some ridiculous loser. The thing is, I'm a sucker for words. Bad men know the best words. 'I only act this way because I'm scared of losing you, Poppy. You're the only one who gets me, Poppy. I don't know why I do the things I do, Poppy. It must be because I love you so much. Be right back, going to go see my side girlfriend while you cry.'" She rolled her eyes.

"You said you haven't dated anyone in a while," he reminded her.

"True. I had a serious boyfriend in culinary school, a real bad boy of the chef world. He's on TV sometimes now. We were together for over a year and…" she broke off, shuddering.

"What?" he snapped. Her tone told him he wasn't going to like what she was about to say.

"It was bad," she stared hard at her plate.

"He hit you?"

"Not a lot, not every day. But a few times he smacked me. It was more than that, though, an entire pattern of systematic abuse and brainwashing. By the time that relationship ended, I was convinced I was nothing and he was everything. The worst part is that *he* broke up with *me*, and I begged him to stay. After he was gone a few months, it was like I began to come back to myself, to come back to sanity and see things more clearly again. That glimpse of myself, of the person I became, of how easily it happened, it scared me. I kind of swore off men after that, and with my schedule, it hasn't been hard to do. I work a minimum of sixty hours a week."

He blinked at her, frowning. In his experience, women who got into those types of relationships always seemed to go for the same type of guy. It became an unbreakable pattern. The information was not good news to Sully. In fact it was a red flag. He would never, ever allow his child to be in such a situation. If it came to that, he would intervene. But to say so now might alienate her when they were making progress with their friendship. So instead he said, "If you ever get in a relationship like that again, I'll kidnap you out of it. And then I'll let your sister kill the guy."

Poppy laughed, albeit uncomfortably. "That's the real kicker. I have this family on standby willing to do anything to protect me, and I never told them. If my dad knew..." she trailed off, looking away. "Anyway, it's over with now, and my foreseeable future has zero men in it."

"Uh, hello," he said, raising his hand.

"You know what I mean. Men aren't exactly beating down the doors of pregnant and single mothers. Maybe I'll become a nun, cloister the baby with me."

"Are you Catholic?"

"Don't rain on my pity parade with facts and information," she said, and he smiled.

"You're too cute, Poppy," he said.

"You're spectacularly adorable yourself, Sully. Like a grownup boy scout or something. So good, and kind, and polite."

He frowned at his plate, not sure why the positive description of his character bothered him, except it felt as though she were categorizing him as safe. No guy wanted to be thought of as safe.

"Oh, no, I've offended you again," she surmised.

"No guy wants to be thought of as Richie Cunningham. We'd rather be the Fonz."

"But, see, when you reference a wholesome '70's sitcom for a comparison, it's really hard to see you as a bad boy," she said.

"I don't watch a lot of TV. I have no idea what's current," he admitted.

"Me neither. You may have noticed the apartment isn't exactly conducive to lounging on the couch, seeing as how there is no couch. And I grew up overseas, so I'm totally out of the pop culture loop."

They finished with their meal and went for gelato at another place run by yet another of Poppy's friends. Strangely, Sully didn't feel stuffed. Maybe it was all the walking they were doing. They must have covered ten miles of the city on foot that day. Poppy was in remarkably good shape from all the daily walking. Toward the end, it was as if a switch got flipped and he could almost see the energy drain from her. He clasped her hand, trying to imbue her with some of his stamina as they made the long walk back to her apartment and up several flights of stairs. The stairwell was another hazard, one that registered in the back of his mind like a beacon. It would be so easy for someone to attack her in there, to pen her in like a helpless calf.

The living room was filled with its usual quantity of sleepers. They picked their way over to her bedroom. Zoe wasn't yet home. The bed was made, and George had left Poppy a box of peppermint tea with a note saying, "Feel better, roomie!"

Poppy smiled as she tucked it into her tote. Sully refrained from comment. He had said all he needed to say about everything. Now it was up to her to make decisions about her life, about her situation here. If that included recognizing the chemistry between her and George, well, he'd face that when it came. He supposed he could do worse than having an NYPD cop in his kid's life, though a stab of jealousy knifed through him at the thought. He wanted to be the only man in his future child's world, not some hotshot city cop.

He and Poppy took turns in the bathroom and then climbed into the tiny bed, lying side by side in oddly comfortable silence.

"It's been fun having you here," Poppy whispered. There was no need to whisper since Zoe wasn't there, but it felt intimate and cozy in the darkness of the room.

"It's been fun to be here. I've enjoyed getting this glimpse of your life, so radically different from mine."

"Differences aren't altogether bad," she said.

"No, they're not," he agreed.

"He or she will have two very different worldviews to choose from," Poppy mused.

"Yes," Sully agreed, trying hard to keep his tone neutral.

The longer they lay there, the more he wanted to touch her. At last he reached out and rested his hand on her stomach. Surely she wouldn't think too much of him wanting to feel what went on in there. She moved his hand lower.

"It's there, south of the belly button."

He smoothed his hand over the spot, trying hard to notice the changes, but since he had no frame of reference, it merely felt like smooth, soft skin to him. Poppy turned to face him. "We're really doing this."

"We really are," he agreed. They shared a tremulous smile and then, slowly, he leaned forward and kissed her, a tender, gentle kiss of shared uncertainty and fear. What they were embarking on was terrifying and huge and hugely terrifying. Poppy rolled toward him and slid her hand onto his shoulder, tipping her face toward his, inviting him to deepen the kiss. He did so, and she responded. Her knee shifted, sliding onto his hip. He reached out a hand and anchored it there, drawing her closer, pressing her to him. As before, things began to spiral out of control when the door was ripped open and Zoe stood framed in the doorway. She stared at them, squinting in disgust.

"I'm showering. Stop that before I get back, or I'll cut you," she promised before she stalked into the room, grabbed her tote, and walked back out again, slamming the door behind her.

"What's wrong with us?" Poppy asked, resting her head on his shoulder. "We're like love-starved animals."

"Or maybe two human beings who find each other attractive," he countered. His hand skimmed down her back. It was an innocuous touch, but she still shivered beneath his fingers. "Maybe, Poppy, we should try to be together, to see where this goes. Clearly we have chemistry." It had been a long time since he had this kind of chemistry with a woman, if he ever had. Physically at least, things felt effortless with her. He didn't have to force any kind of attraction to her; rather he had to force himself not to act on it.

"Maybe we should sleep on it and discuss it in the morning," Poppy said, yawning. "I'm not exactly coherent."

"Sure," he agreed, and she was asleep by the time he finished the word.

CHAPTER 7

Sully had an early flight the next morning. The airport was too far away for Poppy to accompany him, so they settled for breakfast again instead.

"I wonder when all of this will stop feeling surreal," he said.

"It stopped for me the first time I threw up," she said.

"Right. Your reality is a lot clearer than mine. A couple of days ago I was in Texas, and now I'm in New York and I spent the last two nights physically sleeping with the mother of my child, a woman I barely know, surrounded by her multitude of roommates. I have no idea how to go home and act normally after this."

"It will be easy for you to do because I won't be there. Everything will go back to how it was before."

"When are you going to tell Bailey the news?"

She blew out a breath. "I'm going to hold off as long as possible, but I'll definitely give you a heads up before it happens. And I could leave your name out of it entirely. Otherwise you should probably make plans to flee the country and change your identity."

"That seems like the coward's way," he said.

"I am a coward," she informed him.

"I meant for me. Not taking public responsibility? Who does that?"

"Someone who wants to continue to live or, at the very least, keep his friendship with my sister alive," she said.

Now he blew out a breath. "Seems wrong, but we have some time to think on it. Please keep me updated on your health and your progress finding a new situation. I'm worried about you."

"I'm fine," she assured him. "I'm Miss Independent."

It was hard to take her seriously when she was so adorable. With her dimpled cheeks and flowery dress, she looked eighteen again. "I want to give you some money," he said, reaching for his wallet.

She put her hand on his. "I can't accept it."

"Why not? You're bound to have expenses. It could help you get settled in a new place."

She shook her head.

"I'm half responsible for this," he reminded her.

"I know, but taking cash at this stage of things when they've barely begun makes me feel like a surrogate."

"I want to help," he said.

"How about this—I'll do it on my own, but if I get in a bind, I promise to reach out."

"Do you promise, really?"

She nodded. "For now, I'm good, honest."

"Okay." Absently, he stirred his coffee. "About what we were talking about last night."

She leaned forward. "Sully, this weekend has confirmed what I already suspected. I think you're great. I mean, to be friends with my sister, you sort of already waived the preapproval process because, unlike me, she has spectacular taste in men. But here's what I thought. Right now we're on our way to being friends, and we've committed to raising the baby together amicably. If we tried to be something more, it might work. But then again it might not. My abysmal track record tells me it probably wouldn't. We could be left with awkwardness and hurt that might take years to heal, that might massively negatively impact our child. I guess I'd rather hold on to what we know than take a chance on what we don't."

"That's a bit more mature and well-rationed than I gave you credit for," he said.

"It happens occasionally," she said.

"I can't say I'm not a little sad, Poppy. I think we could have something here. But I also can't say I disagree. It's not about us anymore. It's about him or her and what's best. I want to do this the right way, as gently and lovingly as possible. So I think you're right, we'll stick with friendship and work on that. However," they stopped short outside her apartment building. "I can't promise not to be attracted to you. I already was, and the fact that you're carrying my child." He thumped his hand over his heart. "It does something to me, something primal."

She gathered his lapels in her hands. "The good news, Sullivan, is that you're getting on a plane in a few minutes, heading far, far away to Texas, and it's likely we won't see each other again for a while."

"I feel like I've heard this speech before," he said, easing his arms around her.

"My point is that I think a kiss goodbye is wholly appropriate," she said.

"I hope we're always on the same page this way," he said, dipping his head to kiss her. She stood on her toes and kissed him in return before abruptly pulling away and darting around the corner. She returned a minute later looking shaky and pale.

"That was not sexy, sorry," she said, pressing the back of her hand to her forehead.

"I hate leaving you this way," he replied.

"I'll be fine. Lots of other women have gone through this, if the rumors are to be believed." Despite her plucky words, she looked vulnerable, young, and uncertain.

He hugged her and kissed her cheek. "Please call if you need anything, please."

"Promise," she said, resting her head on his chest. He kissed the top of her head, let her go, and forced himself to walk away. No matter how hard he tried to shake it, he couldn't help but feel like he was doing the wrong thing. And no matter what he did felt wrong. He couldn't very well quit his job and move to New York to look after her. That made no rational sense. Neither could he drag her back to Texas with him. He had no claim on her, zero. All he could do was stand helplessly by and hope she would take the vague offer of help he'd given. If she was anything like Bailey, she wouldn't. Bailey would rather die than ask for help or admit weakness. Somehow he thought it was likely a family trait.

With a ridiculous amount of relief, he turned his mind toward work. There were a million and one little things that would require his attention when he returned, and he would gladly dive into them. Anything to avoid thinking of his current situation.

But when he landed in San Antonio, his current situation was there to greet him in the face.

"Surprise," Bailey said as she and Cal met him at the airport. "We had some shopping to do, so we asked Brandt if we could pick you up instead. Do you want to grab a bite to eat, or are you ready to go straight home?"

"We could get something to eat," he said, trying to keep the wariness out of his tone. Now everything felt tainted by the situation with Poppy. He felt bogged down by guilt, like the worst sort of person. Cal and Bailey were two of his closest friends, and now not only had he kept something monumental from them, it also involved them, however indirectly. He had never felt like more of a heel.

He rode in the back seat of their car like they were the parents and he was the recalcitrant teenager. Conversation wasn't easy in heavy traffic, so they didn't talk much until they got to the restaurant, a Tex-Mex place.

"So," Bailey said, eyeing him. Sully tried not to squirm. "Cal informed me you had plans to visit my sister. Did that work out?"

Was he sweating? He felt like maybe he was and resisted the urge to dab his brow. "Yes. We ate together." *And slept in the same bed. Twice. I'm a total sleazeball, please forgive me.* "I saw her apartment," he added for the sake of honesty. "Are you familiar with her living arrangement?" He didn't think she would think anything of his propriety tone. Anyone sane would be concerned.

"Yes, I'm aware. But she has George. Did you meet George?"

He blinked at her. "Yes. Have you met George?"

"I've known George forever. His dad and my dad were roommates at West Point."

"Poppy didn't say she'd known him that long," Sully said.

"Technically she hasn't. Poppy and George are a series of missed connections. I knew him from when they were little, but of course they don't remember each other. After that it never lined up for them to know each other until the roommate thing came into being." She leaned in and lowered her voice. "Don't tell, but we're all secretly hoping they get together."

"Who is this hopeless romantic, and what has she done with my wife?" Cal asked.

"I know it's unlike me. But Poppy has always been one of those kids who has to learn by doing. And usually that comes about in the hardest way possible. And she has terrible taste in men, seriously the worst. She's due for a break, for something good, and George is a good kid." She turned to Sully. "Did you get the sense there was a spark between them?"

"I saw it. I'm not sure Poppy believed it was there," Sully said carefully.

"None of us have interfered because we don't want to tip the scales in the wrong direction but," she held up crossed fingers. "Poppy doesn't like to be told what to do."

"Miss Independent," Sully said.

"Exactly."

"That sounds like no one else in your family," Cal said, turning to smile at her and squeeze her knee.

"Eyes on the road, boss," she replied, poking his ribs.

The topic moved on to other matters. Sully tried to stay a part of the conversation, but he must not have succeeded completely when Bailey gave him a sympathetic smile and said, "You must be exhausted. Let's get you home."

"Sorry, I'm not great company. Lots on my mind," Sully replied.

"Brandt told us a bit about the crime syndicate," Cal said. "Sounds like a doozy."

"It is," Sully agreed, his brain turning to work with relief. They talked for a while longer and then began the long drive home. When they dropped him at his house, Bailey surprised him by turning to pat his knee.

"Thanks, Sul, for seeing Poppy when you were in New York. It was nice of you. I worry about her."

"Bailey, I…" he began but didn't know how to finish. As she stared at him with eyes so full of gratitude, he realized two facts: things were about to get a lot trickier than he ever imagined, and Bailey's eyes were more like Poppy's than he first noticed—surprisingly innocent and full of too much trust in him. "I enjoyed it." It was the most honest thing he could say, and he still felt like the world's biggest fraud. "Thanks for the ride. Night, y'all." He slid from the car and wearily made his way to his house.

CHAPTER 8

For the next few weeks, Poppy made a concerted effort to find a new place to live. Finding an apartment in New York was exponentially harder than finishing culinary school had been, harder than anything she had ever done. Rentals were snapped up almost before they were advertised. One had to have an in with someone to find anything. Poppy talked to everyone she knew, scoured ads and, in desperation, went door to door looking for something, anything better than what she had. But it was always the same. If she found something cheaper with fewer roommates, it was in an exponentially worse location where safety would be a pressing concern. If she found anything closer with fewer roommates, it was at least double her current rent, sometimes more than double her actual pay.

In addition to looking for a new apartment, she also began the search for a new job, albeit quietly. If her boss knew she was looking elsewhere, he might fire her. The food business was fickle. Rumors could make or break a restaurant. If people caught wind of the fact that *Burton's* pastry chef was looking to make a move, it might start chatter over the health of the restaurant. Poppy didn't want that. Her boss had been good to her, and she had no desire to cause him any trouble. All she wanted was a job with better hours and, hopefully, better pay. But if such a job existed, Poppy couldn't find it. In fact most jobs she found were worse than hers, often requiring bakers to work overnight for lower pay. If the search did one thing, it made Poppy realize how fortunate she had been to find a job as head pastry chef at such a young age. Often times it took a new chef years of hard work and proving oneself to get where she already was.

During the day when George slept, Poppy usually rotated between a series of coffee houses and bakeries in order to occupy her time. There she either read or spent time researching new recipes on the internet. But now the smell of everything made her sick. She tried going to the public library instead but found it occupied by too many creepers. Finally, she landed at a few bookstores. When the employees began to give her hard looks for loitering, she bought either a newspaper or magazine to stave them off. That was the first time she began to long for a place where she could relax and hang out, for the sort of living space that would allow such a luxury. Crazy as it was, she hadn't given her lifestyle a second thought in the two years she'd lived in Manhattan. It was what it was, but everyone was in the same boat so it seemed normal. But now she began to remember what it had been like to have her own place, to spend her downtime in her own living room, on her own couch.

One day, two weeks into her search, she clicked on the newspaper for Sully's town and, out of curiosity, looked for apartment rentals. Immediately she knew it was a huge mistake because, eyes bugging, she read listing after listing for not just apartments but houses for rent. And most were under eight hundred dollars a month. Poppy paid more than twice that for what amounted to a place to sleep and store her clothes. A quick look at the job listings showed why the housing was so cheap—jobs were few. The town was small and lacking industry. For most people it was either a place to own a ranch, work on a ranch, or work close to San Antonio but still live a country life. There was a diner in town, however, and it got a lot of customers. Poppy and her family had eaten there twice during the few days they were in town for Bailey's wedding. She could...

She shook her head and closed her laptop. No, she couldn't. She wouldn't. She quashed her thoughts before they could take root. New York was her home. She couldn't possibly leave it for a tiny town in western Texas. Such a move would be career suicide. She would undo everything she had done to get where she was.

It's not about you anymore, a little voice in her head reminded her. It ceased to be about her or her dreams that night in the gazebo a few weeks ago. The tightness of her clothes was a daily reminder of that, along with the continued nausea. Poppy wasn't sure how it was possible her clothes weren't fitting anymore when she was most certainly losing weight. She could barely eat and, when she did manage to stuff something in her mouth, it didn't stay down for long. The last few weeks she had seemingly been subsisting on saltines, lemonade, and multivitamins, despite her best efforts to eat healthy, nutrient-rich foods. She had never been so sick for so long in her life. Each new day was a misery of exhaustion, nausea, and potty breaks.

Tears sprang to her eyes, and she dashed them away. She had also been an emotional train wreck lately, thanks to the bubbling cauldron of hormones now coursing through her body. She did her best to keep it all together, going to work as usual, putting on a happy face for everyone concerned. But in reality she felt as if she were juggling flaming swords. Eventually one of them was going to fall. She had told no one besides Sully about the baby yet, almost as if she didn't admit it, then it wouldn't be true. And if he didn't text her every other day or so to check in, she might have forgotten about the pregnancy all together, minus the slew of ever-increasing symptoms now holding her body hostage.

She needed to talk to someone, a sympathetic listening ear. Her parents and sisters sprang to mind and were quickly discarded. She wasn't ready to tell them yet, not until it became unavoidable and she'd made some sound decisions about her future. Her phone told her it was almost time for work. It also told her George was probably awake now. She texted him and hit send before she could change her mind.

Are you up for breakfast tomorrow before we change shifts? I have something to discuss with you.

Sounds ominous.

When she didn't reply to that, he texted again. *Yes, breakfast sounds great. Have a good night at work, P.*

You, too. Stay safe, she typed.

For you? Anything, he replied.

Poppy smiled as she tucked her phone into her purse. With effort, she heaved herself off the comfy leather couch and walked to work.

⚷

The next morning, Poppy overslept. She always woke in time to vacate and make the bed so George wouldn't have to crawl between warm sheets. Plus it felt less personal if they didn't actually see each other waking up or going to sleep. But now she didn't stir until she felt someone perch on the edge of the bed and run a gentle hand over her head.

Startled, she opened her eyes, and blinked up at George who smiled down at her. "Well, this is a first," he declared.

"I'm so sorry," Poppy said, embarrassed at the lapse.

"No biggie. You must have had a late night last night," he said, his tone questioning. Did he think she had a hot date? She almost laughed at the absurdity.

"No, actually. I came home on time and fell into bed. I don't even remember falling asleep." She sat up, feeling slightly disoriented. For the first time in weeks, she hadn't woken in the night to use the bathroom. Was that a bad sign? Should she be concerned? Then it was as if her bladder was struck by a meteor and she had to pay penance for those few minutes of extra sleep.

"Be right back," she said, practically shoving George out of her way in her mad dash to the bathroom. If it was occupied, she had no idea what she might do but, mercifully, it was open. By the time she had used the bathroom and washed her hands, she had to return to the toilet to get sick as the ever-present nausea also made its usual morning appearance.

Poppy brushed her teeth, gagging repeatedly as she did so, then dashed her face with cool water and returned to the bedroom. "Sorry about that," she whispered, sinking shakily to the bed beside George who surprised her by putting his hand out and rubbing her back.

"I'm worried about you," he said.

"I'm fine," she assured him.

"Look, I've seen the signs before. I know what's going on here." He took her hands in his. "I'm going to ask you a question, and I need you to be honest with me, please. Are you on drugs?"

She snorted and doubled over laughing. "George, no. Oh, my goodness, as if I would even know where to get drugs or what to do with them if I found them."

"You make all these mystery trips to the bathroom, your sleep schedule is off, you're losing weight. What is going on with you?"

In the bed beside them, Zoe sat up. "This ought to be good."

"Let me grab a quick shower, and then we'll go, okay?" Poppy replied to George.

"Oh, come on. I'm vested in this drama, and I don't get to hear the climax?" Zoe said.

"Hush, you," Poppy said. They had been acquaintances in culinary school, but not anyone's idea of close friends. Zoe scared her a bit, if Poppy were being honest. But she'd been a good, solid roommate, and she'd kept a lid on all Poppy's secrets of late. "I'll bring you a bagel."

"I'll take it," Zoe said and lay back down.

As usual, Poppy took a military grade shower, cool and fast. When was the last time she took a long, hot, luxurious bath or shower? The weekend of Bailey's wedding, when she was in Texas.

George held the door for her on the way out of the apartment. They went to another one of her favorite restaurants for breakfast, this one bigger and more well known, though still of incredibly high quality. It was a place famous for its pastries, and Poppy felt a stab of envy for the bakers who worked there.

"You're so quiet, Poppy," George said.

"How do you know, George?" she asked, tipping her head to study him. "It's not like we've spent a lot of quality time together the last couple of years."

"No, but we text a lot and we talk in passing. I feel like I know you pretty well, and I can tell something is bothering you," he said.

She let out a breath. "I need to find a new place to live."

He sat up, alarmed. "What? Why? Did I do something?"

"No," she assured him. "You've been the perfect roommate. Most of the time it's like you're not even there." They shared a wry smile.

"Is it Zoe? Did she threaten to stab you one too many times? Because I'll talk to her. Legally, I could probably confiscate that knife."

She leaned forward. "Frankly, George, I think she could take you. But it's not Zoe. It's me. The multiple roommate thing, it's not working out so well for me. I need something with more space and privacy."

"Where are you going to find that?" he asked.

Their food arrived, saving her from an answer. "Let's talk about you for a bit," she said, purposely changing the subject. "How's work?"

"Good. Prospects are good, I can see the golden ladder before me," he replied. He had his sights on commissioner, and he would probably make it. Not only was he good at his job, but he had a stellar pedigree and people liked him.

"Excellent. How's life on the dating front? Are you seeing anyone special?"

He tipped his head at her. "Poppy, come on."

"What?" she asked.

He sighed. "Nothing. No, I am not seeing anyone special, no one besides the girl who shares my bed each night."

"You'd think I would get tired of that lame old joke but, no, it's still cute."

"What a coincidence, so is the girl who shares my bed each night."

She laughed. "Oh, George, you're a charmer. Hey, thank you for the tea a few weeks ago. That was so sweet. Peppermint hit the spot." Along with lemonade, it was one of the only things she could stomach.

"You're welcome. Thank you for the brownies, and thank you for putting them in plastic so the roaches and rats wouldn't use our bed as a new love nest."

She tapped her temple. "Always thinking ahead."

"You should be a cop. The best ones can see what's coming," he said. "Speaking of which," he leaned forward and took her hand. "What's going on with you? You've lost your Poppy sparkle, and if it's not drugs, I want to know what it is."

Poppy swallowed convulsively, pushing back the tears that seemed to be her constant companion lately. "I think I'm going to move to Texas."

He blinked at her, his jaw going slack. "What?"

"Texas," she whispered, dashing at her eyes.

"What's in Texas?" he asked, his voice sounding hoarse.

"Affordable housing."

"Hold on." He glanced at the check, opened his wallet, and removed some bills.

"George, you don't have to pay for me. I'm the one who asked you, remember," she said.

"Shh," he replied, taking her hand and leading her out of the restaurant. They rounded the corner and leaned on a wall in an alley away from the hustle and bustle of the busy street. "Start over. What were you saying?"

"I think I'm going to move to Texas."

"Do you *want* to move to Texas?"

"Less than anything," she said, sniffling again.

"Then you can't move to Texas," he said, his tone definitive.

"I have to."

"Why? And, so help me, Poppy, if you say affordable housing I'm going to…" he flailed, not knowing what would be drastic enough.

"I messed up, George," she said and the tears began to flow in earnest now.

"What are you talking about?"

"I did something irresponsible. It set off a chain reaction, and now everything is different. I have to leave this life, to start over somewhere different, somewhere affordable with a lot of free space, apparently."

"Are you talking about witness protection?" he asked, confused.

She gave a watery little laugh. "Something like that. I'm definitely planning to assume a new identity."

"Don't do this. Don't leave," he pled.

"I think I have to."

"Poppy," he whispered and then stepped forward and kissed her. Poppy had no idea if she wanted to respond or not. Either way the decision was out of her hands, thanks to her trigger-happy gag reflex. She backed up and bumped the wall behind her.

"I'm pregnant."

He stared at her, and the look on his face was… How was it possible to hurt someone so unintentionally? They weren't together, had never even shared a meal together before this morning. But the news of her pregnancy by another man was apparently more than George could stomach because he turned and stumbled out of the alley without another word.

CHAPTER 9

Sully sat at his desk, scrolling page after page of transcripts. For the last two years, he and his team had been investigating the Cortez family, a local crime syndicate. They were different from the cartels in two ways. For one, they were an old Texas family with roots going back before the Alamo. For another, they were not thugs and gang members. They were sophisticated, intelligent, connected. They dabbled in drugs, of course. It was impossible for a crime family not to, this close to the border. But they were also suspects in multiple other crimes: witness tampering, coercion, forgery, larceny, money laundering, and even murder. The problem, as it so often was with organized crime, was that it was organized. They were good, and they rarely to never messed up.

They had been on the Rangers' radar for decades, maybe even longer, possibly since Steve Austen and the first Texas Rangers. Occasionally over the years one of them would slip and get caught, but it was always something minor, and it always ended with a slap on the wrist. Most of the time they existed on the back burner. The change in priority happened five years ago when a sitting judge in San Antonio was murdered. Everyone knew the Cortez family either did it or ordered the hit. But no one had been able to prove it, and it was maddening. In reaction, the Rangers had begun to take an almost obsessive personal interest in the family, putting them under a microscope, looking for any flaw.

Sully was no different. Recently the son had taken over for the father, and Sully felt sure the new young blood would make a mistake. He was cockier than his father with a chip on his shoulder that said he had something to prove. Sully and his team had taken to baiting him, prodding him toward a screwup that would be like the final card in the deck before the entire house collapsed.

Eventually he became aware someone stood in his doorway. He looked up to see Bailey leaning against the jamb.

"Hey," she said. "Bad time?"

"No, my eyes need a break." He pushed the papers away from him. "What's up?"

"I know a secret," she said.

Thanks to her military training, she was often deadpan and expressionless, closely guarding whatever she might be feeling or thinking. Sully had no idea if she was angry or upset. His heart began to thump with dread, but instead of bumbling into a confession, he played it cool. "Yeah?"

She nodded. "And it concerns you."

"Me?" he echoed, wincing when his voice squeaked.

"Guess who's moving to Texas?" she said, striding forth to take the chair across from his desk.

Sully gripped the desk in front of him. Surely not… "Who?"

"My sister."

"Which one?" he croaked. Surely she would have told him if that were the case. Surely she wouldn't spring it on him as a surprise.

Bailey rolled her eyes. "Poppy, silly. Why would you care if Jane moved here? You don't even know her. I'm only telling you about Poppy because I think you're part of the reason she's moving here."

"I am?" he whispered and cleared his throat.

"She said after you pointed out her living situation, it made her see things with fresh eyes and she realized she needed to be somewhere more affordable with more space. I told her we have all the space she could ever want here, and then some."

"Yes," he agreed, nodding. "Space."

"Anyway, I'll let you get back to work. I wanted to pop in and say thanks."

"Please, please, please don't thank me," he said.

"Okay," she drawled. "Then how about I invite you to go out with us sometime after she gets here. Poppy likes action, adventure, and culture. We're going to have to show her the sights to keep her interested in our neck of the woods."

"Sounds good," he said definitively. They would need to have a sit down with Bailey and Cal. Perhaps together they could figure out a way to break the news and reveal his part in everything.

"I'm so excited," Bailey added. "It never occurred to me I might have a member of my family living here. I mean, Cam and Maggie have vaguely talked about maybe someday, but Jane is married to the Smithsonian, my dad will likely die in his office and continue to keep working, and Poppy loves New York so much..." she trailed off, shrugging with one shoulder. "Sorry, I'm rambling. I guess I'm shocked and overjoyed."

"Me too," he said, and she laughed.

"Now you're making fun of me."

"I'm not," he promised. This would be the solution to so many of his problems, and the start to so many others. He sighed as all the mixed emotions roiled inside him.

"I'll leave you to your work. Thanks for letting me blather on and share the joy," Bailey said, standing.

"Anytime," he said, giving her a little wave as she made her way out of his office. He picked up his work and tried to make sense of it again, but his brain was now mush. Poppy was moving here. His Poppy. No, not his Poppy. His baby, who Poppy now carried.

Oh, what a tangled web we weave, he thought, his head falling to his desk with a mixture of dread and anticipation.

After Bailey's announcement, Sully texted Poppy three times to try and verify if and when she was coming. He never heard back. For all he knew, his texts were going nowhere. For all he knew, she could be anywhere between New York and Texas. Maybe she was making good on her promise to disappear, going into the wind, shucking all responsibility along with modern society. She'd been raised in Africa; would she go back?

He was in the midst of wondering that very thing when he ran into her at the grocery store, literally. She bounced off his chest and would have tumbled over if he hadn't caught her and held her upright.

"I'm sorry," he started then, seeing who it was, amended it to, "What? How?"

"Surprise?" she said weakly.

"I'm going to kill you," he said, but he didn't mean it. He was glad to see her, deliriously so. She was safe; she was here. His eyes scanned her up and down, looking for changes, checking for a baby bump. By his calculations, she was ten weeks along now. But there was no bump. If anything, she looked thinner, practically gaunt.

"I'm sorry. It's been crazy, I mean seriously."

"We need to talk," he said. "Are you free tonight?"

"No. Rain check?"

"Tomorrow," he said.

"Yes." She gave him a nod and a smile and he found himself smiling in return. His hands were still on her biceps, and he became aware that people were likely staring at them.

"Have you ever lived in small town America before?" he asked.

"Does Washington DC count?" she asked.

"No. I feel the need to warn you about what's coming."

"What's coming?" she asked, smiling.

"Gossip, and lots of it. You and I are about to be the center of very public speculation."

"Doesn't bother me, but it's your home turf, chief. Are you braced?"

"Solidly," he assured her. A slow smile spread over his face.

"What's that smile for?" she asked.

"I got this idea to start off the gossip with a bang, but it's going to require a bit of sacrifice on your part," he said.

"It's important to me that you know I'm always game for any shenanigans," she said.

"In that case." He grabbed a nearby employee and handed him the gallon of milk he'd been carrying. "Can you put this back for me? I found something better." When his hands were empty, he bent, tucked his hands behind Poppy's knees and back, and carried her out of the store.

"Go big or go home, huh?" she asked.

"It's the Ranger way," he said. He pushed open the door with his foot, set her in the middle of the sidewalk, tucked her face between his palms, and kissed her. It wasn't a long kiss, nor an especially intense one, but it was enough to make a statement to anyone who was looking. And everyone was looking. "Welcome to Texas," he said and let her go.

"Wow, you park rangers really know how to make a girl feel special," she said, taking a step away from him.

"Come back here and let me show you all the ways I'm not a park ranger," he said.

"Pretty sure you already did that," she replied. She tossed him a wave and turned to head down the street.

CHAPTER 10

The next evening, Poppy arrived on Sully's doorstep with a basket of muffins.

"Peace offering," she declared, handing them over.

"I'm only accepting these because I'm being the bigger person and not because they look amazing," he said, poking his head into the basket. "Maybe you should consider doing this fulltime," he added, pinching a bite of the nearest muffin and popping it in his mouth.

"I'll give it some consideration," she said, following him inside. They went to the kitchen where he made a pot of coffee.

"I bought some decaf for you," he said.

"Thank you, that was sweet, although I have to tell you that I'm still at a twelve on the nausea scale."

"Still?" he exclaimed.

"Everything I've read says it should get better in the second trimester."

"And when is that exactly?" The pregnancy was a confusing mystery to him.

"Two more weeks," she said, crossing her fingers and holding them aloft. "Honestly, if it doesn't get better soon, I don't know how I'm going to survive. I've lost eight pounds."

"Poppy, that's not good. What did your doctor say about that?"

She shrugged. "I haven't been to one in a while. I need to find one here, preferably one who takes cash, seeing as how I no longer have insurance."

"I'll help you look into it. There are a few missions around that provide free or reduced care."

"Thanks," she said, frowning at the table.

"What's that look for?" The coffee finished. He poured himself a cup and offered her something else. She opted for milk, and he poured that before sitting down.

"I hate taking charity."

"Everyone needs a hand up sometimes," he said.

"Have you ever had to go to the free clinic for healthcare?" she asked.

"No, but when I was in school and a rookie trooper, I came close. Instead I just went without healthcare. Not an option in your case."

"I know, but it doesn't feel good. Honestly, Sully, this pregnancy thing has been way harder than I thought it would be. I had no idea I would be so sick, miserable, and exhausted. No idea all the ways it would change my life."

"I know, but you're here now," he said. He meant it as encouragement, but her expression grew dimmer.

"But I don't want to be here. I hate it here. I miss my job, I miss New York, I miss my friends." She sniffled and then it was if the dam burst and she started to cry, hard. Sully stood and pulled her into a hug.

"I'm sorry," he said, "I'm really sorry I got you into this fix."

"You didn't. Please stop apologizing or I'm not going to be able to confide in you, and I *need* to confide in you. You're the only person within a thousand miles who knows what I'm going through, who knows about the baby. We're both responsible, and I don't blame you, not at all, not even a little. It's just really hard right now, and I need a listening ear."

"I'll give you two, plus hugs and anything else you need or want, okay?"

She nodded and pressed a napkin to her face to try to push the tears back. When she succeeded, she sank into a chair again and began picking at a muffin.

"So tell me what's been going on," Sully said. "What brought you here exactly?"

"You were right. I couldn't do it in New York, I couldn't find a better place to live or a job with better hours. I tried so hard. I went everywhere, to everyone. I can't tell you how much I loathe failing at something I've set my mind to. It was fine to be twenty four, on my own, and doing those things. But I'm not on my own anymore, and I can't continue to think about what I want. I have to think about what the baby needs. As much as I hate to admit it, this is probably the best place for us to be for a while."

"It doesn't have to be forever," Sully said. "You can go back someday, restart your career, pick up where you left off."

She gave him a sorrowful look. "I think we both know that's not true. There aren't a lot of careers that work that way. Culinary is no different. You build your resume, take stepping stones to bigger and better until you arrive where you want to be. I was on my way. Now I'm literally nowhere."

"I'm s…" he began, but she gave him another look and he amended the apology. "So happy you're here, is totally what I intended to say. Are you staying with Bailey and Cal?"

"No, I rented a place."

"In town?"

"Yes. I don't have a car, so I need to be within walking distance of a job."

"Oh, a job, right. That might be a problem. I could see if we're hiring. We always need secretaries and clerks. That way we could ride together."

"No, I'm going to work here in town," she said, pointing to the table.

"There aren't any jobs in this town. I probably should have mentioned that when I tried to sell you on it," he said, giving her a sheepish smile.

She shrugged one shoulder. "It's fine, I'll manage."

He didn't comment further, but he doubted it was true. Unless she wanted to be a ranch hand, no one local was hiring. "When are we going to tell Bailey and Cal?"

"As soon as I get my job situation settled. I don't want to go to them being the dumb kid with no means to support myself. I'd like to at least give the appearance of being a capable adult," she said.

"I know it doesn't seem that way, but moving here was a step in the right direction. It was a mature decision, a selfless decision," he said.

"Someday hopefully I'll be able to see it that way. Right now it feels like one more failure." She paused and gave him a rueful smile. "I'm sorry, Sully. I'm terrible company right now. I fully realize I'm wallowing in self pity, but I seem unable to stop it. I'm weak, and exhausted, and nauseated, and it's making it incredibly difficult to do my normal bootstrap pulling."

"Poppy, we're friends now, and being with a friend means never having to fake it. Moving cross country and starting over is reason enough to feel unsettled and adrift, but you're also adding pregnancy in there. And it's all happened in a shockingly short amount of time. I don't think you're failing; I think you're doing great, far better than I would if I were you. I don't do change well."

"You're being very nice to me," she said.

"It's the least I can do after I knocked you up."

"The very least," she agreed, and he laughed.

"Let's move to the couch, it's more comfortable." He put their dishes in the sink and led the way to his sofa. "Where are you going to try and get a job? I might be able to offer some insight."

"I don't want to tell you. That way if it doesn't work out, I won't feel as disappointed," she said.

"How did George take your leaving?" he asked, but it was apparently the wrong thing to say because tears returned to her eyes and she shook her head.

"Not well. I haven't seen or spoken to him in the two weeks since I told him. I left him a letter, saying goodbye and sorry, but I don't know exactly what I was sorry for. He and I weren't together. We never had a date, never expressed feelings for each other. We handed off the bed, left each other the occasional note, and texted most days. But our texts were always fun, friendly, lighthearted teasing. I could show you, to prove to you we were nothing more than friends."

"I believe you," he said.

"Then why do I feel so guilty, like I cheated on him and broke his heart?" she asked, sniffling and dabbing at her eyes with a napkin to stop any tears from escaping. She was turning into a crybaby, and she hated it. Stupid pregnancy hormones.

"Because it's highly likely you have unrealized feelings for him, and I'm positive he has them for you. I get the sense he believes you're his destiny, and now his destiny has been ripped away. That has to hurt. I'm sure he's not upset with you personally, just hurt over the change in the plans he had for your future."

"What plans for our future?" she asked, baffled.

"Transitioning your weird roommate thing into an actual relationship, falling in love, getting married, living happily ever after."

She gave up the pretense of trying not to cry and burst into loud, weepy tears instead. Sully pulled her into a hug and rubbed her back soothingly while she cried for a while. Eventually the weeping died down to hiccups, until he realized she was asleep. She had to be exhausted, and he felt terrible. Despite her protest to the contrary, he knew it was his fault she was in the shape she was in. If he hadn't gotten her pregnant, she wouldn't be so sick and miserable. She wouldn't have had to quit a job she loved or move to a place she detested. But she had, and now it was up to him to help take care of her, to help make the best of a bad situation for her. Meanwhile he got to remain healthy, unchanged in the job he loved, in the town he loved, surrounded by all the people he loved. The imbalance was incredibly unfair, but he had no idea how to fix it.

After a while she curled into a little ball, her head resting on his leg. He covered her with an afghan, thinking, his hand making soothing passes over her hair. He wasn't merely responsible for his child now; he was responsible for Poppy. There was a part of him that recoiled from the knowledge. She was twenty four, not done growing up yet, admittedly headstrong and impulsive. And from now on they were inexorably linked. Whatever she did would be a reflection on him, on his reputation and relationships with people in the community. Though they had made strides in their friendship, they still barely knew each other. What if she had some horrible personality disorder and couldn't get along with others? What if her impulsive decision making led her into something destructive, something that might even affect his job? Part of his job was maintaining the image of the Rangers; he had to be above reproach. It was bad enough he'd gotten a woman pregnant out of wedlock. What if that woman turned out to be crazy?

There was a not so small part of him that wished she hadn't left New York, even though he was the one who'd suggested she come. When she was there, she was out of sight and out of mind. He could give her money and ease his conscience because it was all he could do. But now here, in his town, in his *home,* he was going to have to be a hands-on provider, and he was beginning to realize that meant more than monetarily providing for her. He was going to have to be her keeper, to make sure she was doing okay, both physically and emotionally, probably much the same as if they were husband and wife. It was a massive responsibility, one he felt ill prepared for. He sighed under the weight of it. Poppy stirred and sat up.

"Oh, geez, I'm sorry," she said.

"It's fine," he assured her, but he wondered if some of what he'd been thinking was still on his face because it felt as if she withdrew from him, and not just physically. She sat up and handed him the afghan.

"I think I'll go home," she said. "Thanks for the milk and sympathetic ear. And shoulder. And lap, apparently."

"Don't go. We'll watch a movie or something."

"Thanks, but no. I have a lot to do." She stood.

He stood. "Let me walk you home." He felt doubly guilty now, both for her misery and for his thoughts about her. Did she actually know what he'd just been thinking? That, for the briefest second, she had felt like an albatross? He hoped not. He was all she had here. Until she knew about the pregnancy, Bailey didn't count. It was all on him, and he was already failing.

"That's sweet, but I'm good. It's only a few blocks, thanks to this small town thing you've got going on." She patted his arm. "Have a good night, Sully."

"You too, Poppy. Call if you need anything."

"Will do," she said, but the words rang hollow. Somehow he had the feeling he had managed to alienate her, to push her away and he both wanted her to go and wanted her to come back. In the end he did nothing but stand by and watch her leave.

CHAPTER 11

Poppy had exactly one chance to get things right, but she couldn't let herself believe that or she might have some kind of breakdown. So she feigned enthusiasm and went to the town's only diner, a small place eponymously named *Huck's* after the owner, Huck. She took a seat at the counter and asked to speak with him.

He was a big, hairy guy, but unlike the ubiquitous image of cigarette smoking hash slingers, he was immaculately clean, as was his restaurant. Poppy liked that a lot. She wouldn't be able to stomach working anywhere dirty, quite literally. Her stomach pitched and rolled with nausea, but she had learned how to mostly ignore it over the last several weeks and she did so now.

"What can I do for you, darlin'?" he asked in a strong Texas twang. He rested his massive forearms on the counter and offered her a smile that was fatherly and wholesome, further putting Poppy at ease.

"It might be a matter of what I can do for you, Mr. Huck. My name is..."

He put up a hand and interrupted her. "I know who you are, sweetie. You're Poppy Dunbar, Bailey Ridge's sister, Sully's new girl."

Poppy blinked at him. "Sully and I are just friends. The rest of it is correct, though. I'm here because..."

He interrupted again. "You're here because you're a good cook and you need a job. Darlin', I'd love to help you out, truly, but I do all the cookin', and I got enough waitresses. There just isn't enough work or money to go around." He looked regretful, heartbreakingly so. Poppy could read the pity for her in his eyes and tried hard to ignore it. She was not a charity case; she was a businesswoman with a business proposition. She sat up slightly, stiffening her shoulders.

"Have you ever heard of a pop up restaurant?" she said it fast, lest he interrupt her again.

He blinked at her. "No, can't say as I have."

"It's like a restaurant within a restaurant. Usually they operate at differing hours, but they share the kitchen. Either the second restaurant pays the first one rent or sells items on commission."

He squinted. "I cain't hardly see what you're gettin' at, sugar. You want to open a restaurant here in the middle of the night? You might get a few truckers, but not much else."

"I don't want to open an entire restaurant. I'm a pastry chef. I propose opening a bakery within your restaurant, selling baked goods that would complement the menu you already have. I'll keep to that portion of the counter down there where you have the pies." She pointed. "I'll use the kitchen in the wee hours of the morning and have it cleaned and ready for you by the time you open. Then I'll sell my baked goods and get out of your hair. I'll buy my own supplies and give you a percentage of my profits."

He squinted, thinking. "That sounds real nice, but I have to be frank with you. This is a small town with a lot of regulars who are set in their ways. I don't have a lot of faith they'll be willin' to take a chance on a newcomer, even if she has town connections."

"That may be so, but it would seem you have nothing to lose by letting me try," she said.

"Now that part is true. Go ahead and try, and I wish you well." He gave her a big smile that warmed her lonely, secretly insecure heart. He stood upright to move away, but she hailed him back.

"There's one more thing."

Now he gave her an amused look. "Knowing your sister, I shoulda figured there might be."

"Who does your pies?" she asked.

"A place in San Antonio," he replied.

"They're horrible. Let me do them instead. It can be the one thing you buy outright from me, and it will allow you to advertise that they're made fresh daily in house."

He tilted his head at her. "Can you actually make pies? People around here are picky about them."

This time when she smiled she wasn't faking her confidence. "Oh, I can make pies."

"Well, then, it looks like we got ourselves a deal." He held out his hand for her to shake.

She did so, standing to reach him better. "Excellent. Go cancel your pie orders for tomorrow. I'll start tonight. And I'm going to need a key to the restaurant."

"Anything else?" he asked, his tone wry.

"I'll let you know." Feeling ridiculously happy over the small gain, she waltzed out of the restaurant and removed her phone, wanting to text someone, anyone with the news. She paused, thumbs aloft over the phone. The development was fresh, and it felt vulnerable. Poppy's gut reaction was to text George, and she stopped short. Somehow she hadn't realized that he had become that person for her, the one she shared her inmost heart with. But she couldn't text George. Not only was he not hers, but he was no longer speaking to her. She blinked back the tears and considered texting Sully. She might have, if not for the look on his face last night after her mental breakdown and subsequent nap. It had been too much for him, the revelation into her inner struggles. She shouldn't have laid all that on him, but she was so desperate for some sort of reassurance that she wasn't throwing her life away by giving up everything and moving here. The look on his face last night had been the opposite of reassuring.

However, she did need information, and he might be the only one who could provide it. So she texted him a generic question.

Can you give me the name of a good pecan guy?

He replied a second later. *Pecan guys are notoriously bad husbands and fathers.*

She laughed. *Thank you for your continued belief in both my desperation and promiscuity.*

He texted a few seconds later with the name and number of a local pecan farmer and, happy to concentrate on work for a while, Poppy made the call and arranged for a delivery.

While her situation was a bit direr than she'd like, it wasn't as if she had no money in savings. Her parents had been clear on the need to save money, to prepare for the future and emergencies. Poppy didn't own a car and she didn't have health insurance, but she had seven thousand dollars in the bank. It would have to be enough to start her fledgling business, to buy the supplies she needed.

She already had the tools, things like pans, measuring cups, etc. Those were items she had been accumulating since culinary school. They and her clothes were the only items she owned, the only items she brought from New York. All she needed were ingredients, and that proved to be tricky. The local grocery store had some basics, but they didn't carry the large quantities she would need, and they didn't have the high quality she desired.

The pecan guy led her to a local dairy that would provide her with butter and cream. She went to the library and used the free internet to order vanilla and Belgian chocolate, planning to make do until they arrived in a few days. She already had a menu in her head, but today she wrote it down. She had researched what the locals ate, knowing instinctively that Parisian baked goods probably wouldn't go over well in tiny, small town Texas. The pecan was king here, and Poppy planned to use it liberally, both with a pecan pie and pecan sticky rolls. Kolaches were something new, a local favorite she had never made before. She loved trying new things and experimenting. She had spent the last couple of days researching recipes, trying them out until she perfected her own twist. Along with the pies, sticky buns, and kolaches, she planned to make brioche jam-filled donuts and a coffee cake with pecan streusel. In time she might add more to her menu, such as brownies and cookies, but for now that would be enough.

Once she got to know people better, she also hoped to add some cake orders to her repertoire, both wedding and birthday. Those she could do in her own kitchen on her off hours, padding what would likely be a meager income. If she didn't have to worry about health insurance, she would probably be okay. Rent was cheap here, and so was the cost of living, especially without the cost of car ownership, maintenance, or gasoline. But the need for health insurance loomed on her horizon like a thundercloud. Having a baby in a hospital was exorbitantly expensive. Without insurance, she might spend the rest of her life trying to pay for it. But how could she afford insurance on what she would soon be making? For a self-employed woman her age who needed maternity coverage, it would be over a thousand dollars a month, and it barely covered anything. She had no idea how much her new job would bring in, if anything. It might be an utter failure, but as it was all she had, she had to try.

CHAPTER 12

Sully hadn't heard from Poppy in a few days. Their last meeting ended on a weird note, and he felt the need to give her some space for a bit. Or maybe he needed space. He wasn't certain. All he knew was that things with her were going to be more complicated than he first realized.

His job was busy, but he liked it that way. It kept him from thinking too much. Most of his day was spent on patrol, but occasionally he was in the office working on the Cortez investigation. They were so close, he could feel it, could sense the impending crack in the case. If they kept up pressure on Diego Cortez, the new heir apparent, they were sure to get something usable.

Sheila, his secretary, set a plate on his desk. "Thank you," Sully said distractedly. She was only a decade older than him, but she was the motherly sort, always making sure he and everyone else in the office ate and took proper care of themselves. He took a bite of whatever it was almost absently and then set aside his paperwork and did a double take. Before him sat a massive pecan roll, dripping with sticky syrup and overflowing with pecan halves. Sully devoured it in four bites and then went to find some answers.

It took him a while to track Sheila down; the woman was seemingly always on the move. "Sheila, did you make that sticky bun?" he asked, an appropriate amount of awe in his tone. Her former home-made baked goods had been, er, lacking to say the least.

She laughed. "Are you joking, Sully? You know I can't cook like that. I got it from the new bakery."

He stared, his brain stuttering over the information. "New bakery?" Surely not, there was no way she could open a whole bakery here, no way one would survive.

Sheila gave him an exasperated once over. "Child, come out of your own world once in a while and take a look around. There is a new bakery inside *Huck's*."

"Inside *Huck's*," he repeated dumbly.

"Inside *Huck's*," she affirmed, tilting her head at him. "I might have thought you would know this already, seeing as how it's Poppy Dunbar who opened it."

"Uh, no," he murmured, feeling slightly embarrassed over his lack of foreknowledge. His almost omniscient secretary understood there was something between him and Poppy, though she couldn't yet puzzle together what it was. Come to think of it, neither could he. How could she open an entire bakery without even telling him? Then again, he hadn't exactly reached out to her since that last night at his house, when she had seemed to read his thoughts about her. "How's it doing?"

"Like gangbusters. I mean, you tasted it and you know how we feel about our pecan rolls here. She has other things, too. It's all the buzz in town, both her appearance and the new food. She's sold out every day she's been in business."

"She has?" Sully said, shocked.

Sheila nodded. "Boy, maybe you need to get on over to the diner for lunch today."

"Maybe I do," he agreed.

"Have the pie. Trust me."

"I've had *Huck's* pie," Sully said, grimacing.

Sheila rolled her eyes. "Sometimes you are really dense, Sullivan.

It's not *Huck's* pie anymore. It's Poppy's pie, and it will change your world. Much like the girl herself, if you take my hint."

"The rocks outside in the driveway take your hint, Sheila," he said.

"Well, then, let's hope you're smarter than a rock. You missed out on the sister. Don't let this one get away from you, too."

"It's not that simple," he said.

"Honey, it never is," she replied, turning her back on him and resuming her copies.

Sully wandered back to his office and tried to make his mind focus on work, but he couldn't. He stared at the far wall, thinking. Mostly he thought about Poppy, and he thought about himself. He had been a heel. Again, this time in thought, if not in deed. He asked her to come here, and then when she arrived he had second thoughts, selfish thoughts about how her presence and pregnancy would reflect on him. So she struggled; so she was messy. So what? It reflected worse on him if she was those things and he didn't take care of her than if she was those things and he did take care of her. He made up his mind that, no matter what, she would be a vital part of his life, regardless of who she was or what she did. It was the sort of commitment he thought he made when he found out she was pregnant, but it turned out that time had been in theory only. This time he meant it in practice. Poppy was his responsibility. He would not let her down again.

With that resolved, he put on his hat and walked to the diner.

Huck's had been the same for as long as Sully could remember. When Huck assumed it from the former owner, whose name Sully couldn't remember, he had left all the decorations in place, swapping only the sign out front proclaiming his name instead of the last guy's. The decorations were and had always been a faded assortment of Texas paraphernalia. But now the far corner had been transformed by a colorful display of glass cake stands. They were fresh and pretty, much like the woman herself who stood behind the counter wearing one of her floral dresses, her hair held back in a scarf and tucked to one side, tumbling gently over one shoulder.

Sully was so focused on her it took him a minute to realize she was immersed in a smiling conversation with one of Cal's ranch hands,

Jonah, the eldest son of his foreman, Jinx. One day soon Jonah would likely take over for Jinx as foreman. He was a good guy, and Sully had always liked him. Not today, though.

He strode to the counter and stood close beside Jonah, waiting to be noticed. Jonah did so eventually and jumped slightly as if he'd been caught, which he had. "Hey there, Sully," he said, adding a sheepish smile.

"Hey, Jonah. Fancy seeing you here in the middle of the morning on a workday," Sully said, a not so pointed reminder that he should be far away on his ranch.

"Cal sent me for a baked goods run. Bailey requested a few dozen chocolate chip cookies," he said, holding a box aloft.

"Her favorite," Poppy added helpfully.

"It would seem you have them now. Give the Ridges my best on your return," Sully said.

"Will do," Jonah replied. To Poppy he added. "Thank you for these. Good talking to you."

"You, too. See you on Sunday."

"See you," Jonah said, a bit perkier now. He tipped his hat before turning to walk out of the diner.

Poppy faced Sully. "Would you like to come around here and lick me, just so everyone makes sure to get the point?"

"Yes, in fact I would," he said, and she laughed.

"I'm beginning to understand why everyone in this town keeps referring to me as your girl."

He leaned forward slightly. "You are my girl."

She leaned forward, too. "I think not, Park Ranger Sullivan."

He nodded. "It's factual information. Everyone says so. Have dinner with me and we'll solidify it in people's minds."

She leaned closer and whispered. "I'm sorry, but I have this rule that I can only have dinner with a man when I'm carrying his child."

He grinned. "It would seem today is my lucky day all around. First I had the world's best sticky bun, and now I get to have dinner with its creator. PS. Thanks for filling me in on your life. I always appreciate hearing news secondhand from my secretary."

"I prefer to keep my cards close and, I don't know, it would seem I've spewed a bit too much in your general direction lately." She busied herself straightening a cake stand that was already perfectly aligned.

He shook his head. "Don't say that, Poppy. We're in this together, all the way. I want to know what's going on with you, and I plan to be involved in everything, even if I have to force my way in like an unwanted puppy."

"Is there such a thing as an unwanted puppy? Not in my world," she said.

They shared a smile, and he tapped the case. "I've been told to try the pie. Which do you recommend with my lunch?"

She glanced at the clock. "Do you always eat lunch at eleven in the morning, Ranger Sullivan?"

"I was especially hungry today, Baker Poppy."

"Baker Poppy makes me sound like we live in Salem in the seventeenth century. Might as well call me Goody Housewife and chastise me for dabbling in witchcraft."

"If that's what you're into," Sully offered, and she laughed.

She reached beneath the counter and presented him with a plate. "Lucky you, this is the last piece of pecan pie."

It was massive, at least three inches tall and loaded with an overdose of unbroken pecan halves. Sully whistled appreciatively. "I can definitely see why this pie has been the talk of the town. How much do I owe you?"

"Buy me dinner tonight, and we'll call it even," she said.

He leaned in to whisper. "I only buy dinner for the women I've gotten pregnant."

"What a creative way of being a tightwad," she said, and he laughed as he took the pie, purposely brushing his fingers on hers. "You are shamelessly proprietary."

"I feel a little shame, but mostly for the deprivation I'm causing other men," he said.

She rolled her eyes. "Are these the lines you actually use on women?"

"Yes. Are you they not working on you?"

"A smidge," she admitted.

"Well, I have a few hours between now and tonight to see what I can do to crank that up a few notches. Thank you for the pie, Baker Poppy."

"God be with thee, Ranger Sullivan," she said, pressing her hands together prayerfully.

Laughing, Sully turned and went to find a seat.

CHAPTER 13

Freight robberies weren't common in the United States. They were in China and gaining popularity in Europe. But now Texas had joined the party. It was an invitation Sully wished he could rescind. A moving crime scene, sixty miles per hour to be exact. What a nightmare. He might wonder if the danger was worth the reward, but so far nearly a million in freight had been stolen—jewels, tech, even shoes. There were thousands of trucks on the road at any one time. Predicting which one would be hit next was an exercise in futility. Worse, they knew it was the Cortez family but, like always, couldn't catch them at it.

Their best bet was to stage a semi and hope for attack, which was how he now found himself in full tactical gear, stuffed in the back end of a semi, barreling down a lonely stretch of highway. It was even hotter and more airless than he thought it would be. Sweat poured off his face and soaked his shirt.

"Man, I wish I had my ukulele," Garcia, to his left, whispered. Every cop had a persona. Sully was Sanguine Cop, mellow and cheerful until he wasn't and then look out. When he turned mean, everyone knew it was because he had a reason to be. But Sanguine Cop was a far cry from Class Clown Cop. That was Garcia, always butting in with a stupid or inappropriate joke to make them laugh. Or annoy them.

"Man, shut up," Lopez hissed. He was Perpetually Annoyed Cop. Far from being a hothead, he'd merely seen enough of humanity not to want to see it anymore. Not surprisingly, he was a decade older than everyone but the lieutenant who maintained the privilege of calling their plays from an air-conditioned mobile unit. "One thousand frickin' degrees in here, and you're talking about a guitar. Wish I had a guitar right now. I'd garrote you with it."

"I'd sing us all a song right now," Garcia continued undaunted. "Like Kermit."

Across the trailer, Harris snickered. Harris was Laughs Inappropriately Cop, the one who found the humor in the worst situations possible at the worst possible time. Somehow he and Garcia always ended up together, joking and laughing until steam came out of Lopez's ears. And Sully, Sanguine Cop, watched it all with a passive smile.

"Kermit played a banjo, you frickin' moron," Lopez hissed.

"Kermit lover says what," Garcia pretended to cough and Harris lost it, doubling over, shoulders shaking with silent laughter.

"Ah, man, I hate you morons," Lopez groused, but everybody knew he lied. For better or worse, they were a brotherhood. Why else would they be cramped in the back of an airless, windowless semi, hoping against hope they'd be attacked?

"Movement," the lieutenant hissed in their ears, and everybody went silent and sat up, gripping their weapons.

The semi slowed suddenly, exactly as if someone had cut in front of it and tapped the brakes. *This is it,* Sully thought. He could feel it. As if to prove his theory, the back doors of the semi swung open. Two men rappelled down from the truck's roof. There was a breathless second when the Rangers stared at the thieves. Sully made direct eye contact with one. The man wore a balaclava, obscuring all of his face, minus his eyes. They were eyes Sully recognized. Cold. Lifeless. Black. The eyes of Diego Cortez. *Gotcha,* Sully thought.

Except he didn't. There was a swirl of activity, a burst of gunfire from both sides, and then the intruders were gone, as quickly and easily as they'd arrived.

"Freakin' ninjas," Lopez said, tossing aside his cap in disgust.

For once, Harris didn't laugh.

"You sure it was Cortez?" his lieutenant asked Sully for the third time.

"I'd stake my life on it," Sully replied. He knew those eyes. He'd spent the last four years tracking them. The problem, as always, was the lack of concrete proof. He couldn't take a man into court and tell the jury he knew it was him by his psychotic eyes.

The lieutenant sighed, expressing their combined frustration. The Rangers were elite, the best Texas had to offer. Being one step behind a notorious crime family was a blow to their well-deserved pride. "Next time," the lieutenant said, trying to rally spirits.

Sully was usually the first to rally, but today he stared into the distance, feeling more than frustrated. He felt disturbed. In that moment he recognized Diego Cortez, he could swear Diego Cortez recognized him in return. And both of them seemed to be thinking the same thing. *Now it's personal.*

CHAPTER 14

Poppy was pleased. Her first week in business, she grossed a thousand dollars. Of course she had to pay for her supplies, and taxes, and the commission to Huck. She had tried to give him the industry standard of thirty percent, but he had generously waived it down to ten. "You hardly cost me a thing except a mite of electricity in the middle of the night, and you're bringing a lot of people to the diner." That part was true. Many people had arrived merely out of curiosity, though most of those bought her baked goods and not diner fare. But people were ordering a lot of pie, sometimes whole pies to take home, and that was a win for both of them. The pecan pie was especially popular, drawing an almost cult like following already. Poppy could hardly make enough of it.

She had been doing her part to advertise the new venture, putting pictures on social media and sending word of the new restaurant to her food contacts in New York. She also sent some photos to a food writer in San Antonio, along with several local food bloggers. So far she hadn't heard back from any of them, but it had only been a couple of days.

The following Sunday Bailey invited Poppy and Sully for lunch. Poppy and Sully agreed it was the perfect time to spring their news, though they were both incredibly nervous to do so. Now that Poppy's nausea showed the first signs of abating, she began to develop a tiny bump. Their secret wouldn't stay hidden much longer.

"Everyone's going to know immediately if you don't stop staring," Poppy warned Sully. He was fascinated by the tiny little swell, barely able to keep his eyes off it, or his hands when they were alone. Things between them were still planted firmly in the realm of friendship, but the new bump tested those boundaries as it had seemingly amped up Sully's attraction to her. Poppy tried to hold him at bay for both their sakes. It was a reaction to the change in her body and not a desire to be with her on any sort of permanent basis. She knew, even if he had a difficult time remembering.

"It's so miraculous," he said, his right hand resting on her bump while his left hand gripped the steering wheel.

"You know what's miraculous? The fact that food is beginning to smell and taste good again," Poppy said. She both looked and sounded healthier and stronger than she had in months. The pale, sickly pallor of her cheeks was gone, replaced by a rosy flush. He wondered if it was the pregnancy glow he'd heard about. If so, he could see why it was called such. She practically shimmered with health and good cheer, a far cry from where she'd been even a couple of weeks ago.

"It's amazing what sustenance can do for a body," he agreed, his hand making a little pass over her abdomen. He wanted to pull the truck over, to reach for her and…

"Easy there, park ranger," Poppy said, pushing his hand away from her belly.

He sucked a breath and put both hands on the wheel. "Right, sorry." She drove him crazy. The feel of her, the smell of her, the nearness of her. It was like a physical craving he couldn't satisfy because of the many barriers between them, not least of which was the fact that she was already carrying his child, but that only made him want her more. He knew it was a physical reaction to the pregnancy. Maybe it was biological, a primal protective thing. Maybe males were hardwired to respond to their pregnant females. All he knew was that he had never had this sort of addictive reaction to anyone, and if it didn't find some relief soon, he might actually die from it.

Mercifully, they arrived at the ranch a short time later. Sully opened the door and inhaled deeply. It smelled of manure, but he was thankful. Anything was better than being trapped in the cab of his truck with the overwhelming scent of Poppy, so close, so off limits. As always lately, his eyes found her and zeroed in her belly, the itty-bitty bump visible only to someone who knew to look for it, someone like him, the maker of said bump. His heart kicked into high gear, and he forced his eyes away, to Cal who was now advancing on them with a smile.

"Come into the barn and see our new feeder calf. You can give it a bottle," he said to Poppy who clapped her hands in delight.

"I'll nip into the kitchen, see if Bailey needs help," Sully said, glad to put some space between himself and Poppy, the mother of his child, the bearer of his seed, the...*Stop, you pathetic moron.* Shaking his head as if to clear it, he went toward the house in search of Bailey.

"Hey, I'm here to help," he announced, stepping to the sink to wash his hands.

"Great, want to pour the tea?" she said, not bothering to turn from her task at the stove.

"Is it caffeinated?" he asked, knowing Poppy wouldn't want it if it was. She was doing well at sticking to a healthy diet and limiting her caffeine intake.

"No, I made decaf," she said.

"Huh," he said, musing over the odd coincidence of Bailey making decaf tea when her sister was unable to have caffeine.

"I'm hearing lots of rumors about you and my sister," Bailey said in the usual deadpan way that gave nothing away and sent Sully into shivers of panic.

"You are? Like what?"

"Like that you carried her out of the store and kissed her in the middle of the street," Bailey said.

He smiled over the memory. "Oh, right. That one's true." Now she did turn to look at him. "What? She's hot and highly kissable," he added, his tone defensive.

"Oh, I know, and I'm not surprised at you because you're like that." She tipped her head and gave him a derisive look, a reminder of when he had tried to hit on her and failed horribly. "I'm surprised by her."

"She thought it would be funny to fuel the town gossip," he explained.

"That part sounds like her, but you are so not her type."

"Why not?" he asked, and now he was definitely defensive.

"You're too clean. She goes for artists, chefs, singers, guys with piercings and tattoos."

"What about George? He's none of those things," Sully pointed out.

"I know, that's why we all wanted it to work. We thought maybe she would grow up a bit, get over her pull toward bad boys, and go for someone nice. Someone like George." She sighed. "I wonder what happened there. Poppy hasn't mentioned him. Did she mention him to you?"

"Yes, she mentioned him. Things didn't end well. George didn't take kindly to the move."

"Poor George," Bailey said.

"Poor George," Sully agreed.

"I'm glad you guys have hit it off and become friends, in any case. She needs someone young to hang out with. What have you been doing together? Have you taken her to San Antonio? The rodeo? Anywhere fun?"

"I…" he faltered. He had done none of those things with Poppy. Why not? If she were any other girl, he would have. *Because you've become complacent, that's why.* He knew Poppy and he were indelibly connected now because of the baby, so he hadn't tried to impress her, hadn't done anything really, other than eat supper with her on most nights. "No."

"What do you guys do together? If rumors are to be believed, you're together most evenings."

"We eat supper." That had been his idea. She had once said food was the basis of community. Sully thought they should try to eat together every night, to build up their friendship before the baby arrived. "She's usually pretty zonked because she gets up at three every morning."

"Wow, okay. Try to keep it to a dull roar, party animal. Way to ring out the end of your twenties. With *supper*." She rolled her eyes.

"I'll try to step up the entertainment factor," he promised.

"You'd better or someone else will swoop in and do it for you," Bailey warned.

He laughed. "Not likely."

She put her hands on her hips. "Just what are you saying about my sister?"

"Nothing," he said, backing away slightly. "I don't think she's in the market for love right now is all."

"Take it from someone who knows, Sully. That's when love finds you, when you're not looking."

"I'll second that," Cal said, pausing to pick her up and plant a kiss on her cheek as he entered the kitchen, followed by Poppy who came to Sully's side and gave him a smile. He resisted the urge to kiss her cheek and then thought, *why not,* as he leaned forward and did it.

"What's that about?" she asked, reaching around him for a carrot stick.

"Because you fed a calf. Texas law says after the first time you feed a baby calf, you get a kiss," he said.

"Wait until you see what happens after the first time you pull one," Cal said.

"She's too young for that," Bailey said, and Poppy and Sully studiously avoided each other's gaze.

Lunch was a nerve-wracking event, at least for Poppy and Sully. At the end of it, they would tell their news. They were both prepared to flee for their lives, if it became necessary. They cut the cake Poppy had brought and had just finished the last bite when Bailey spoke.

"So, Poppy, we're so ecstatic you're here," she said.

Poppy looked at her, blinking in surprise. Her sister wasn't one for a lot of gooey emotion. "Thank you. I'm settling in as well as can be expected."

Bailey nodded. "I'm glad to hear it."

Poppy took a breath. "Actually," she began. Sully rested his hand on her leg beneath the table, giving it an encouraging squeeze. She clasped his hand and held on tight, but Bailey preempted her.

"You're going to be an aunt," she blurted, then clamped both hands over her mouth.

"I'm…I'm…what?" Poppy said.

"You're pregnant?" Sully said in the same disbelieving tone.

Bailey nodded enthusiastically, tears flooding her eyes. Cal reached for her and held her close.

"Oh, my…when are you due?" Poppy asked.

"July fifteenth," Bailey said.

Poppy and Sully shared a look. They were due July fourteenth. Poppy started to laugh and then stood and hugged Bailey. "Congratulations. Oh, this is wonderful, amazing news. I am so, so, so happy for you. Isn't it great, Sully?" she prompted him because he remained frozen staring into space.

He snapped forward and stood, hand outstretched toward Cal. "Congratulations, Dad. I can imagine how you're feeling right now."

"Ecstatic doesn't begin to describe," Cal said, looking at Bailey with all the love in his heart, perhaps all the love in the world.

"I know," Sully blurted. "I mean, that's what I imagined you'd be feeling."

"Why'd you wait until your second trimester to tell us?" Poppy asked.

"Wow, you did some quick mental calculations there to figure out how far along I am. I waited because I didn't know for a long time."

"You had no symptoms?" Poppy said, incredulous. She'd known practically since conception. Everything in her body had been off, wonky, and frankly horrible.

Bailey shook her head.

"No sickness?" Poppy said, her voice rising with affront.

Bailey cocked her head at her. "No, it doesn't happen for everyone. I finally took a test, and when I went to the doctor I was already ten weeks along."

"A honeymoon baby," Sully said. He put his arm around Poppy and gave her a squeeze because she still looked like she wanted to pop her sister in her face for her unfair lack of nausea.

"It would seem so," Bailey said.

"This is so wild," Poppy said. "So, so wild."

Bailey laughed. "It's just a baby. People have them all the time."

"Yes, but…" she trailed off, giving Sully a helpless look. He shook his head slightly. Now was not the time to impart their news. Let Cal and Bailey wallow in their unmitigated joy.

"But we know how long Cal's been waiting for this, and that makes it that much better," Sully said, giving Cal a slap on the back. "Congratulations again, we could not be more thrilled."

Bailey looked between them. "You're speaking of each other in the plural now. Are you guys actually together?"

"No," Poppy and Sully agreed at the same time.

"Friends," Sully said.

"Just friends," Poppy added.

"I wouldn't say 'just,'" Sully countered.

"Really, incredibly not helping," she said, linking her arm with his.

"I'm so confused right now," Bailey said, her assessing gaze traveling slowly between them.

"We bonded, and we're good pals," Poppy said. "Now let's get back to the baby. Are you going to find out the sex?"

"I don't know, we haven't decided. I want to but Cal wants to be surprised."

"Definitely seems like the kind of thing a couple should talk about," Sully said, darting Poppy a glance. They hadn't had that conversation yet.

"I'm guessing we all know who's going to win this one," Cal said. "And, really, I don't care. I'll be happy with whichever. And we'll have lots more chances for whatever comes next."

Poppy felt the pressing need to get away, to process the new information. Also Sully eyed her belly again, and she needed to get him out before he started touching it. She was going to have to buy bear spray to get him to keep his distance. "So, so happy for you," she said, hugging her sister again before gathering her purse to take her leave.

Sully opened the door to the truck for her and waited until she was safely inside before closing it. He jogged to his side and started it. They waited to talk until they were a couple of miles down the road.

"That was unexpected," Poppy said at last.

"You know what I keep thinking?" Sully said.

"What?" She hoped he would have some insight into the new twist. Or at least an idea of when and how to tell them their news, in light of Bailey's pregnancy.

"I wonder if we were making these babies at the exact same time."

"Ew." She pressed her hands to her ears. "What kind of weird sicko wonders that?"

"The scientific kind. I mean, come on, chances are high that…"

She reached out and pressed her hand over his mouth. "Never finish that sentence, and I'll let you touch the bump again."

He nodded, his lips pressed tightly together. She dropped her hand and he reached out, settling his hand possessively over her belly. "You're going to have a cousin," he whispered, and her heart turned over. She talked to the baby all the time, but it was the first time he'd done so.

CHAPTER 15

The next week several things happened. The first was that Poppy realized she could no longer fake it in her old clothes. She had already moved her bra to the last clasp and cut slits in several pairs of underwear. On Monday when she woke at three AM, groggy and disoriented, the bra wouldn't even stay on the last clasp. She had to safety pin it and hope and pray it didn't pop open and jab her. The dresses, too, were incredibly tight, causing her cleavage to pop over the top way too aggressively for a small town baker. Much as she didn't want to, she would have to break into her savings and buy some maternity clothes.

The second thing to happen, later that same morning, was that she received a text from George.

I miss you, P, he wrote, and that was all.

I miss you, too, she replied. She waited for more, but nothing came. She wanted to text him back, to go over the letter she'd written him, the one apologizing for things she couldn't articulate, simply a vague sense of guilt at having hurt him. But that wouldn't help. George apparently needed time and space. Even her moving away to Texas wasn't enough for him to yet recover, telling her the wound had gone even deeper than she knew. She sniffed and blinked back a few tears.

Her emotions had evened out in the last couple of weeks, and she wouldn't be sucked back onto the rollercoaster or give in to yet another crying jag.

The third thing that happened came in the form of a new customer to the bakery. By now Poppy began to familiarize herself with the regulars. In addition to those who came every day for their morning muffin or doughnut or sweet roll, there were a few who put in larger orders for a pan of rolls, an entire pie or cake, a dozen donuts. Those she didn't see as often as the daily set, but she could still mostly recognize them and remember many of their names. When a new woman strode purposefully to the counter, Poppy was certain she had never seen her before.

"May I help you?" she asked with a cheerful smile.

"I'm Waverly Bishop, Sully's mother," the woman threw out the words like a challenge, and Poppy accepted them the same way, her eyes rounding with something like terror. She hadn't met Sully's family yet. He hadn't mentioned it, and neither had she. She wasn't certain they knew about the baby. The look on his mother's face said yes. "Maybe we could have a conversation outside."

Poppy nodded and slipped wordlessly from behind the counter. Sully's mother took her arm, almost but not quite frog marching her out of the diner and around the corner to the alley where she let her go. They both leaned against the wall, seemingly both in need of support.

"You look different than I imagined," the older woman began. "Sweeter and more innocent, less like…" she trailed off.

"A scheming harlot?" Poppy guessed.

Waverly snorted a laugh. "Yes. I had it in my head that you tricked my innocent boy, trapped him in a pregnancy. But that's not true, is it?"

"We're in it together," Poppy said. "But I don't want anything from Sully, more than for him to be a good dad to the baby."

"He will be," Waverly declared. "He's a good man."

"The best," Poppy agreed.

Waverly tipped her head. "Are you in love with him?"

"No, but I love him, if that makes sense. We're trying hard to be good friends, to do this together with as little collateral damage as possible."

"I suppose that will have to do," Waverly said, resting her head on the wall. "This is not how I wanted my first grandchild brought into the world. I thought there'd be a wedding first."

"Me too," Poppy admitted. "I thought I'd be older than twenty four."

"I was only twenty when I had Sully. It was hard, and I was married. Motherhood has a way of changing you, of exposing every last drop of selfishness and rooting it out. You'll realize you're stronger than you ever knew and weaker, too." She sighed. "I'm probably not helping, but I intend to. If you'll let me." She added the last part meekly, hopefully.

"I would love that, really. I never lived near my grandparents. I dearly want better for this baby."

"Oh, gosh, it's really real," Waverly said, dashing at her eyes.

"It really is, and it's about to get serious because I'm not going to be able to hide it for much longer."

"Do you have maternity clothes?"

Poppy shook her head. "I don't have a car, and nowhere in town sells them. I was going to try and order some things off the internet when I get off work."

Waverly's eyes narrowed and hardened. "Don't do that. You need to go shopping like a normal woman and try things on."

"I don't know how that would be possible," Poppy said.

"I do. You'd better get back in there, looks like a line's forming," Waverly said, glancing at the front of the diner.

"Oh, right," Poppy said, snapping to attention. "I'm sorry this has been shocking and difficult for you."

"Please don't apologize to me. I'm really looking forward to getting to know you better, and regardless of how it came about, we are thrilled, *thrilled* about the baby. You call if you need anything, even if it's for me to tell my son to get his act together."

"Will do," Poppy said. She smiled and, impulsively, hugged Waverly who returned it fiercely a second before letting go. Someday Poppy would have to tell her own mother the news, and she hoped the reaction would be a hug like that one.

Later, Poppy received a text from Sully.

My mom says I'm to take you shopping. Let's grab dinner. Five OK?

Five works, but you don't have to.

Tell that to my mom. I must be the only Ranger in Texas whose Mommy shows up to tell him to take his baby mama shopping or else.

So sweet when you call me your baby mama. Not creepy or demeaning at all.

Glad we agree. XO.

He collected her from her house at five, waking her from a nap. She rose at three in the morning now and, though she wasn't as tired as she was during the beginning of the pregnancy, her new hours took a toll. By the time her day was said and done, she put in twelve hours, taking off only Sunday to rest.

"Want to hear something ironic?" she asked when Sully greeted her at her door.

"As long as it's not being sung by Alanis Morissette, yes," he agreed.

"I left New York to try and find a better job, and I'm putting in more hours here for less money and no benefits," she said.

"Oh," he drawled, not sure how to respond.

"However, I have greater autonomy here, and I like it. It's fun to be the boss, to decide what to make each day. I think maybe I was born to be an entrepreneur."

"Miss Independent," he said.

"Exactly. And the rent is blessedly cheap and," she paused and regarded him, "can you believe there's going to be an and?"

"It had better be me," he said.

"It's not. It's about space and relaxation. Unlike New York, I can sit in my own living room. I can walk around in a complete state of undress."

"Why don't you have me over more often?" he asked, and she laughed.

"Stop it, I'm trying to say good things about life here in Texas, looking for that silver lining."

"Am I not silver?" he asked.

"The silverest," she assured him. "Let's go, I'm starving."

"I'm not used to hearing that from you," he said.

"Get used to it because I have a lot of lost time to make up for. Food and I have made up in a major way, and I feel it has a lot of reparations to make up for, so where are we going?"

"Um…" he said, stalling until he could think of something. Unlike her, he put almost no thought into future meals. "What are you in the mood for?"

"Tex-Mex, the best Tex-Mex on the planet. Something with lots of spices."

"Um…" he drawled again. "Let's see, hmm."

Poppy sighed and texted her brother-in-law, asking his advice. While not as much of a foodie as she was, he still somehow usually knew the best places. He replied a minute later with the name of a restaurant.

"Oh, right, I forgot about that place. It is good. Let's go because at the mention of food I'm now starved as well."

"Aw, I feel so sorry for you, being hungry these five minutes. It must be hard, almost like growing a human or something," she said.

"This bitterness does not suit you, Poppisandra," he said, picking her up with one arm and carrying her to his truck.

"You'd better enjoy this while it lasts because now that I'm able to eat again, it's not going to be possible much longer."

"You can carry me then," he said, and she laughed. He set her in the truck, leaned in to plant a kiss on her belly, and closed the door.

"Sully, you're so adorable," Poppy declared when he slid behind the wheel.

He gave her a look. "What's got you so lovey dovey?"

"It might be because I'm being flooded with oxytocin, the bonding hormone that makes me want to reach out and connect with others. Or it might be because I'm so excited to eat food again I can't stand it." She squeezed his leg. "I can't wait to eat. You have no idea."

"I'm beginning to," he said, covering her hand and giving it a squeeze.

"Promise me you won't feel differently about me after you see how much I can put away," she pled.

"Poppy, at this point, I don't think there's a thing in the world that could make me feel differently about you," he said, and then he started his truck and headed for food.

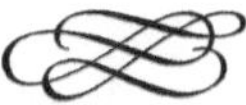

CHAPTER 16

Poppy wasn't joking. For a few minutes, Sully sat and watched her eat, savoring each mouthful as if it were her last.

"I feel like a prisoner who has been let free," she said, reaching for the bowl of salsa on the table between them. It was the fourth time the waiter had refilled it, and so far Sully hadn't had any. She dunked a chip in the salsa and caught sight of him staring. "You're horrified, aren't you?"

"I'm the opposite of horrified," he assured her. Watching her sensuously enjoy her food was...he needed a distraction, pronto. "What's new?"

"I got a text from George," she said, and Sully almost choked on the chip he'd just stuck in his mouth.

"What? When?"

"This morning and then again right before you showed up."

"What did he say?" He tried to keep his tone neutral.

"That he missed me. And then later that he hadn't replaced me because it felt too weird with anyone else. And he thought Zoe missed me because she added an extra knife under her pillow." She paused. "He talked about my note. He said I didn't owe him an apology because I didn't do anything to him. He was merely sad I went away and he didn't handle it well. And then he apologized for not talking to me before I left, for being standoffish when I needed a friend."

"Chatty text," he said. "Did he ask who the father is and if we're together?"

She shook her head.

"Huh. Thank you for telling me."

"Do you really want to know every time I text with George?" she asked, wrinkling her nose.

"No, not every time. Just if it develops into something more."

"We're two thousand miles apart. What could develop?" she asked.

"Something magical," he said, naming his unnamed fear. What if George actually was Poppy's destiny? Sully had been searching for his, had always felt the right woman was out there and someday and he would find her, as if in a dream. All the stars would align, and he would know without a doubt that it was his perfect partner. From everything Bailey had told him, George seemed to be that for Poppy. And he had seen them together; they had undeniable chemistry.

"All I know is that I miss him, but I don't know how I miss him, as a friend or something more. I left before we could explore that possibility, and now it seems too late." She gazed into the distance, across the crowded restaurant, staring at nothing.

"If it's meant to be, it will come back around," he said, laying his hand on hers.

"But if I end up with George, who will we find for you? Someone who is okay with our crazy, mixed up situation?"

"Any woman who wants to be with me will have to accept a package deal. I now come with a Poppy." He brought her hand to his lips and kissed it.

"You'd better hope she has a sweet tooth," she said.

"I'll add it to my list of demands," he agreed. "Now come on, Cinderella, let's buy you some maternity clothes."

They were on their way to the store when Poppy pressed her nose against the truck's window, gasping. "Ice cream. I haven't had ice cream in so long."

"Poppy, would you like some ice cream?" he asked, refraining from asking how it was possible. In addition to all the chips and salsa, she had polished off her meal and what was left of his.

"Yes," she said. "But there's a huge line."

"I have a spectacular idea. I'll drop you at the store, go get your ice cream, and bring it back to you. Hopefully you'll have accomplished all your shopping by then and I won't need to be present." He pulled into the store's lot and put the truck in park.

Poppy unbuckled, but instead of opening the door, she slid across the seat and put her arms around him. "You are the sweetest baby daddy ever." She kissed his cheek. "I'll have a peanut butter milkshake. Medium. No, large. Don't judge me, the baby needs iron."

"I'll be back. Have fun shopping." He grasped her chin in his hand and kissed her on the lips, albeit softly and gently.

Poppy sat back slightly and swallowed hard. "Dangerous territory, park ranger."

"I know," he agreed. "But sometimes I can't resist."

"And sometimes, like when we talk about George, you feel the need to leave a lasting imprint," she guessed.

"Look how well you're beginning to know me already. Now scoot so I can get your ice cream."

"Don't you mean 'git,'" she asked.

"Make fun of me one more time, and there will be no ice cream," he warned.

She pretended to zip her lips and scooted out of the truck.

Once inside the store, she was easily distracted. Her mind was like that, quick to focus on pretty things and forget what needed to be done. She tried hard to think what exactly she needed. Undergarments were essential, and because she had no idea what size she wore now, she took a few to try on. Once she had those, she began building layers, adding a few shirts and skirts and finally some dresses, her favorite, though the ones on display left a lot to be desired. Maybe she would merely buy some necessities now—the skirts and shirts she could mix and match—and save the beauty buys for when she had more time to look. Plus there was the money factor. She was basically buying an entirely new wardrobe. It would be best if she spread it out a little at a time so as not to blow her entire budget on the serviceable items on display.

She made a few selections and took them into the fitting room to try on, noticing as she did so that her bump was now on full view. Her hiding days were over, and her heart fluttered nervously. She had become quite attached to the patrons at the diner. How would they react when they learned she was a soon-to-be single mother? To say nothing of her sister, whom she still hadn't told.

After gathering her final selections, she opened the curtain, stepped out, and came face to face with Bailey.

"Poppy, what on earth are you doing here?" Bailey asked. "Did you see our car in the lot and stop in to say hello or something?"

"Uh…" Poppy stammered, unable to have a coherent thought or sentence. Her glance fell helplessly to Cal.

"Oh, boy," he muttered.

"What?" Bailey said, looking back and forth between them.

"I…" Poppy began, but had no idea how to finish the sentence.

Cal stepped forward and took Bailey's hand. "Honey, your sister is pregnant."

"Jane's pregnant?" Bailey exclaimed, and Poppy fought the mad desire to giggle. It was all so absurd, and her panic mechanism was beginning to kick in. She had wanted to sit down, to have a rational and prepared conversation.

"No, baby, not Jane." His eyes fell purposefully on Poppy, now clutching the new clothes like a lifeline.

"No," Bailey said.

Poppy nodded.

"George?" Bailey whispered.

Poppy shook her head.

"A boyfriend?" Bailey tried.

Poppy shook her head.

Bailey's expression shifted from shocked to stern. "A stranger?"

"Uh…" Bailey stammered. She glanced to Cal again for a rescue, but he had none to give. He seemed as curiously flustered as his wife.

"Mine," Sully said, emerging from the clothes rack to her left.

Bailey blinked at him, uncomprehending. "What?"

"The baby's mine. I'm the father," he said, and Poppy gave him credit for maintaining eye contact in the face of Bailey's expression. She looked so…gutted.

"From when you went to New York?" she asked, her voice a bit airy and breathless.

He shook his head. "From when she was here before."

"When was she here befo…" Bailey froze again. "My wedding?" The whisper dropped even lower.

"Yes. I'm sorry," Sully said.

"You…my baby sister…my wedding," she stammered.

Sully blew out a breath. "Yes."

"I…I can't. I can't." Bailey hung whatever was in her hand back on the rack, turned, and walked out the door. Cal remained, regarding them with an unreadable expression.

"You two sure know how to make a ruckus," he said at last.

"I'm sorry, Cal," Sully said.

"I'll talk to her. She'll forgive you," he added to Poppy. "You, I'd sleep with one eye open." He thumped Sully on the shoulder and followed his wife outside.

Sully and Poppy remained silent for a few beats. He handed her the milkshake and took the clothes out of her hands. "Are you ready to check out?" he asked softly.

"Yes," she said in the same soft tone. They went to the checkout where she attempted to shift the milkshake and her purse in order to pay.

"I've got it," Sully told her.

She frowned at him. "You're not supposed to…"

"I've got it," he said, almost but not quite snapping at her.

"It's going to be expensive," she warned.

He shrugged and plopped the clothes on the counter, shaking his hand out when the bra hanger snagged on his watch and dangled.

"Could have lived without that," Poppy said, and he laughed.

The cashier rang them up. Sully carried the two bags to the car and opened the door for her, holding her milkshake as she climbed inside.

He opened the truck's door, started the engine, but seemed unable to make the necessary steps to put it into gear and go.

"It was always going to be bad," Poppy said, resting her hand gently on his leg.

"Did you see her face?" he asked.

"Yes."

"I don't think I've ever made anyone's face look that way before," he said.

"I have. That was how George looked when I told him I was pregnant. So betrayed, like all his faith in me was wasted effort."

"It feels horrible," Sully said.

"Yes, yes it does," Poppy agreed.

"Do you think she'll get over it?" he asked.

"She'll have to eventually. You're her niece or nephew's father," Poppy said. "We're family now."

"Yes," Sully agreed, but the drive home was long and silent.

CHAPTER 17

It happened. Word began to spread about Poppy's bakery, like proverbial wildfire. People were trickling in from farther away, foodies on a mission to try new things. Each day she saw new faces at the diner.

The cat was also out of the bag after her encounter with Bailey. Sully showed up as usual for lunch that day when Poppy signaled him over.

"You look especially ornery today. What gives?" he asked.

"You think this look is orneriness? It's anxiety," she said, giving him a nervous smile.

He froze. Had something happened? Something more than Bailey's adverse reaction? "Why? What's wrong?"

"Nothing per se, it's just...you remember how much I ate last night?"

"There's no right answer to that question, is there?" he asked.

"The point is I think I gained about five pounds."

"Okay," he drawled, still not following.

"Brace yourself," she said.

"You're starting to scare me a little," he said.

"I'm going to come around the counter," she warned.

"Are you going to stab me? Because your demeanor says yes." He watched as she walked from behind the counter and, even after her warning, had to fight against the urge to gasp and stare. Her belly had popped, the new maternity shirt highlighting it like a beacon. No longer was it a barely discernable mound, easily hidden under flowing dresses. It was now full and rounded and on display for all the world to gawk. And gawk they did. If anyone had guessed before this moment that she was pregnant, it hadn't made its way into the gossip mill. But now word was out in a major way.

"Oh boy," Sully whispered, forcing his eyes up to her face, a face that was filled with uncertainty. "I like the new shirt."

"Thank you. This boy I know bought it for me," she gave him a nervous little smile. People seemed to be awaiting his reaction, as if maybe they thought he hadn't known she was pregnant, as if they thought maybe she had been pulling the wool over his eyes. Time to dispel that notion. He pulled her close and kissed her, resting his hands on the bump, his heart doing the cartwheel flip-floppy thing it did whenever he touched her stomach.

"Have lunch with me," he said.

"After that little display, I'd do anything you ask," she said.

He quirked an eyebrow at her.

"Almost anything," she amended. "And I saved you a piece of pie."

"Totally worth the price of admission," he said. She slid into a booth. He sat beside her, and she looked at him askance.

"What are you, a serial killer? Who shares the same side of a booth?"

"Two people who are in need of some moral support," he said.

"Oh, right." She rested her head on his shoulder for a second, and he slid his arm around her, his lips skimming her temple. Conversation was abuzz in the restaurant, and they both knew it was about them. "Wonder what they're saying?"

"Well, I don't think they're discussing the weather," he said.

"No, I mean I wonder if they think it's yours or if you've simply taken pity on me in my lowly state," she said.

"I don't know, let me see." He stood and faced the crowded diner. "It's mine, y'all."

"That was subtle," she said as he sat down again and slid his arm back around her.

"Best to face these things head on, get in front of the rumors," he said. He reached for the pie she'd saved for him and took a bite. "Oh, my lands. Girl, this pie is going to make you famous, mark my words."

"I could be the pregnant pie lady," she mused.

"You *are* the pregnant pie lady," he said.

"What'll you have?" Marjory asked, pausing by their table. They placed their order. She wrote it down, stuffed her pad in her pocket, and faced them. "Y'all getting married? You know folks are going to ask me."

"Co-parenting as friends. Spread the good word, Marjory," Sully said, handing her their menus.

"Not sure it's good. Y'all ought to get married," she said, but not unkindly.

"Getting married would solve a lot of problems," Sully said to Poppy after Marjory was gone.

"Solving problems isn't a reason to get married," she reminded him.

"What is a reason to get married?" he asked.

"Because you fall in love with a person and want to spend your life together, having children, making a family," she said.

"We already made a child and we're becoming family," he said. "Maybe the love comes after."

"You're confusing me in my vulnerable state," she said, reaching for a bite of his pie.

He moved it away from her. "Mine."

"I can't possibly marry a man who won't share his pie," she said.

Sighing, he shoved the pie closer to her. "Just think about it," he said.

"I'll think about it, but, Sully, isn't the fact that we're having a rational discussion about it kind of a clue? Aren't we supposed to be two crazy kids head over heals in love? I believe that was what you said to me that night, that you were looking for magic."

She loaded a piece of pie on the fork, but instead of eating it held it out for him. His eyes fell on her soft and rounded body, her pretty face with eyes alight, the fork full of pie she'd made held out to him. For a second, he thought maybe he'd found the magic he'd been looking for, but it was a wispy thread, a gossamer thought, gone before he could grasp onto it. The mouthful of pie saved him from an answer, and when it was finished, their food arrived. After that, they didn't return to the topic of marriage or magic again, and Sully wasn't sure if he was relieved or regretful.

The next day when Sully arrived at the diner, Poppy was not behind the counter as usual. Instead she sat in a booth, the same booth they'd shared yesterday, talking and laughing with a man he didn't recognize. He wasn't a local, that much was certain. He wore the preppy clothes and round glasses of an intellectual and, right away, Sully was both suspicious and jealous in equal measure.

He tried to be casual when he approached their table but failed miserably when Poppy looked up at him with a knowing smile. "Is it marking time already?" she asked.

"Looks like," he said, forcing her aside as he sat down next to her. He held out his hand to the man. "Sully Langford."

The man shook his hand in return, showing no hesitancy or trepidation. "Ash Gallagher, San Antonio Express-News."

"The News?" Sully echoed.

"Yes, we caught wind of Poppy's bakery here, and I'm doing a story," Ash replied.

Sully faced Poppy. "Well, aren't I the idiot?"

"There's no right answer to that question, is there?" she replied, clearly amused by his misplaced jealousy.

"It was nice to meet you, Ash," Sully said, ignoring her. "I'll leave you to get back to it." He started to stand, but Ash put out a hand.

"Could I get a picture of you two? It's sort of part of the story, New York girl meets Texas Ranger, falls in love, opens a bakery," Ash said.

Sully turned back to Poppy. "Is that the story we're going with?"

"It would seem so," Poppy said, and Ash took a picture while they were mid-conversation. They turned to him in question.

"Sorry, sometimes the candids are better. I'll take a posed one now." They put their heads together. He took a picture, checked it, and nodded in satisfaction. Sully eased out of the booth, and the interview continued.

The story ran a few days later and was picked up by the *USA Today*. Poppy was ecstatic with the exposure. Sully was enamored, both with the glowing article and with the picture of him and Poppy. Ash had used the candid shot, the one where they were looking at each other and talking. They were smiling at each other, Poppy's finger resting on her chin, her dimples in full effect. It was the sort of picture they'd be able to show their child someday, and he loved it so much he contacted the paper and bought a copy of the photo. Unknown to them, however, the story would spark a series of unforeseeable events.

The first such event was a phone call from Poppy's father. She hadn't yet told her parents she was pregnant.

"Hey, Sugar Bear. I saw your picture in the paper," he said, and Poppy smiled.

"Hey, Dad. I thought you hate that paper."

"I do, but I bought ten copies. Even a stopped clock is right twice a day, Poppy, and this paper got it right about you. Sounds like things are going well there with the new venture."

"I'm not going to be a millionaire anytime soon, but I'm surviving. How are you? How's Mom?"

"That's what I wanted to talk to you about. I'm at Laughlin."

Laughlin Air Force base, in Del Rio, was even closer than Lackland. "You're local?" she said, her world shifting suddenly from a pleasant interlude to total panic.

"Yes, I am, and I want to see my girls. Bailey has to have a baby bump by now, right?"

"Uh," Poppy drawled. "I can't honestly say, Dad. It's like Bailey lives in a whole other town, the ranch is so far away. And I've been so busy with the new business."

Her father paused, an ominous sign. "What's going on, Poppy?"

"Bailey and I had a bit of a falling out," Poppy explained. It wasn't so unusual for the two sisters to butt heads. They were extremes in temperament. Growing up, their middle sister, Jane, often played peacemaker between them. But they hadn't argued in years, not since they both left home.

"I don't like that," her father said.

"Neither do I," Poppy agreed. "I'm sure it will be fine eventually, but she needs some time and space from me."

"What did you do?"

It irked Poppy that he automatically took Bailey's side. He said he didn't have a favorite, but sometimes it was hard to remember when he and Bailey were so much alike they could always read each other without words. "It's hard to explain, Daddy. We'll talk about it over lunch. Have you talked to Bailey yet?"

"No, I called you first."

"Could you do me a favor and see us separately, me first? I think you'll understand after that."

"If you like. I want to see your place. I'll come there first and meet Bailey after," he said. "But, Poppy, I don't like separation between my girls."

"I don't either, Daddy. Bailey and I will be okay eventually, I promise."

He sighed. Poppy could imagine he thought, that it was a lot easier to manage the world's problems than those of his three daughters. "All right. See you in a bit."

Poppy withdrew her phone and texted Sully. He was on patrol all day today, some top-secret assignment he couldn't tell her about.

My dad is coming. Now is a good time for you to head south of the border and hide out for a while.

She hoped he got the message, and she hoped he realized she meant it.

CHAPTER 18

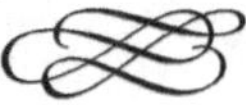

When Poppy's father arrived, a half hour ahead of schedule, she was at the bakery. She was supposed to be at home where they could have a quiet, private conversation. Instead he showed up and stood beaming at her in the middle of the diner.

"It looks so good," he declared. "Honey, Mom and I are so proud."

"Hold on to that," Poppy said.

"Come out here so I can hug you," he said. He was in full uniform, making him even more intimidating than usual, as if he needed any enhancements.

"What can I get for you, Dad?" she asked, stalling.

"You know I'm partial to pie," he said.

"I do, actually, and I already set aside a piece for you." She held the plate aloft but remained standing behind the safety of the counter.

"Come out here," he prompted.

Poppy looked around. Everyone stared at him, at them. It was likely because her father was that sort of man, the kind people stared at. He exuded power, the kind that could only be attained through hardened experience. There was not one situation her father couldn't or hadn't faced, possibly save learning his baby daughter was four months pregnant in a room full of strangers.

"Dad, I need you to channel all your military reserve for a minute," she warned.

He stood straighter, his smile gone in an instant. "Why?"

"Just remember you're a colonel and people are watching us," she said.

His lips disappeared, pressed together in a hard line. Never a good sign. "Poppy, step out here right now." He didn't say it loudly, but the diner came to an absolute hush. No one dared to speak or move or seemingly even breathe.

Poppy took a breath and stepped out. Her dad's expression remained resolute except for the eyes which blinked once and stared at the center of her body and the protruding baby bump. Poppy took his arm and led him from the diner. They rounded the corner into the alley and both leaned on the wall, exactly as she and Sully's mother had done.

Her father said nothing for a solid four minutes. Poppy knew because she counted. "Who?" he bit out at last.

"Sully Langford."

"The Ranger," he bit out, his fists clenched until his knuckles popped.

"Yes. Dad, he's a good guy and you'll like him."

"Where is he?" he growled.

"Hopefully in Tijuana by now," she said. He softened slightly, a flicker of amusement passing over his features.

"When are you getting married? Or are you already married?"

"No we're not married, and no we're not getting married."

He stood away from the wall. "He's not marrying you?"

"I'm not marrying him," Poppy said. "He asked. I said no."

He closed his eyes. "Poppy. Why?"

"Why do I always have to do everything the wrong way, you mean?"

He opened his eyes. "Why do you have to do it the hard way?"

"I like to do things my own way. It's coincidence that it ends up being hard or wrong," she said.

He barked a harsh laugh and unclenched his fists. "And this is why Bailey's mad, because you're pregnant?"

"I don't think it's that so much as the timing of everything and the fact that Sully is her good friend. She feels like he let her down."

"He did," her dad said.

She frowned. "Don't take sides, Dad. Sully's a good guy, and we are equally responsible here."

Her dad let out another breath. "When did you grow up?"

"About four months ago," Poppy said.

"I never gave you that hug," he said, pulling her into his arms and holding her close. She hugged him in return and rested her head on his chest. "I got a call from Ben."

She tensed. Ben was George's father. "Yes?"

"He has a fairly despondent son on his hands. Said the boy's been moping about like crazy since you went away. Does he know about this?"

"Yes, I told him. I didn't know he felt anything but friendship for me," she said.

"How could he not?" her father asked. He kissed her head and let her go. "Now, let's go eat my pie and you can show me your house."

They returned to the diner. Absently Poppy wondered what they did for entertainment and conversation before she arrived in town. She had certainly provided enough of it to last a lifetime the last few weeks. They sat in a booth. Marjory arrived with coffee and a menu, and her father began eating his pie.

"Let's talk business. How's it going, champ?"

"Pretty well. Rent here is insanely cheap. I'm putting a lot in savings because I won't be able to work for a bit after the baby comes. Everything else is going toward insurance."

Her dad's lips pressed together.

"Dad, if you do that any harder you're going to swallow them," she said, and he put his napkin to his mouth to keep from spitting his coffee. "Just say it."

"If you married the boy, you could be on his insurance. You

wouldn't have to pay separate rent. All your extra income could go into savings."

"That's what I've been trying to tell her," Sully said, now looming over their table. He was dressed head to toe in black tactical gear, making Poppy wonder how he'd managed to get away.

"I told you to go to Mexico," she said, exasperated.

"And I told you to marry me," he replied in the same exasperated tone. He held out his hand to her father. "How do you do, Colonel, sir?"

Her father stood. "I've been better, Ranger Langford." Nonetheless he held out his hand and the two men shook.

"Yes, sir, sorry about that," Sully said, bumping Poppy aside as he sat down.

"I take it you plan to be an active part of the baby's life, physically, financially, and emotionally," her father said.

"In as many ways as Poppy will allow," Sully said.

"It's not up to Poppy. A father's duty is not determined by the mother," The Colonel said.

"Yes, sir," Sully agreed.

"It's feeling very midcentury in here," Poppy said.

Her father turned to scowl at her. "Don't give me that garbage, Poppy. There are some things bigger than your independence or feminist initiative or whatever this is you're referencing. A father's love and responsibility to his child are eternal and unchanging." He pulled out his phone and gave it to her. "Go outside and call your mother and Jane and tell them your news while the Ranger and I have a conversation."

"But..." Poppy started to protest. Her father's expression didn't shift, but he had a way of changing moods without his face reflecting what was happening, the same as Bailey. Meekly, Poppy accepted the phone and slid from the booth.

The Colonel waited until she was safely outside to speak again. "Ranger Langford, I realize I am a man born out of time. I have old fashioned notions about things, including duty, honor, sacrifice, service, and family. I do not like that this cart has come before the horse. However, I cannot control my daughters, and wisdom says it's better not to try.

"What I can control is my actions in regard to you. So I will tell you the same thing I told my son-in-law before he married Bailey. If you prove yourself to be a good, responsible, upstanding man and father to my grandchild, I will welcome you to our family with open arms. But if I ever hear of you mistreating my daughter or grandchild in any way or shirking your responsibility to Poppy or your child, I will make you suffer in unimaginable ways. Are we clear?"

"Yes, sir," Sully said. He might think the man was exaggerating, but knowing Bailey had taught him otherwise. Neither of them said anything they didn't mean or weren't willing to back up with actions. "You should know, sir, that I intend to do everything in my power to take care of Poppy, not that she'll make it easy."

"There's the matter of George to discuss."

Sully blinked at him in surprise. "George, sir?"

"It's my opinion that George still intends to make a play for Poppy. It's always been my secret hope they would get together. But I also believe families should stay together. Regardless, I won't take sides beyond giving you this fair warning. I don't know you, but I know my daughter and I know George and I am telling you that if you want Poppy, you'd better step up your game because he'll try hard to woo her from beneath your nose."

Sully's hands balled into fists on the table. "We'll see."

"I suppose we will. Either way, your responsibilities don't change."

"We're clear on that," Sully said.

"Well, then. What have you been up to today because it looks like it was fun," The Colonel said, nodding at Sully's tactical attire.

Sully found himself telling the older man all about the Cortez family and the years of pursuit and investigation. The Colonel listened intently, asking pertinent questions that sparked new insights in Sully's brain. If not for the terrifying part regarding the warnings over Poppy, it would have been a delightfully interesting and productive lunch.

CHAPTER 19

The next morning a new customer arrived at the diner. Poppy noticed him immediately because he was young but, unlike all the other young men she'd seen around, clearly not a ranch hand. He wore all black and when he reached for his piece of coffee cake, she saw words written on the inside of his wrist. Before she could read the words, he removed his hand, grasping his coffee and muffin, his fingers lightly skimming hers as they made the handoff.

It wasn't unusual for her to accidentally brush a customer. She spent her day handing them food and receiving money in return. It was bound to happen occasionally. The difference this time was that she felt a little thrill of attraction when it happened. The only man who had affected her that way in recent memory was Sully. But the last few months of unending nausea had driven all thoughts of romance or attraction from her mind. Now that she finally felt better, she began to notice men again, both Sully and others.

Sully she continually categorized as off limits. Things were good between them; they had established a familial sort of friendship, a mutual dependency on each other and growing excitement over their pending bundle. So it took her by surprise to find the handsome stranger attractive. For a second, she allowed her mind to advance, to picture having a flirtation and maybe even a date with him. Then his dark eyes landed on her belly bump, and she quickly came back to earth.

Oh, right, I'm pregnant. Despite taking over her entire life, the pregnancy still felt so new that sometimes she forgot. When she saw the handsome man, she had one of those moments. It wasn't until his gaze landed on her belly that reality came crashing back. She was not in any position to find a man attractive and certainly not to act on it. So she forced a bland smile as she told him to have a good day. He nodded, not commenting. He sat and began to eat his cake and drink his coffee, but every time she happened to glance at him, he was looking at her. As soon as their eyes caught, he looked away.

For three days in a row, the man returned, ordered the same thing, and sat in the same place. And every time Poppy's eyes landed on him, he glanced away, caught, almost guilty.

On the fourth day, his fingers were covered in paint. Without thinking about it, Poppy latched onto them and pulled them closer, inspecting. "Do you paint?"

"I dabble," he said. "Are you a painter?"

"No," she said, letting his hand go with a flush. The gesture had been one of surprise, not flirtation. Not that anyone could tell the difference. "I'm merely an art enthusiast."

"Ah, I guess that makes me a baking enthusiast," he said, holding the treats he'd bought from her aloft.

Poppy smiled and tapped the tattoo on his wrist. "What does that mean?" The words were written in Latin script.

"Family first," he replied.

"That's sweet," she said. "You must be close to your family."

"The closest," he agreed. He glanced to make sure no one was behind him and rested his hip against the counter. "What about you? Are you close to your husband?"

Her cheeks flushed again. "No husband."

"Boyfriend?" he queried.

She shook her head, the blush deepening.

"You're alone?" he asked, a hint of a grimace darkening his handsome features.

"No, but we've decided to be friends."

His answering smile was wide. "Friends are nice to have."

"Yes, they are," she agreed.

"Can I ask you a question?" he asked. His dark eyes were the sort that always had some hidden expression, the kind that made her want to find out what he thought. He was exactly the kind of guy she always went for—mysterious, complex, artistic. He was certainly unlike anyone else she'd met so far in Texas. He looked better suited to big city life than rural middle of nowheresville.

"Absolutely," she said.

"Would you be interested in attending an art exhibit in San Antonio with me?" he asked.

She blinked at him, shocked. "You understand I'm pregnant, right?"

He laughed. "Yes. Am I not allowed to ask you out?"

"No, I mean yes, I mean I guess. Sure. We can go to an art exhibit." The request seemed casual enough.

"Great," he said, smiling wider. "One more question."

"Yes?"

He leaned in to whisper. "What's your name?"

She leaned, too, holding out her hand for him to shake. "Poppy Dunbar. And you are?"

"Diego Cortez," he said, grasping her hand. He gave her the mystery smile again. "You have no idea how happy I am to meet you, Poppy Dunbar."

"Don't tell me you've been searching for a pregnant baker your whole life," she said.

"You know what they say. Timing is everything." He winked at her, took his treats, and went to sit down at his table.

Poppy did her best not to watch him, but she couldn't help but feel slightly anxious. If he didn't leave before Sully arrived...But he did. Ten minutes before Sully showed up for lunch, Diego tipped his head to Poppy and disappeared. Poppy breathed a sigh of relief. She was in the clear, at least until she had to try and explain to Sully that she had somehow gotten a date.

S he still puzzled it over as they ate supper later that night.
"What's the matter, hon? Are you not feeling well? You're so quiet," Sully noted. They were at his house, as usual, sitting on his couch watching TV with their arms linked. Poppy didn't get reception and she had only a decrepit couch. Sully, on the other hand, had satellite reception and a comfy leather couch with matching recliners. His house was strangely well decorated for a bachelor, Poppy thought. But it was comfy and cozy enough that she didn't mention it.

"What do you do when I'm not here?" she asked, forcing him to pause the game he watched in order to face her.

"Sleep."

"No, I mean what did you do before I showed up?"

"Got home from work and showered," he said, reaching for the pause button again.

Poppy put her hand on his. "Sullivan, what did you do for fun before I arrived in town and this became our life?"

"Oh," he drawled, finally understanding. "I worked a whole lot more. I've been making a conscious effort to get out at a reasonable time, to practice for fatherhood. I don't want to be one of those 'Cats in the Cradle' dads."

"What's that?" she asked.

"You know, that song about the absentee father? Every man's nightmare," he shuddered.

"But what did you do during your off hours? For fun?"

"I went out with friends or on dates sometimes, but mostly my life was work. Work and sleep and then work again."

"What kinds of things did you do when you went out?" she asked.

"The usual," he said, unpausing the TV again.

"You could go out, if you wanted," Poppy offered a minute later.

"Ungh," he muttered, only half listening as someone was tackled on TV. Poppy waited to speak again until the commercial.

"Like on a date," she added, and finally his attention turned to her.

"Honey, what?"

"You could go on a date. It would be okay," she said.

"Thank you for that, but who would this mystery date be? I've pretty much cycled through all the girls in town," he said.

"You could go out with friends," she suggested.

"If it ever comes up, I'll let you know," he said as the game resumed.

Poppy sighed, reached for the remote, and paused it. "Sully, I don't want you to feel tied down or restricted by me. You are free, free to go out, to have fun. We only have five months until this baby arrives and our lives will change forever. We might as well enjoy it."

Smiling, he reached for her and pulled her into his lap. She rested her head on his shoulder, and he eased his arms around her. "Why are you being so solicitously concerned about my social life?"

His soft twang was so pleasant, as was the feel and smell of him. All in all, Sully Langford was quite a haul. And yet Poppy was keenly aware that he wasn't actually hers, might never be hers. Did she want him to be? She tried hard never to peer too closely at that.

They sat in peaceful silence for a while. Sully seemed to accept her silence as some sort of answer and resumed the game. Poppy petted his chest, absently at first, as one might a beloved pet. But then he swallowed hard and tensed and she realized her touch might be misconstrued. Or perhaps it was merely being construed because the more she touched him, the more she wanted to touch him. They had been careful, very, *very* careful not to fall into a situation where they replicated their first encounter. At this moment Poppy felt as if they were teetering on the edge of that, that if she put her face up to be kissed, Sully would respond like a lit match in a box of firecrackers.

His left hand began a soothing little circle at the base of her spine. Poppy, who had always been particularly sensitive to touch, could feel herself begin to slip under. So she said the only thing she could think of to pull herself back out.

"I have a date."

CHAPTER 20

Meanwhile, an hour away at Ridge Ranch, Calhoun Ridge saw a whole new side of his wife. For as long as he'd known her, which was admittedly not long in the scheme of things, she had been a rational sort of person, one who eschewed emotion and stuck to thinking and planning instead. She was cool, calculated, and fastidious in her reserve and good judgment. So it came as something of a surprise to him when, a few weeks into her pregnancy, she suddenly turned into a quivering mass of inconsolable weeping.

The first time it happened, he walked into the house, saw her prostrate on the kitchen floor, and thought something dreadful had happened to her or their unborn child. When he was finally able to get the story out of her, it turned out that the barn cat killed a mouse and left it on the doorstep. She felt sad for the mouse, this woman who, as a Marine Major, had personally killed eleven enemy combatants and beaten several more into unconsciousness. As he picked up a shovel and prepared to bury a dead mouse for the first time in his life, he had the thought that perhaps this pregnancy, while joyful and much wanted, might not be all rainbows and sunshine.

The second time she burst into tears was because she burned a pan of biscuits. "I can't do anything right," she wailed, and he stared at her, the most capable woman he had ever known, amazed and speechless. She caught his look and cried harder. "I know, I hear it, but it's like something else has taken over my body and I can't stop all these words and tears from pouring out of me." She scrubbed her face with a wadded napkin. "If this is what it's like to be a normal girl, I hate it." Then she laid her head on the table and sobbed until Cal finally rallied, picked her up, and held her close. After that the tears dried fairly quickly and instead of feeling helpless, Cal had been left feeling a cocksure sort of power. When his wife wept for reasons that made no sense, he and he alone seemed to be the cure. It was a heady sensation, one he didn't think he would grow tired of quickly.

But when she saw her sister in the maternity store and realized her good friend had been the one to get her pregnant on a whim, even Cal hadn't been able to console her or bring her back from her surge of angry passion.

"How could they? Our wedding," she had fumed.

"Honey, they're human," Cal had inserted, and the look she gave him was enough to make him stay silent for the long drive home.

He thought her anger would abate, and it did at her sister. But the simmering ire toward Sully never dimmed. She seemed to take it as a personal attack, as if Sully had purposely preyed on Poppy during a weak moment. She stopped mentioning it, but he knew she still held on to the resentment, might hold on to it forever, knowing her. Bailey was a woman who demanded perfection, both from herself and from those around her. When someone let her down, especially by breaking her unspoken code, she was both unwilling and unable to forgive. As someone who had struggled with that very thing, Cal felt he was able to help her, but he had to wait for the perfect moment.

It came a couple of weeks after they learned the news of Poppy's pregnancy. "Bailey, come in here a minute," he called from his office.

She smiled in anticipation as she stepped into the room. He had been teaching her the ropes of the ranch since her arrival, and she took to it eagerly, always ready and willing to learn and listen. For Cal, who never imagined having the sort of marriage that would give him an equal partner in everything, her interest and enthusiasm were like a gift. But today ranching wasn't on his agenda. He reached for her, pulling her into his lap.

"Look at his," he said, motioning toward the computer when she remained staring at him. "It's an article in the paper about Poppy and her bakery."

"Oh," she said, turning to the screen with interest. Despite any lingering irritation with her sister, she was proud of her new venture. And, after their father's visit and resulting lecture, she was ready to make amends and heal the rift, at least with Poppy. Cal had purposely scrolled down, hiding the picture at the top of the page while she read.

"What a great article," she commented. "She's doing so well. Honestly, Poppy's always been so soft and fickle. It's both amazing and a little shocking to see her putting so much focus and dedication into something." She paused. "I'm going to call her."

"Hold on," Cal said, reaching for the mouse. "Look at this picture." He scrolled up, revealing the picture of Poppy and Sully at the top of the page.

"Oh," Bailey said, gasping a little as she leaned in for a better look.

"You see it, don't you?" he asked.

"I don't see anything," she stubbornly insisted, turning her head to look at him instead of the faces on the screen. He took her head and turned it toward the picture.

"Look at his face and tell me he's not in love with her."

After a few seconds of stubborn silence, she sighed. "I can't. I see it, he is. But he…"

"Yes, he did. He was wrong, and he is sorry. But he's only a man, a mere mortal. He's our friend, and he's your niece or nephew's father, and you need to forgive him and move on."

Defeated, she rested her head on his shoulder. "I really hate it when people screw up and let me down, when they make me disappointed because they're less than I thought they were."

"I know," he said, gently rubbing her back where he knew it ached. "But, honey, as much as we might try to be, none of us is perfect. Everyone has the potential to fail or mess up. With that in mind, which is worse, messing up to begin with or refusing to give grace and forgiveness to those who need it most?"

"I've been such an emotional basket case lately. Thank you for believing you can still appeal to my logic and I'll hear you," she said, sitting up to cup his face in her hands.

"Does that mean you're ready to forgive Sully and move on?" he asked.

"Yes. Now kiss me quick before the pregnant crazy lady makes a return and starts weeping," she said.

"I have a confession for you, darlin'. I like the crazy pregnant lady as much as her rational counterpart. It's like sexy Dr. Jekyll and Mrs. Hyde," he said.

She shifted, straddling him in the chair so her little belly was pushed against his. "You know what I'm going to do today?"

"Call your sister and Sully?" he guessed, his heart thundering as always from her nearness.

She shook her head and slid her arms around him. "I'm going to declare today Sunday. You're going to take the day off and be with your wife. You know why?"

He shook his head, speech failing him.

"Because, buddy, we're on the clock. A few more months of you and me, and then forever after we'll be at least three."

He swallowed hard as she eased forward and kissed his neck. "When you put it like that, let's make every day Sunday."

"Whatever you say, boss," she agreed, and kissed him again.

***

The next day Sully looked up from his computer and did a double take when Bailey stood in his doorway.

"Are you here to kill me? Because there are witnesses who saw you arrive," he said.

"Witnesses can be erased," she said, helping herself to the chair across from his desk.

His eyes took note of her belly, bigger than Poppy's. Bailey's stomach had been hard and flat to begin with; the baby had nowhere to go but out. Poppy was softer, fuller, her body readier to absorb the newcomer. He got caught up a moment thinking about Poppy's softness so that Bailey had to tap his desk to get his attention.

"Anyone in there?" she asked.

"Sorry, didn't sleep well," he said, scrubbing his hand over his face. "Let me state once more and for the record that I'm sorry."

"I know, and I'm sorry for my reaction," she said.

He blinked at her. "Wow, Cal's had quite the effect on you."

"I'll say," she agreed, patting her belly.

He chuckled and leaned back, lacing his hands behind his head as he stretched. "So I guess we're family now."

"How about we make it official?" she suggested, She started to lean forward, realized it was too uncomfortable, and leaned back instead.

"There's a slight hiccup with that plan," he said.

"What's that?" she asked.

"Your sister has a date."

She blinked, digesting the news. "With who?"

He shrugged. "She won't tell me, doesn't want me to interfere or 'hover jealously.'"

"What are you going to do about it?" Bailey demanded.

"What can I do about it?" he asked.

"*Something*," she said hotly. "Geez, Sully, get in the game here."

"Uh…" he stammered, confused by her impassioned tone.

She took a breath. "Sorry, apparently I fly off the handle now. Has Poppy been emotional?"

"No, except maybe a bit euphoric now that she's able to eat again," he said. "I have no idea what to do or what you mean by 'do something.'"

"What have you done so far?" she asked. "Something fun."

He picked up a pen, twirling it. "I got her pregnant. That was fun."

"How would you like me to give you a tracheotomy with that pen?" she offered.

"I don't know what you want from me here. We talk, we hang out, I'm trying hard to be there, to be supportive."

"Are things still, you know, physical between you?"

"No, we've taken that off the table."

"Put it back on."

"What?"

"I merely mean that Poppy is freakishly responsive to physical touch. She's a cuddler. If she's not getting it from you, she's going to seek it somewhere else. Rub her back, it has to be killing her, if she's anything like me. She stands all day—rub her feet. Hold her hand. Hug her. Kiss her. She'll melt."

"I'm not sure if this is incredibly awkward or incredibly helpful," Sully said. He had come to view Bailey as one of his guy friends, one with whom he shared a lot of similar interests. But his guy friends never talked to him this way.

"Maybe it's both. And take her somewhere."

"We go out to eat," he said, his tone turning defensive.

She quirked an eyebrow at him. "The diner?"

"Maybe," he admitted.

"The diner where she works, where she spends her entire day from three in the morning on?"

"I always pay," he said.

She shook her head. "Poppy doesn't care about stuff like that. She's not into money or material possessions. She's experiential. Have you not learned that by now?"

He blew out a breath. "I don't know. It's all so messed up."

"If you're looking for disagreement, you're looking in the wrong place. But it's a done deal. So if you want the desired outcome, you have to do the work. What is the problem here, really? What is holding you back?" she asked.

"Fear of failure and, I don't know, I always thought there would be some kind of mythic sign or something," he said.

"You want a sign? You got a girl pregnant, there's your sign," she said.

"I don't know, Bailey. When you met Cal, didn't you *know* he was the one?"

"No. I was attracted to him right away, I fell in love with him eventually, but if you'll remember, I was prepared to walk away when he didn't step up. There's no such thing as a magic, friction-free relationship. There's merely a whole lot of hard work and, if you're lucky, a whole lot of reward."

"I don't know," he muttered.

She picked up the box of tissues from his desk and bounced it off his head. "You're hopeless."

He grinned at her. "Good to have you back. Now go away. Some of us still work for a living, Mrs. Ridge."

"For some of us, growing a human is harder work than you could ever imagine. Something to remember as you relate to the woman in your life."

"You've gone from not speaking to me to giving me unsolicited advice in a shockingly short amount of time," Sully said.

"We're family now," Bailey replied. "The insufferability is only beginning."

CHAPTER 21

Sully showed up at Poppy's house uninvited and unannounced. "Hey," he said, trying and failing to sound innocent and unrehearsed.

"Sullivan Langford," Poppy said, shaking her head in exasperation.

"Yes, Poppisandra Dunbar?"

"You're ridiculous," she said.

"What?" he asked, feigning innocence.

"You know what. You showed up here hoping to catch a glimpse of the guy. You plan to stand in the background and be intimidating, forcing me to explain your presence," Poppy said.

"My child is going on a date, and I'm curious to see who the culprit is. You could marry this guy. In reality, I'm checking out my baby's potential stepfather. This is not me being jealous and possessive; this is me being a good dad."

"The joke's on you, Papa. I'm meeting him there."

"Where?" he asked.

"You're delusional if you think I'm going to tell you that information," she said.

"Do you think I'm going to get in my car and follow you like some sort of deranged stalker?" he asked.

She didn't answer. He picked her up and gave her a squeeze. "You're right, I totally would. I am much more okay with this in theory than in practice."

"If you don't want me to go, I'll cancel. But," she held up her hand before he could speak, "you should know this is completely casual. I know almost no one here. I haven't been out much since I arrived. I'm not looking for a mate here; I'm looking for a friend and a bit of entertainment."

He sighed. "Fine. But I am only a text away. If he turns out to be some kind of creeper who preys on pregnant women, I will come get you at any hour no matter what."

"Duly noted. You can set me down now," she said.

"Can I?" he said, continuing to hold her close. "You vastly overestimate my willpower."

"As the recipient of your last lack of willpower, I really don't," she said.

"Hilarious." He kissed her cheek and finally set her down. She reached for her purse. "Do you have your phone?"

"I have my phone." She opened her purse and double checked it. "You know it's highly likely your job has made you paranoid. Not everyone in the world is a psychotic criminal out to get each other. The guy in question in a perfectly nice individual who happens to enjoy art as much as I do. The end."

"Fine. Go, but don't have fun. Enjoy a bitter night of misery without me so you appreciate how good you have it."

"'Kay," she said, not bothering to rise to the bait he attempted to set before her. She walked to the grocery store, double checking that Sully wasn't behind her. She wouldn't put it by him to follow her. His protectiveness seemed overblown, and she wasn't certain if it was jealousy or cop instinct that made it so.

Diego waited for her in his car, as they'd prearranged. Poppy didn't know much about cars, but even she recognized the Jaguar symbol jutting forward from the top of the hood. She slipped into the car and he gave her a little smile.

"I have never met a woman this way on the sly before," he said.

"It's ridiculous, I know but," she motioned to the tiny town. "Such is life in a small town. Thank you for agreeing to meet this way."

"I wouldn't have missed it." He faced forward and then looked at her again. "You look stunning."

"I look overfed, but thank you," she said, patting her bump. She wished she could be like Bailey, whose weight gain remained centered on her midsection. No such luck as her already round cheeks appeared even rounder lately. Sully said it made her dimples look deeper but Poppy thought it simply made her look chubby. The extra weight made her feel insecure, so it was doubly odd that she found herself on a first date at her heaviest and most uncertain. *This is my life now.*

"Do you care to talk about it?" he asked. "I don't wish to be intrusive, but it seems odd somehow that a woman such as you is in this situation alone."

"I'm not alone. I'm just not romantically involved," she said.

"So you and the, uh, baby's father broke up?" he asked.

His curiosity was natural but she so didn't want to talk about Sully tonight. "We agreed we're better off as friends. What about you? Do you have any children?"

"Yes, I have two young sons. I love them dearly and wish things had worked with their mother, my ex-wife. As you said, sometimes thing don't work out."

Poppy's first reaction was to pull back, to shut down. A man with an ex-wife and children, yeesh. So much baggage. Then she realized that from this moment on she would always have a child and a Sully, her own baggage. These little moments when she gained sudden insight into how much her life had already changed, how much it would continue to change, induced nothing less than panic. How did she get here? She wasn't ready for this; she wasn't ready for any of this.

"Why did you become a chef?" Diego asked, saving her the continued horror of staring into the scary abyss of grownup decisions her life had become.

"Because of my dad's job. We moved a lot. A lot a lot, to different countries. Food was the one constant, the universal language of love. I developed an affinity for it, and my mom encouraged my interest by letting me cook and bake. I've never wanted to do anything else. What about you? What do you do?"

"Family business," he said, tossing her a little smile that looked self-deprecating. "It was what was expected of me. If I'd had my way, I would have been an artist."

"Did you ever try to do that instead?"

"No, no, no," he said, shaking his head. "This is not one of those situations where I could even try. It is enough that I dabble, that I have a hobby."

"Seems a little sad to me," she said.

"You are young. Dreams are for youth. Responsibility, duty, honor, they are for the wise."

A few months ago, Poppy would have argued with him, would have insisted dreams were worth following no matter the cost. Now she realized that wasn't true. Some things were worth more than dreams and, in fact, dreams could do harm, they could be selfish. More often than not they had to be put away. She faced the window again, the salty taste of tears in her mouth.

Her dream of being a renowned New York pastry chef was in tatters now. All her hard work, all her training, gone in the time it took to kiss Sully in that gazebo. Why had she been so foolish, so stupid, so utterly reckless with her life? It hadn't even been for love. It had been for a moment of adventure, for the thrill of kissing a handsome stranger in a far off place, a stranger who wore a cowboy hat and spoke with a sweet twang that had made her heart thrum.

"I'm sorry, did I offend you?" Diego asked.

Poppy forced a smile and faced him. "No. I suppose I'm merely coming to terms with the fact that I agree with you, that I'm no longer that girl who would have argued passionately in favor of dreams and rainbows and happy endings."

"Let's not throw the proverbial baby out with the bathwater. Just because we can't always follow our dreams doesn't mean we can't have passion and happy endings," he said. He gave her the kind of slow smile that likely would have made her heart turn over if she hadn't just been thinking of Sully and the way his smile had made her heart do the same thing.

"I suppose the trick is in finding the balance," she said, facing forward.

"That's the trick to everything, I think."

He took her to a new restaurant, something trendy and expensive. It was the first time since Poppy left New York that she felt the same thrill of being caught up in the food scene, of being surrounded by people who cared about trends and what was new in the food world. They split an appetizer of roasted bone marrow on sourdough toast points. The marrow was done perfectly, but Poppy secretly thought her sourdough was much better.

"How long were you and your wife together?" Poppy asked. She scraped out the last of the marrow, spread it on the toast, and handed it to him. He smiled as he took it, somehow realizing what a sacrifice it was for her to do so.

"We were high school sweethearts. We've been divorced two years," he said.

"I'm sorry. Somehow it always seems worse when high school sweethearts split," she said.

"I take it you split with your high school sweetheart," he said.

"I never had one. I didn't go to traditional school. My mom home-schooled us because we moved so much. What happened, if I may ask? Though, sorry, I'm insatiably curious. Please tell me to butt out if you'd rather not talk about it."

"No, it's okay. Usually I think most people would be hard pressed to pinpoint one thing that went wrong, but with us it's very easy: my family."

"She doesn't like your family?" Poppy said.

"My family is...very entwined. We work together, we socialize together. We're closer than most families, I'd wager. It got to be a bit too much closeness. She felt I always chose them over her."

"Did you?" Poppy asked.

"Yes," he said. He peeled back his sleeve to remind her of his tattoo.

Family first. Unconsciously she reached out and traced it with her index finger.

"I thought when you get married, that becomes your new family," she said.

"Most of the time, yes. In my case, no."

"Hmm." She realized she still traced absently over the tattoo and withdrew her hand, cheeks flushing. She was a highly affectionate person. Sometimes it came out in all the worst ways. The upside to having a baby soon was that she could cuddle it as much as she wanted and no one would judge her for it. Smiling, Diego reached for her hand and kissed the back of it. He was charming and sophisticated. But Poppy wasn't certain she was in the mood to be charmed. *If I ever get a tattoo, it will say "bad timing,"* she thought. If she'd met Diego before Sully, she would have jumped in with both feet, flirted, tried to impress and amuse him. As it was now she felt almost wary and more than a little pessimistic over their prospects as a couple. On the other hand, they seemed to have similar tastes. It could be fun to have someone to try restaurants with, to go to galleries with. She had been feeling bored and restless lately and Sully certainly had no interest in those things. He was a homebody, thoroughly content to sit on the couch night after night watching sports. Poppy had read more books on his couch lately than she had read in all the years since high school.

The gallery was as fun and interesting as she thought it might be. Most of the artists were local and most were people Diego knew. He also knew the owner of the gallery. Being there, immersing herself in the art world, meeting new people, filled a need Poppy had tried hard to suppress. She had to get out more, even if she had to borrow a car and do it on her own. Her mom used to say she was aptly named because she was like a flower; she needed certain things to survive or she would wither and die. Affection, fun, adventure, and culture. Those were the things she needed, and those were the things she had been lacking since she arrived in Texas.

"You look happy," Diego whispered as they walked to his car.

"I am," she said. "Thank you for this evening. I can't think of one part of it I didn't enjoy."

"You are most welcome," he said. They reached his car and paused. Poppy thought he might kiss her, and she wasn't certain if she wanted him to. Despite the enjoyable evening, despite the fact that he was handsome and pleasant, she still felt a certain reserve. If she had to put a name to it, it would be Sully. They weren't together, they'd been clear on that. But still…

He didn't kiss her, and Poppy was both relieved and disappointed. He patted his pockets, almost absently, and frowned.

"Something wrong?" she asked.

"I gave up smoking a year ago and I've been filling the void with chewing gum. It's a nasty habit but one that will ensure more life with my kids. Only now I seem to be out of gum and in desperate need. Would you mind very much if we stop at a gas station?"

"Not at all," Poppy assured him. He held the door for her, closing it behind her after she slid inside. They drove to a gas station a few blocks away.

"I'll only be a moment. Do you need anything?" he asked.

She glanced at the gas station. It was the kind that made the good milkshakes. Could she reasonably request a milkshake at the end of a first date? "Nothing, thank you."

He nodded and disappeared inside. Poppy rested her head on the seat behind her and then realized now was a good time to check her makeup and reapply some gloss. She pulled down the mirror, and that was when she saw it. Sully's white work truck was parked a hundred feet away. She couldn't see his face, but she could make out the outline of his hat. She withdrew her phone, ready to fire off an angry text.

"Forget it," she mumbled. Stuffing the phone back in her purse, she pushed open the door, stomped to the truck, and yanked open the door. "What on earth do you think you're doing?"

"Ma'am?" A man stared back at her, shocked, alarmed.

"Oh," Poppy said, her cheeks filling with heat. Was pregnancy making her crazy? She had been so certain this was Sully. Same truck, same white hat. "I'm sorry, please excuse me. I thought you were someone else."

He gave her a little smile and a polite nod as she closed the door and walked away. She stopped short, whirled, and went back, knocking on the door this time. He lowered the window. "I'm sorry, but are you a Ranger?"

"Yes, ma'am. May I help you in some way?"

"No, I…" she shook her head as if to clear it.

"Are you in danger? Do you need help?" He nodded toward the gas station.

"No, everything is fine. He went for gum. I just…" she rested her hand on the bump, suddenly missing Sully with something like physical force. "Rangers are so iconic." She smiled again, tossed him a little wave, and returned to Diego's car to wait.

CHAPTER 22

"Well, lookie who we have here. The Rangers' most famous loverboy."

Sully tipped his hat to the speaker, his friend, Oliver Bebout who liked to give him a hard time. Who was he kidding? They all liked to give him a hard time, not that he didn't give as good as he got. But ever since that blasted article about Poppy came out, the one with his picture attached, his coworkers had been having a field day making fun of his newfound (and profoundly unwanted) fame.

"Can I have your autograph?" Oliver continued, handing Sully his pen.

"I have another suggestion for this," Sully said, turning the pen around and holding it like a weapon.

"You kiss your pretty girlfriend with that mouth?" Bebout continued.

Sully had spent the first week after the article came out trying to explain that Poppy wasn't his girlfriend. When that became too complicated, mostly because no one listened anyway, he gave up. So they thought Poppy and he were actually together. What was the harm?

"No, I kissed your Mama," Sully said, and everyone snickered. Being one of the younger members of the team, Bebout's mother actually was a nice looking woman and often wound up the topic of conversation, much to his aggravation.

"Shut up about my Mama," Bebout replied, predictably annoyed. He pounded the top of Sully's hat, making it flip up in the back. Sully took it off and laid it on the table beside him, shaking out his head to try and fluff up the mashed pieces of hair. It was time for the meeting to start and the other Rangers in the room did the same until the table was crowded with hats and pens and laptops.

The lieutenant sat, and the meeting began. "First up, Cortez family."

"Man, I'm so sick of the Cortez family," Lopez groused. For once Sully agreed with him. They'd been hitting the family hard lately, trailing them day and night, waiting and hoping for them to trip up. "I see more of him than I do my wife. Shut it, Garcia," he added, jutting his finger at Garcia, who held up his hands in supplication. Predictably, Harris laughed.

"There was a new development," the lieutenant said, and everyone leaned forward in interest. Anything new had the potential to be explosive. Cortez was a man who always followed the same pattern. He was extremely careful with every aspect of his life. The lieutenant who, for once, seemed to be enjoying the drama, didn't hasten to explain.

"Is he waiting for one of us to ask him what it is?" Garcia whispered in a loud aside. Harris giggled like a thirteen year old girl.

"Cortez had a date," the lieutenant said, leaning back and clasping his hands behind his head.

Lopez let fly an expletive. "Co-sign on that," Garcia said, sounding void of humor for once. In all the time they'd been tailing Cortez, they'd never seen him with a woman outside his wife. With enough motivation, mistresses could be flipped. It had been another frustration in a series of frustrations that Diego Cortez didn't have one.

"Can we flip her?" Sully asked the question everyone thought.

"Dunno. Let's look at what we've got," the lieutenant said. He nodded to his assistant. The lights went off, and everyone turned their attention to the opposite end of the room, waiting for the pictures of Cortez and the new mystery woman to begin.

CHAPTER 23

Poppy was mid-conversation with a rancher's wife when Sully opened the door of *Huck's* and made a beeline for her. As much as she tried to keep her focus on the woman in front of her, it was diverted to him when he steamrolled up to her, bypassed the counter, and clasped her hand, tugging her alongside him toward the exit.

"I'm with a customer," Poppy said, trying futilely to resist his leading.

"Excuse us, Mrs. Marsh. She'll be back in a minute," Sully said, relentlessly leading Poppy out the door and around the corner.

"I'm going to have to have my name engraved on this wall space," Poppy said, leaning there now.

"Don't joke right now, Poppy," Sully said, his tone angry and dangerous.

"What is your problem?" she asked.

"You went out with Diego Cortez," he said. He had been at his morning briefing when the picture of her came up, startling him so badly that he jolted forward and nearly upended his coffee. If they hadn't had a tail on Cortez, he might never have known until it was too late.

She blinked at him. "Right, and? You knew that. I told you I had a date."

"You said you had terrible taste in men, and I thought it was hyperbole, but it wasn't. You literally walk into a room and find the lowest specimen humanity can offer," he said.

She blinked at him, hurt. "I didn't deserve that."

He blew out a breath and reminded himself she had no idea. "I'm sorry. I know you don't get my job, but I am not the kind of cop who sits in my car all day and hands out tickets to old ladies going five miles over the limit. I'm an investigator, the sort who handles big cases, the biggest cases in the state, really. Diego Cortez is part of my work. He's a bad man."

Her face looked like she tried not to smile. "Are we talking about the same Diego? A man who held every door for me and kissed my *hand* goodnight?"

He put his hands on her biceps, resisting the powerful urge to shake some sense into her. "It doesn't matter, none of that matters. What matters is who he is, and he is a bad man, the worst sort of man. His family has been an organized crime syndicate for generations, involved in racketeering, witness tampering, kidnapping, theft, drug running, money laundering, and murder."

She swallowed hard. "Murder?"

"Yes, Poppy, murder. I have reason to believe, good reason, that Diego has personally done a few to earn his street cred. He's the head of the family now. You don't get there merely by nepotism. He had to earn his spot. He purposely targeted you because of me."

"Oh," she said, her face going slightly pale.

She looked exactly like someone whose innocence had just been shattered, and Sully felt immediate regret that he'd been the one to do it.

"He seemed so kind, so gentle, so intelligent and cultured," she said.

"He is intelligent and cultured. That's what makes him lethal. He'd be a whole lot easier to catch if he were ignorant and stupid."

"So he doesn't actually like me. It was all for pretend."

On the one hand, he couldn't believe that was her primary concern at the moment. Did she not understand how much danger she had been in, might still be in? On the other hand, she was pregnant and vulnerable and a man she liked had used her. "If it's any consolation, I like you, and it's not for pretend." His arms slid around her and drew her closer. Her bump pressed against him, and he swallowed hard, a wave of desire hitting him like a fist to the gut.

"It's fine," she said, forcing a smile. "We had one little date, not some epic romance. It's not like I'm carrying his child or anything."

"No, not his," he agreed. Her face tipped up to his, trying to smile to cover the hurt. His knuckles brushed her cheek, and then he kissed her, fear and relief and attraction all mingling together into some powerful force that erased any reserve from the kiss. Poppy responded as if she'd been waiting for it, standing on her toes and slipping her fingers into his hair to urge him closer. He picked her up, bringing her within easier reach of his face, pressed her to the wall, and kissed her again. She kissed him back, hungrily, as if she had been starving for his touch. A horn beeped, and they broke apart, breathless, startled to realize they were still in an alley in the middle of the afternoon.

"What was that?" Poppy asked, her voice whispy and unsteady.

"I don't know, I just...Marry me, Poppy." She opened her mouth to reply, and he pressed his thumb to her lips. "I want you in my life, in my house, in my bed. Let's put aside everything else and be together."

She kissed his thumb. He smoothed it gently over her swollen lips and moved it aside, allowing her to answer. "No."

"Why?"

"Asking me out of a knee jerk reaction because you're jealous and afraid is no way to start a marriage," she said.

"You know that's not the only reason, and it's not as if I haven't asked before when I was both reasonable and rational," he said.

"That's true, but that time was too reasonable and rational. This time was too emotional and reactionary. There has to be a balance, Sullivan."

He ran a hand wearily over his face. "I don't understand what you want from me."

"It's not what I want from you, it's what I want for you, and for myself as well. I want magic for both of us. Sully, we have something here, some attraction and some friendship, but is that enough to sustain a lifetime of togetherness? I don't want either of us to wake up five years from now and realize we're together only for the sake of the baby. I want us to feel like, regardless of our child, we would want to be together. Can you honestly say you'd want to spend your life with me if I weren't pregnant with your baby?"

He opened his mouth, but the words wouldn't form.

"Exactly," she replied, but her tone was more sad than triumphant. "I really need to get back inside." Despite her words, she stood on her toes and kissed him again, gently and sweetly this time. "If life were only about kisses, I'd marry you in a minute, Sully, because I think I could kiss you every day of forever and never lose heart."

He pressed his face to her neck and inhaled. "Poppy."

"I bet I'm making you crazy, huh?" she asked, her tone sympathetic as she ran a hand soothingly over his head.

He nodded and clutched her closer, her bump nudging his abdomen.

"I'm not trying to," she said.

"I know," he said. He forced a deep breath. "You need to tell me if Diego contacts you again."

"What should I tell him if he asks me out again?" she asked.

"Tell him you have a crazy jealous partner who will literally lose his mind if you so much as talk to him again," Sully said.

"Is that really what you want me to say?" she murmured as his lips began absently kissing her neck.

"No." He stood upright away from her. "Tell him it's not going to work out, something innocuous and gentle. You don't want to provoke him."

"Okay." She pressed her palm to his cheek. "Are you doing okay?"

He nodded. "But, Poppy, I don't think I can stand the thought of you with another man right now. It's too much." His hand settled possessively on her bump.

"It was probably too much to hope that I could date someone else while pregnant with your child. The good news is my prospects in that regard are pretty dim, minus the psycho who was only interested in me to get to you."

"That's not the only reason he was interested in you. It was an added bonus. He was interested in you because you're beautiful and sweet and charming and pregnancy has somehow made you insanely more appealing."

"Only to you, I think," she said.

"Maybe so, but isn't that enough?" he asked.

She took his hand and gave it a squeeze. "I don't actually enjoy the thought of you dating anyone else right now either."

"I just asked you to marry me, and you think I'm going to go trolling for another woman?" he asked.

She shrugged. "You can't remain a monk forever."

"That's not on my radar. Not now, not any time in the near future. I'm solely focused on you and the baby."

"You're a good man, Sully Langford, and I'm lucky to have you in my life. You're going to be an amazing father." Despite her insistence that she needed to get back inside, she hugged him, resting her head over his heart.

He slid his arms around her and rubbed a gentle little circle in the center of her back. "I know neither of us chose this path on purpose, Poppy. But if I had to do it with anyone, I'm glad it's with you." He kissed the top of her head.

"That feels so good," Poppy said, leaning into his touch. "My back hurts all the time."

The words made Sully feel guilty on a number of levels, first because he was the one who had done this to her, and second because Bailey had told him Poppy's back must be hurting, had told him how much physical touch meant to her. He had held off touching her because he hadn't wanted to push their relationship somewhere it wasn't ready to go. But Poppy needed him, now more than ever.

"Tonight, after work, I will rub your back for as long as you want, okay?" he said.

She made a little sound, somewhere between a grunt and a sigh.

"I should get back," he said, but he made no move to go. The feel of her against him was doing confusing things to his senses. His hand still made a little circle at the base of her spine. With each pass, Poppy melted into him a little bit more. His heart began to thud painfully as his breathing became shallower. How could he possibly let go of her and walk away? Not just today, but ever?

"Hey, y'all, I'm sorry to bother you, but Poppy's getting quite a line." Mrs. Baker stood at the end of the alley, watching them with a wry smile. Sully had no idea what the town said about them, but he could imagine what they'd say now after Mrs. Baker got done relaying their canoodling session.

"Thank you," Poppy said, easing away from him without making eye contact. She still held his hand, and she gave it a squeeze. "I'll see you, Sully."

"Supper tonight," he said, holding on to her hand as she took a step away.

For a moment he thought she might refuse, might try to run away from whatever was now brewing between them, but she nodded instead. "Supper tonight." She pivoted back to him, stood on her toes, and kissed his cheek, pausing to whisper in his ear. "You have magic fingers."

He laughed. "Clearly," he said, motioning to her burgeoning belly.

Her eyes widened and she shook her head. "Oh, my, Sullivan Langford."

"You think I need to go back to Sunday School?" he asked.

"Clearly," she said, motioning to her bump again. He laughed again, the last vestiges of attraction clearing away.

"I'll see you tonight. Try to stay out of trouble in the interim."

"No promises," Poppy said, tossing him a little wave as she disappeared from view.

CHAPTER 24

That evening began a new normal for Poppy and Sully. They weren't together, they were clear on that. But another layer of intimacy had been added between them. No longer did they confine themselves to separate ends of the couch and a friendly wave goodbye. Now they spread out on the couch, their legs overlapping as they took turns rubbing each other's feet. No one Sully dated had ever rubbed his feet before. It turned out he liked it as much as Poppy did, which was to say a lot. Sometimes they shifted positions. He lay behind her and rubbed her back, but more often when they were in that position one or both of them fell asleep, cleaved together like yin and yang, his arm around her waist, one hand tucked between both of hers.

Poppy had become as familiar to him as his own body. He could tell with a grimace or a twinge when a part of her hurt, when she felt exhausted or stressed or frustrated. And yet it was a false intimacy, forced by the bond of mutual and surprising parenthood. At the end of the evening, she still went home to her own place, still maintained a barrier between them, still held on to whatever kept them from being together, kept them from being one. Sully could never figure out if he was relieved or upset by that. In some ways, he had the best of both worlds. Poppy was there when he wanted her and went home when he didn't. Except the more time they spent together, there were fewer instances when he didn't want her. Increasingly it hurt to see her leave at the end of the day. He began to dread the point in the evening when she would glance at the clock and unfurl herself from his couch, intending to head home. It hurt, physically hurt, to see her walk away. On the other hand, he had no idea how to make her stay. He had proposed twice. What more was there?

He still pondered as Easter approached. They would spend the holiday at Cal and Bailey's ranch, along with Sully's family. It wasn't such an unusual thing that his family had been included in the celebration, seeing as how they'd all been friends for years. But he knew it was Bailey's sneaky way of pushing everything together. Sully wasn't certain if he should be grateful or resentful. Poppy, who took orders of pies, cakes, and cookies for the big day, was too stressed to do anything more than roll her eyes when Sully addressed the issue of Bailey's matchmaking between them.

"Why do you think I resisted moving closer to my family for so long?" she said, making what had to be her fifteenth batch of cookie dough for the evening and sticking it in the freezer. "Oh, hey, guess what?"

By her buoyant tone, he knew it was going to be something good. He smiled in anticipation. "What?"

"One of my best friends is coming to visit for Easter."

"That's awesome. Who is it?" he asked, swiping a blob of dough from the mixer paddle before she could wash it.

"Sasha," she said absently, turning her back to him.

He studied her back. By now he knew all her body language. By the tense set of her shoulders, he knew there was more she held back. "Poppy, what?"

She swallowed hard. "Nothing. It's just...Sasha is George's sister." She let out a shaky little breath. "I wasn't sure she would still be speaking to me, considering how much I apparently hurt him. I'm relieved and trepidatious."

"You think she's coming here to ream you?"

She shrugged. "I don't know. Sasha travels a ton, doesn't get a lot of time off to be with family. It feels a little ominous that she's choosing to spend Easter with me."

It felt ominous to Sully, too, but for different reasons. He didn't believe this Sasha person was coming to let Poppy have it. Rather it felt like she was coming to try and fix things. That's what he would do if something went wrong in his sibling's life; he would travel as far as he needed to go and do whatever he saw fit to make it right. Sasha was coming to go to bat for George; Sully could feel it in his bones. The question in his mind was what Poppy's response would be.

Danger, danger, danger. He could feel it, suddenly, as if someone were waving a red flag in front of him. Something was coming, something with the power to take Poppy away from him, possibly forever. Hadn't The Colonel warned him that George wasn't done with Poppy? Maybe this was his pitch, sending his sister in to soften her up before he made his own move.

Swallowing down a lump of dread that tasted like acid, he eased forward and began rubbing the small of her back with both hands. She turned to mush, as she always did, setting aside the bowl she'd been cleaning and leaning both hands on the counter for support.

"You're going to get tired of being my masseuse," she whispered.

"Not likely," he said, his hands smoothing from her back to her front, offering support to the ligaments there that were also starting to pull taut and ache. "Besides, it's good practice for labor."

"Sully, I don't know," she whispered, eyes still closed. "It's so incredibly intimate."

"I was there for the making of this baby; I should be there for the delivery, too," he pointed out, easing his hands back to her spine and then toward her navel again.

"I'm going to be..." she started and trailed off.

"Going to be what, honey?" he asked.

She swallowed hard and faced him. His hands had been smoothing toward her navel again, so that when she turned they met at her spine. He kept them there, circling her in his embrace. He tucked his elbows in and eased her closer, lining her body up with his. Her arms had goosebumps, as they always did when he massaged her. He eyed them and pressed back a smile. He had as much of an effect on her as she had on him, even if neither of them was willing to admit it.

"I'm going to be exposed and helpless, more than I've ever been before. If we do that, if we go there, what if there's no coming back?"

She looked so incredibly vulnerable. In that moment he realized anew how easy it would be to break her, to do permanent damage with his words or actions. He had to tread carefully, more so than ever before. Now was not the time to play around. He brought his hands forward and used them to cup her face. His thumbs smoothed gently over her cheekbones.

"I want to be there for me, obviously, but mostly I want to be there for you, to support you and care for you in every possible way. And, Poppy, I have a feeling you're going to need and want me there, hard as that may be for you to imagine. You and I have built something these last few months. I don't know exactly what it is, but I know it's real and deep. We're in this together, all the way. I want to be the person you hold on to, the person who gives you strength, at least in that moment."

"In that moment," she repeated, turning the words over as if they held some significance. Then she drew in a sharp breath and pressed her head to his chest.

"What is it?" he asked.

"Braxton-Hicks, I think. Ouch."

His hands migrated to the baby. He felt her body contract and become hard a couple of seconds and then release. And then the baby kicked against his hand, bubbling little flutters.

Sully froze. "Did…"

"You felt that, right?" Poppy said, now beaming at him.

He nodded, his face a mask of wonder. Both hands were on the bump now, skimming over it, waiting and hoping for another nudge. One came, and then another and another.

"He has the hiccups," Poppy said, smiling. Her hand covered his.

"He?" Sully said.

"Or she. It's easier to say he than try and make a genderless distinction each time." She stared thoughtfully at her stomach. "I guess next week we'll know for certain."

Sully's heart sped up and turned over. "Wow."

"Very much wow," Poppy agreed. She beamed down at their little miracle, both dimples so deep he could probably poke his fingers in her cheeks and make his knuckles disappear. Her hair tumbled forward, obscuring his view, and he pushed it jealously out of the way. Poppy was sparkle and sunshine, a riot of color and warmth. Sully felt like vanilla pudding when he was in her nearness. How had he never realized how bland his life had become?

"After the doctor appointment next week, let's go out," he said.

Now her smile tipped in his direction, turning coy. Poppy was all the adjectives: coy, bright, vivacious, sparkly, vibrant, fizzy. She had none of Bailey's steely reserve. Sometimes he thought one of their eggs must have been switched in the nest but, not knowing their mother, he couldn't say for certain which one.

"What did you have in mind, Ranger?"

What he had in mind and what he could safely say to her were vastly different things. "I'll plan something, Baker Poppy."

Her eyes brightened, her slightly tipped nose tipping farther with pleasure. Her face was an exaggeration of everything feminine: lush mouth, dazzling eyes, deep cupid's bow, upturned nose. The smattering of freckles across the bridge did nothing to lessen his fascination with her features. His fingers itched to touch her freckles, and so he did, easing his finger gently along the apex of her nose.

"Make it epic," she whispered, and he grinned.

"Why must you challenge me in all the ways?"

Her smile dimmed, a lid extinguishing a candle flame. "My lot in life is to challenge the people I hold most dear."

"Want to know a secret?" he asked, using this thumb to tip her face back to his.

"What?" she said, some of her sparkle making a return.

He leaned closer and whispered in her ear. "I love it. Keeps me on my toes."

"These toes?" she asked. Together they stared down at his leather cowboy boots. They were a source of constant amusement for her. *We could not be more different if we tried,* she was fond of telling him. *We're the city mouse and the country mouse. Opposites in every way.*

Sully thought it was a good thing, the differences between them. "Opposites attract, Poppisandra."

She glanced up at him, her smile sliding away again and ending in a little shudder. "Until they don't, Sullivan."

CHAPTER 25

Sully's day started bad and went downhill. In law enforcement, holidays could go two ways. Either it was deathly silent while people took time off being stupid to celebrate, or people used the time to fuel their stupidity with alcohol. Today was a combustible day. He'd been sent to tag along on five domestics with the state patrol, and it wasn't even noon. Domestics were notoriously the most dangerous calls, emotion and alcohol merging to create an unstable powder keg. And there were always weapons in the home, adding another element of danger. Cops never knew if they were about to walk into battle, if a few well-placed words would be enough to diffuse the situation, or if they'd have to use force. In three of the scenarios, Sully and Len, the state trooper he was backing, were able to talk the couple down. In two it ended in a brawl. At the last house, there had been young children on standby, watching their screaming father get tackled, a gun wrestled out of his grasp while their bleeding mother stood nearby, pleading with the officers not to hurt him. Until Poppy, that was the thing Sully hadn't understood—how a woman could take a beating and defend the man who beat her. But he got it now, at least a little. They'd been conditioned, trained to take it and move on. It was a horrible way for a woman to live, wrenching when children were involved.

In addition to the draining, disheartening domestics, he had his regular investigative work, work that had ground to a standstill after Poppy's date with Diego. The man was taunting him, Sully could feel it. Every time he thought of how close he'd gotten to Poppy, close enough to touch her, he wanted to erupt in a pile of hot lava rage, to literally hunt the man down and lay hands on him. But then he would calm himself with the remembrance that it was what Diego wanted. So much of being a cop was an issue of mind over matter, of not reacting to enraging emotional stimuli. It was why so many cops ended up divorced, because they became so used to cutting off their emotions they started doing it with their wives.

Sully tried imagining ever being cold and aloof with Poppy and laughed out loud. It would be like not reacting to picking up a live wire. She was so electric the response was beyond his control, all passion, sparkle, and sass. And they weren't even together. How much more potent would she be if they were?

"You all right?" Len asked, darting him a glance when he remained silently staring into space, his mind on Poppy.

"Fine," Sully said, dragging his attention back to the vehicle, a good thing since he was the one driving.

"Whatcha got going on tomorrow?" Len asked. "You working?"

"No, working Christmas. Tomorrow's off." Since crime never stopped, cops didn't either. It was Sully's first Easter off in six years. "We're going to my, ah, Poppy's sister's house."

Len's eyes bugged. "Wait, that's Calhoun Ridge, right? Man, sometimes I forget you know him, and now you're practically family."

"We were always practically family," Sully said, tugging his collar. "We go back a ways, grew up in the same town, I played ball with his brother."

"Yeah, but now it's official. Well, almost. I mean, he's going to be your kid's uncle. Although I guess you won't be his kid's uncle, not really."

For some reason the comment annoyed Sully. It seemed unfair

somehow that Cal got to officially be his child's family while Sully orbited on the periphery, alone and unofficial. Not that he planned to be uninvolved, but he also wouldn't be Uncle Sully. He would remain Sully, baby daddy. His hand gripped the wheel and he cleared his throat.

"Man, your girl sure is pretty. I can see why Diego went for her. Even pregnant, she's…"

"Len, shut up," Sully said, his voice low and dangerous. Len did a double take. Even though Sully was a tough, no-nonsense Ranger, he was affable, congenial, friendly, almost always smiling or laughing. It was the first time outside the job Len had ever heard him sound so…menacing.

"I didn't mean anything by it, Sul. It seemed out of character, you know, you getting a girl knocked up. We were all pretty shocked by it. But then we saw her in those pictures with Diego and it was like, oh, that's why. Because sweet and hot together. And even pregnant you can tell her body is…"

Sully slammed on the brakes so hard Len's body would have flown through the front windshield if he hadn't been wearing his seatbelt. "Not another word, or I swear you will walk back to the station."

Len made a show of pressing his lips together. Sully resumed driving, heart thundering. It was bad enough the guys had been talking about Poppy, speculating over what kind of woman she was because she'd gotten pregnant, over what kind of man he was for making her that way. But then he brought up the pictures with Diego, and it was all Sully could do to keep a lid on his temper. A murderer had gotten within inches of his heart, next to his baby and his, well, his Poppy. And all his coworkers had witnessed it. Sully wanted to throw up.

The remainder of the day did nothing to improve his mood. By the time he let himself into his house, he wanted nothing more than to run off his anger and then shower. But the scent of butter and sugar greeted him on the porch, tempting and confusing him at once.

He followed his nose to the kitchen where he saw Poppy working frantically, a dozen pie tins spread over his kitchen table. She didn't look up when he entered. He wasn't certain she'd even noticed him.

"Poppy?" he said, curious and only a tiny bit annoyed. She had never let herself in uninvited before.

She glanced up, a streak of flour on her cheek. "Oh, hi," she said, and then she burst into tears.

He hadn't seen her in tears since her arrival. He vowed then that his reaction the next time would be better. The vow galvanized him to action. He went forward, gathered her to him, and led her to the couch, settling her into his lap as they sat down. The thing he had finally realized about Poppy was how important, possibly even necessary, human touch was to her. She needed it the way she needed food and air. He petted her, rubbing her back, kissing her hair, squeezing her shoulders, soothing her with his words, whispered little endearments, *sweetie, honey, baby,* and her favorite, *darlin'.*

At last she was calm, her head resting tiredly on his chest, her body shuddering with leftover snuffles.

"Can you talk?" he asked, his thumb sliding gently up and down her neck.

"It's nothing," she said, and he laughed. His laughter made her smile. She took a deep breath and let it out slowly. "It's really nothing, in the scheme of things. A pipe burst in my house. The landlord had to shut the water off. Sasha will be here any minute, and now I have nowhere to stash her. I have about a thousand pie orders for tomorrow, which is great, but I was a bit optimistic in my ability to get everything done. I've been up and baking since three. My feet hurt, I'm exhausted, and I'm nowhere near finished." She inhaled deeply again. "You smell amazing, by the way."

"Thank you. How many pies do you have left?"

"Thirty six," she said. "I had to do the cakes first because of frosting." She explained as if this made sense to him when, really, it didn't. What he knew about baking could fit on an index card. He was merely the one who got to enjoy the fruits of her labor, hence the reason he had now started running five miles every night when he got home from work. Life with Poppy was a delight, but it had the power to make him soft as a butter cow. He checked his watch. It was six.

"I'm going to help you get your next batch of pies in the oven, and then I'm going to grab us some BBQ takeout. And then we'll do the next batch and the next until we're all finished." He kissed her temple. She snuggled closer, nestling.

"What about Sasha?" she asked, sounding sleepy.

"She'll stay here, you both will."

"Your house is better anyway," she admitted, sliding her arms up to wrap around him. "Thanks, Sully. I owe you."

"I think you'll pay me back forever when you push this thing out," he said, tapping the bump. Poppy giggled, pressing her face to his neck to absorb the laughter. Sully squeezed her tighter and closed his eyes, wishing to freeze the moment. Life with Poppy always felt like a small series of stolen moments that never seemed to last. Always the reminder intruded: *She's not really yours. Soon this will all be over. Someday she'll belong to someone else.* In the beginning those intrusive little thoughts had been annoying. Now they were nothing less than panic inducing. At this point in their relationship, if he had to see Poppy with another man, he might actually die from the pain and injustice of it.

"I should get back to it," Poppy said, sounding as reluctant and tired as he felt. They both dragged themselves to the kitchen where they made an assembly line. Poppy had already put the crusts in the tins. Sully measured equal amounts of the filling into each one while Poppy went behind him adding the pecans. They put six pies in his oven. He carried four pies to her oven while Poppy cleaned the kitchen. Sully went to get their supper while Poppy began prepping the next batch of dough.

When he returned, she glanced up at him with something like adoration in her eyes, and he felt a spark of hope. If this was all it took, this taking care of her, he could do it. He was a natural caregiver, and Poppy made it easy by being so receptive. They shared a smile, one not devoid of sparks, and ate as they worked. Between bites of brisket, Sully cracked about a million eggs while Poppy rolled dough and pressed it into tins. The first batch of pies came out of the oven, and one more batch went in.

"Hey, my Mom's got an oven," Sully said, smacking his skull like the dunce he was. "Let's put some in hers, and we'll almost be done."

"For a park ranger, you're kind of a genius," Poppy said, standing on her toes to steal the pickle out of his fingers and eat it before he could protest. He grinned at her, his eyes following her fluid movements around his small kitchen. It was like watching a dancer in her element—pivot, dip, slide, spin, repeat, over and over as she repeated the prep work for each pie. Sully was amazed, both by her ingenuity and her skill. Everyone loved her pies, everyone loved *her*. She had made a success of her popup bakery in a town that didn't like strangers, a town that could barely keep any business alive.

They were too tired and tense to talk much as they worked, both exhausted from their long days. But even so, a funny thing began to happen in that kitchen. It became filled with a kind of glow, sparks of electricity that multiplied into one giant current of attraction. The room was charged with it. Sully stared at Poppy, dropping his eyes when she looked up to catch him. And then, when he couldn't take it any more, his eyes would stray in her direction again, in time to catch her averting her stare from him.

She put the last pie in the oven and turned her attention to the sink, her back to him as she began to wash the dishes.

"What are you doing?" he asked.

"Cleaning up," she said, not bothering to turn around. Her tone sounded normal, but there was a tightness in her shoulders, more from exhaustion than anything else.

"No, I mean what are you doing to me," he said. He pressed against her, pushed her hair aside, and kissed her neck. Poppy melted, as she always did, going up in flames as a sigh leaked out of her. He was about to spin her to face him when a loud knock sounded on the door. They both froze.

"Sasha," Poppy whispered, sounding guilty, likely because she forgot. Sully forgot, too, but then he tended to forget everything but Poppy when she was in the room.

They eased apart. Poppy dried her hands and faced him. "How's my hair?" Her fingers reached to smooth the flyaway strands. Sully noted the way they shook and beamed at her.

"Beautiful," he said and then, because he couldn't resist, he tipped her face and skimmed his lips over hers, ever so lightly. She tipped forward on her toes, leaning into him, urging him to continue. "Sasha," he said, his lips moving against hers.

"No, it's Poppy," she said, pulling back to give him an ornery grin and a boop on his nose.

They walked to the door together, side by side. Sully had offered to pick the friend up from the airport, but she declined, choosing to rent a car and drive instead. Apparently all the women in Poppy's world were the strong and independent sort.

Excited now, Poppy flung open the door in delight. "Sasha!"

"And George," he added, stepping into view beside his sister.

CHAPTER 26

Sully and Poppy stood side by side staring at Sasha and George who stood side by side on the other side of the threshold. They were like mirror images of each other, except Sasha and George were beaming while Sully and Poppy remained speechless with shock. In those tense few seconds before anyone spoke, George's eyes flicked quickly over Poppy, wincing with pain at the sight of her bump, before fastening accusingly on Sully.

You did this to her, he seemed to say.

Sully, who suddenly sensed he was about to enter the fight of his life, narrowed his eyes and sent a message of his own. *That's right I did, and I'd do it again so back off.* Outwardly of course he smiled as he eased his left arm around Poppy's shoulders and gave them a squeeze.

"Welcome to Texas, Sasha and George."

"Yee-haw," Sasha replied, already nosily glancing around him to spy the interior of his house.

"What am I doing?" Poppy asked, finally unfreezing her tongue. She sprang forward and hugged her friends, Sasha first and then George who lingered a bit too long in the hug for Sully's taste. Sully stood very nearby, scowling his displeasure, in case anyone had doubts. Poppy let go of George and grabbed Sasha's hand, dragging her inside.

"You haven't officially met Sully. Sully, this is Sasha."

Sasha was tall and willowy with the same dark hair and eyes as her brother. But unlike George, there was no hostility in her eyes. Her smile was warm, if frank and a bit sarcastic. She thrust forth her hand and gave him a hearty shake.

"The baby daddy, we meet at last," she said. "I believe you know George."

George and Sully exchanged heads up nods while Sully reassessed his opinion of Sasha. She wasn't there to run interference for her brother or play matchmaker; she was there to cause trouble. If possible, Poppy now seemed like the temperate one in their relationship.

"The two of you together must have gotten into a heap of trouble," he noted, glancing between them.

"If only," Sasha bemoaned. "Believe it or not, this is our first time meeting face to face."

"What? You didn't tell me that," Sully said, darting Poppy an accusing glance that made George snort in delight. "How is it possible? You said she's one of your best friends." *See, George? I know things. Poppy and I talk.*

"Pen pals," Sasha volunteered. "Since the time we could both write. Poppy and I have a lot in common, our dads to begin with, but so much more."

"And what do you do?" Sully asked. It occurred to him he should probably know. He refused to look at George and give him the satisfaction of realizing it was one more thing he and Poppy hadn't discussed.

"I'm an assassin," she said, so deadpan Sully didn't know if she was joking. He thought she was, but given what Poppy's dad did for a living, he couldn't be certain.

"A *corporate* assassin," George volunteered, sensing his confusion. "Sasha goes into troubled companies and takes care of all the dead weight."

Sasha made a slitting motion across her throat, not bothered in the least by her brother's dim assessment of her job.

"So," George continued, clapping his hands and rubbing them together as if in gleeful anticipation. "What have you got planned for us, P? Some rotten adventure, I'll bet."

"Yes, I have this new game called, 'Helping Poppy Survive Poverty.' We're all going to take a pie and wrap it in cellophane," Poppy declared.

"Bring it," Sasha said. Sully was willing to bet she had it tattooed somewhere. They headed toward the kitchen while Poppy gave them each a pie and instructions on how to wrap. Despite the heavy tension in the atmosphere, it was fun. Then again, there wasn't much Poppy couldn't make fun. Even so, she was practically dead on her feet by ten, and they still had more than two dozen pies left to go.

"Poppy, go to bed," Sully said.

"When we're finished," she said, hiding a yawn in the crook of her elbow.

"I'm sorry, did you think that was somehow optional?" He came to stand beside her and turned her to face Sasha and George. "Say goodnight to the nice people. We'll finish wrapping the pies, and I'll get them settled. You'll see them in the morning and the next few days after that."

She wanted to argue, he could tell by the way she attempted to hold herself stiffly away from him. But she'd also been awake almost twenty four hours, and her body couldn't take it anymore, not with a baby growing inside her. "I'm sorry," she explained to Sasha and George. "I have no control anymore. It's a misery."

"Yeah, you're suffering for certain," Sasha said, her eyes sweeping approvingly over Sully from head to toe. "We'll see you in the morning, chipmunk. Get some sleep."

"I'm really sorry," Poppy added to George who had been quiet and watchful all evening. Sully guessed they would need some time to clear the air between them, but it definitely wasn't going to happen tonight.

"Get some sleep, woman," he said, rolling his eyes with a smile that only looked half forced.

Sully put his arm around her and half-carried her up the stairs. Now that she realized she was headed to bed, she began to shut down. "I need to wash my face," she protested when he bypassed the bathroom and ushered her to the bedroom.

"I'll wash it for you." He rifled in a drawer and tossed her one of his t-shirts. "Change and I'll be right back." He disappeared, loaded a washrag with some fancy soap his mom had purchased for him, and returned to the room. Poppy was just slipping between the sheets, his t-shirt still too large for her, even with the bump. The sight of her in it gave his stomach a jolt, as did the vision of her in his bed.

"This is your room," she whispered as he sat on the edge of the bed and commenced scrubbing her face with the cloth.

"Yep," he agreed.

"Are you planning to stay in here with me?" she asked, half-joking, half-concerned.

"You'd like that, wouldn't you?" he asked, smiling in anticipation of her comeback. When one failed to emerge, he pulled away the cloth and studied her face. She gave him the look again, the adoring one. He decided on the spot he wanted to see that look again, possibly for the rest of their lives. "Would you?" he whispered.

"I…" her glance slid to the door and she shook her head. "Probably better not. The town will flap its gums off."

"I know," he agreed, absently folding the washcloth to give his hands something to do. "That's why George and I are going to stay with my mom."

"George won't like that," she said, biting back a smile.

"Ask me if I care," he said, and she burst into a giggle that made his heart drop to his toes and pitch back up.

"Hey, Sully," she whispered.

"Hey, Poppy," he whispered in return, smoothing her hair off her too-sleepy face.

"Thanks for tonight. I couldn't have done it without you."

"I've got your back," he said.

"I'm starting to believe it."

He gave her one more smile and turned toward the door, intending to stand. She clutched his shirt in her hand, pulled him close, and kissed him senseless until he broke off with a shaky gasp.

"As I said, thank you." She tapped his cheek and smiled at his breathless discomposure.

"That was so much better than a card," he said, causing her to laugh.

"You should go back to our guests. Sasha gets in trouble if left alone too long," she warned.

"In a minute. I'm just going to…"

"To what?" she asked, her thumb sliding over his bottom lip.

"Sit here and stare while you fall asleep," he said.

"Won't take long," she whispered, and it didn't. Three blinks later, she was out. Sully eased to the door, turned off the light, and leaned against the wall in the hallway outside. What just happened? Was it his imagination, or did things with Poppy feel like they were finally on track? Then again, it had become their M/O to take one step forward and two steps back. He had stopped trying to convince himself they were anything more than they were—good friends drawn inexorably together by the baby they'd created.

He shook his head and pushed away his thoughts. There were two guests downstairs, friends of Poppy's, currently wrapping her pies. It was up to him and him alone now to play host and make a good impression. *And make good and certain George understands he's here as a pal and nothing more.*

When he reached the kitchen, George looked up at him and a current of understanding passed between them. *Game on.*

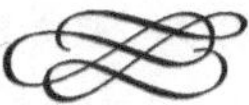

CHAPTER 27

Bailey Dunbar Ridge had never made Easter dinner before. In fact she hadn't celebrated Easter properly since she was a kid. And even then she'd been living in Africa. This was her first American Easter, her first Easter as a wife, her first Easter as a hostess, her first Easter with both sides of her family in attendance, as well as Sully's relatives. The quick onslaught of realizations should have paralyzed her with fear, but Bailey was one of those people who found insurmountable odds inspiring.

For that reason it was no surprise that when Poppy arrived at the ranch, her sister ran her kitchen like a well-ordered factory. Everyone had been recruited and given a station. Cal was in charge of the meat. Because it was Texas, he had decided to deep fry a turkey, smoke a ham, and grill steaks. He and the menfolk were outside when Sully pulled up, laughing and talking loudly. Even so, everyone came to a standstill when George emerged, adding a surprised element to their party.

"George, my boy, how are you, son?" The Colonel asked, sounding delighted. Poppy wondered if it was because he liked George that much or because he was enraptured over the reminder of his best friend and former roommate.

"Colonel Caruthers, Sir," George said, extending his hand for a hearty shake.

"Sasha," The Colonel added, opening his arms for George's sister.

"Uncle Bear," she replied, tossing herself at him and returning his hearty hug.

Uncle Bear? Sully mouthed to Cal who shrugged in response. The Colonel wasn't the sort to lend himself to nicknames, but he didn't seem to mind this one. Poppy made the introductions to the newcomers and went to the kitchen to check on Bailey. Sasha decided to remain with the men, unsurprising since her friend probably possessed as many Y chromosomes as any of them. Not a wilting flower, was Sasha, and yet in a completely different way than Bailey. While Bailey could flatten a combatant with a punch and slit his throat without batting a lash, around normal people she was the soul of feminine politeness. Not so Sasha. She never met a bawdy joke she didn't enjoy, and she could make grown men cry with the power of her words. Relished it, in fact. Poppy had the feeling she was one of Sasha's only female friends, and if not for their family's close acquaintance and many years of correspondence, they might not be. If they met now for the first time, would they get along? Would Poppy be able to see beyond the hard façade to the sweet girl within? Doubtful.

"Mama," Poppy said, ignoring all the women in the room in favor of her mother, whom she saw far too little since becoming an adult. No one would know she was an adult now as she dropped her parcels on the table and snuggled into her mother's embrace like a toddler.

"My baby girl," her mother replied, tossing aside her paring knife to snuggle Poppy in return. After a long time being cuddled and coddled by her mommy, Poppy took a step back. "Let me inspect you."

Poppy stood at attention, their family joke. After seeing so many men salute their father so many times over the years, the three girls had started doing it also, as a way to tease him. And though he pretended to be annoyed by the action, he always bit his cheek to hold back a smile.

Her mother was the one to walk around her in a circle now, scanning her body up and down for changes. At last she held Poppy's cheeks between her hands and looked deep in her eyes. "Are you doing okay? Really?"

"Yes," Poppy said, with a definitive nod. After a good night's sleep and the money she made after delivering her pies this morning, she felt like a new creation, all of last night's exhaustion faded to mist.

"And when do I get to meet this Sullivan Langford?" her mother asked, tone serious and intent.

"How about now, Ma'am?" Sully stood in the doorway, his shoulder pressed to the jamb. He had followed Poppy inside, unknown to her, for no other reason than he couldn't seem to stay away. And now he finally glimpsed her mother, her beauty and softness stark contrast to her husband's hard exterior. She had the kind of face that always seemed to be smiling or about to smile, as if everything was an inside joke only she knew. Unconsciously at his appearance, she put her arm around Poppy's shoulder and drew her protectively close, and Sully got a sudden premonition. The father might be tough and scary, but it was the mother he'd have to watch out for. Hurt her child, and she'd cut you to pieces. He straightened and moved forward, hand outstretched.

"Mom, this is Sully," Poppy said, linking her arm companionably with his.

"Ma'am," Sully said. He resisted the urge to rifle his fingers through his hair, fluffing it after taking off his hat, feeling unaccountably nervous, or maybe not so unaccountably as her eyes shifted slowly between him and Poppy, assessing, searching for he didn't know what.

When she finally extended her hand, it felt like a peace offering. "Sullivan, I'm Juniper Caruthers. I'm very pleased to meet you."

He wondered if he'd passed some unwritten test, a suspicion confirmed when Poppy sagged against him slightly, as if in relief. Reflexively his arm eased around her and rubbed the painful little spot at the base of her spine, the one that always seemed to ache. She leaned into him farther, clutching at his arm as she arched closer. Juniper's eyes took it all in, flicking from her daughter to Sully and back again.

Cal arrived with a tray of turkey to stick in the warming oven. "Here you go, Little Bit," he announced. "We're almost ready out there, although we're going to have to add another place setting."

"Oh? One of the hands joining us?" Bailey asked absently.

"Didn't Poppy tell you? It's George."

The kitchen came to a stand still as everyone looked first at Cal and then at Poppy and Sully. "Surprise," she said weakly.

"Hear that, Mom? George is here," Bailey called, barely able to contain a laugh.

"The elusive George. Hmm," Juniper said, one side of her mouth quirking so Sully caught sight of a Poppy dimple. Her gaze bounced between Poppy and Sully again, curious and amused this time.

"How are you holding up there, Sullivan?" Bailey asked, her hand never pausing on the gravy she whisked.

Sully took Poppy's hand and gave her a sweet smile. "Any friend of Poppy's is a friend of mine."

"I'd say he's holding up mighty fine," Cal said, stealing a deviled egg on his way back out of the kitchen.

Poppy wasn't needed in the kitchen, mostly because she'd brought all the desserts, a sum total of four pies, two cakes, a pan of brownies, and two massive trays of cookies. Texans seemed to like to eat pastries as quickly as she could bake them; in this way they were a perfect match. Once outside, she and Sully separated, reluctantly on Sully's part, it seemed. His eyes strayed to her more than once, questioning and possessive. Poppy couldn't decide if she was heartened or annoyed by those glances. Sully was an alpha. George's surprise appearance would no doubt cause him to perform a bit of chest beating.

George and Sasha were still enmeshed in a conversation with her newly chatty father and Cal's brother, Cam. George's eyes followed her much the way Sully's did. Poppy made her way over to her other sister, Jane, and Jane's fiancé, Blue, hovering at the periphery of the group, seemingly lost in their love-struck little world.

"There she is," Blue said, cheerful for someone surrounded by so many members of her family. Poppy tipped her head closer and sniffed his drink. "Sweet tea," he added helpfully.

"From Long Island?" she asked.

He laughed. "No, but I think the sugar is being sucked up through my molars and going straight to my brain. Cal must sweeten this according to his body size." He tipped back another sip and grimaced at the overt sugariness.

"How are you holding up, Poppinfresh?" Jane asked, circling her in a hug. Jane was older than Poppy, but smaller and more delicate, a pixie next to her own Mrs. Butterworth frame.

"George is here," Poppy said, not needing to add anything else. Her family rarely saw each other, but they tried to keep current on each other's lives. Jane knew the tricky situation with George, his devastation, and Poppy's subsequent guilt.

"How's Sully taking that?" Jane whispered. Their trio glanced at Sully who quickly turned away, having been caught staring.

"Really well, apparently," Blue observed. "Any better and he's going to toss a net over Poppy and blow dart her with love potion."

"I actually know how to blow dart," Jane volunteered.

"Of course you do, baby mine," Blue said, giving her hand a squeeze.

"Blue, your assignment is to stick close to me and be a buffer," Poppy hissed, grabbing his arm and giving it a tug.

Blue studied her, his eyes uncharacteristically serious. "One condition."

"We're practically family, and you're giving me conditions?" Poppy asked, abashed.

"That's why I'm giving you conditions. Stop calling me New Nick." Old Nick was Jane's last boyfriend. Poppy and Bailey said it was too much trouble to learn a new name. This moment marked the first time Poppy had ever called him Blue, a sign of her desperation.

"You're sucking the joy from my holiday," Poppy pouted. Blue quirked an eyebrow at her and she huffed a sigh. "Fine, *Blue*, I will stop calling you New Nick."

"All right then," Blue said happily, patting her gently on the head.

"Would it help you make a decision between them if I told you their credit scores?"

"Maybe," Poppy said, sounding intrigued.

"Poppy," Jane exclaimed, letting go of her to shove Blue's shoulder. "Don't encourage his cyber stalking."

Poppy rolled her eyes at Blue. "She makes it so easy," Blue said, hooking his arm around Jane and pulling her close for a kiss on her temple.

"Oh, you were teasing me that time. So you didn't actually hack both of my sister's suitors," Jane said, pinning him with a stare.

Blue cleared his throat and downed the remainder of his tea, buying time. When he finally swallowed, he clinked his ice in the glass. "Look at that, I'm in need of a refill. Anything for you ladies?"

"No chance, it's go time," Poppy said, grabbing his arm to detain him as Bailey stepped forward and clanged the dinner bell.

CHAPTER 28

Cal's ranch was massive, with a dining room and table big enough to accommodate the guests, all eighteen of them, including Cal and Bailey. Both of their immediate families were there, Cal's brother, Cam, and his wife, Maggie, Cal and Cam's parents, The Colonel and Juniper, Blue and Jane, Poppy and Sully, George and Sasha, and Sully's mother and stepfather, the man she married after Sully's father was killed in a freak farm accident when Sully was eight. And then there were Sully's younger brother and sister, fifteen year old Cooper and thirteen year old Lucy. Poppy loved that he had siblings so young, but she hadn't had much chance to get to know them yet. Maybe when everything settled down and became less chaotic, they'd have more time.

She glanced around the gathering, feeling her throat close with emotion. Almost all the people she loved best were in this room, something that rarely happened. For the last few years she'd remained in New York for Easter, celebrating the day with her coworkers at the restaurant. Bailey had been overseas with the marines, leaving Jane and her parents in DC. Now they'd added Cal, Blue, Sully, George and Sasha. She even felt a warm rush of affection for Cal's brother and sister-in-law, and she hardly knew them at all. She'd never talked to Cameron, though she'd spent forty minutes at the wedding having a brass tacks discussion with Maggie about which buttercream was best, American or Swiss. Next year three new little lives would be added to the table, her baby, Bailey's baby, and Maggie's.

Cal said the blessing, saying a special prayer of thanks for each person who was there. Poppy wondered if everyone felt as filled to the brim as she did, or if it was merely her pregnancy hormones making her weepy. When she couldn't hold back a little sniffle, Sully reached under the table and squeezed her leg. She rested her hand on his, and he flipped his palm, twining their fingers together. Her heart flipped at the unexpected little gesture. Sometimes Sully was too sweet for his own good. She had no idea what to do with that goodness. The men she'd been with in the past had started out well and gone downhill fast. One stole her money, another stole her identity. The last one came close to stealing her soul. And then there was Diego Cortez, a murderer. She really had the absolute worst taste in men.

The prayer ended. Sully gave her hand a squeeze and let her go as the food began to pass. Across from her, George stared. *I've missed you,* he mouthed. He was so handsome, with his dark hair, dark eyes, and rosy cheeks. And then there was Sully who nudged her arm and handed her a bowl of mashed potatoes, golden haired with lively green eyes, one of the handsomest men she'd ever seen in real life, and a Texas Ranger to boot.

So maybe my taste isn't all bad, she thought, suppressing a wry smile. She passed the potatoes to Blue who'd observed the entire exchange— George's message, Sully's secret touch.

"I'm going to need more sugar in my tea. Too much buffering," he said, holding his fingers to his temple in his best James T. Kirk impression. She snorted a laugh and both George and Sully turned toward her with a smile.

It's going to be a long day, Poppy thought.

After lunch some of the men and Bailey decided to shoot while the rest of the ladies accompanied them to watch. Sully was glad for something to do to burn off his angry energy. The nerve of George. He couldn't quite get over it. Sully was a calm, even-tempered guy. Being a cop had trained him to keep a cool head but, unlike some, it came easily to him. His mother said he'd been pleasant from birth, rarely fussy, never had a ragey tantrum. Now might be time to change that. Poppy was carrying his child, *his*. How did a man walk into that situation and start flirting? Though, to be fair, George hadn't been flirtatious, at least not yet. He'd been quiet and friendly, but his eyes followed Poppy with a sorrowful sort of possessiveness. It was like looking in a mirror.

The walk to the shooting range was long and rocky. Sully clasped Poppy's hand and she leaned into him a bit. It was like a gift, that lean, and he wanted more. When had he become this person who looks for the nuance in every tilt of a woman's body? He'd dated. A lot. Starting in early high school, he realized girls thought he was cute. He'd worked hard to hone his flirting skills early so that by the time he became a Ranger, he was lethal. If the hat and boots didn't get them, the twangy, "Aw, shucks," attitude did. But none of them had ever stuck, and not for lack of trying on Sully's part. He was a romantic at heart, always searching for Ms. Right, but it never seemed to happen. And now somehow the most unlikely girl in the world had burrowed under his skin like a chigger.

They were all wrong for each other, at least on paper. Sully had always thought he'd fall for someone like Cal's former wife, a beauty queen type, a former cheerleader and pageant girl. Someone who'd reached perfection in her beauty but, unlike Isabel, was still nice. Someone like his mom. She'd done the beauty pageants and been a cheerleader before she married his dad. But then she gave everything up and became a mother, had devoted her life to her family and only now that her kids were independent had she started to pursue photography as a hobby. These days it was odd to see her without a camera strapped around her neck.

But Poppy was...she was so aggravating he wanted to spank her most of the time. She looked soft and adorable, even smelled like sugar, but appearances were deceiving because she had a mind and a will of her own and they were both unbending. She was a steel rod in a pretty candy coating. She did what she wanted, always. She was the person who would ignore the steps and pull herself up the side of a cliff by her fingertips. Her stubborn insistence on maintaining her independence was a constant source of annoyance to him, she was so career driven he had no doubts she would bundle the baby up like a little papoose and bring it along on her job, probably far before she was physically ready to resume baking. She teased him mercilessly, leaving no areas of his life unpoked. She hated routine, always wanting to be wherever the wind took her. Was citified and metropolitan through and through. She drove him nuts, from the moment he woke to the time he went to bed, challenged him on everything, seemed to thrive on making him lose his ever loving mind, and yet he couldn't get enough of her. Even now in the midst of all their friends and family, he wanted to draw her close, drink her in, inhale her scent, and cover her face with kisses. And not because George watched their every interaction for signs of a connection, but because the more he touched her, the more he wanted to touch her, the more time he spent with her, the more time he wanted to spend with her. She made him absolutely out of his mind, and he couldn't get enough.

"Sully, you're breaking my fingers," Poppy said, and he realized he'd been squeezing her hand.

"Sorry," he said. He relaxed his grip and brought her hand to his lips, bestowing a kiss.

"What are you thinking about over there, so serious?" she asked.

"How much I want to lock you in a tower, like Rapunzel's mother," he said and her face exploded in a laugh, causing several heads to swivel in their direction, smiling. Poppy's laugh was as infectious as everything about her.

"For what reason specifically?" she asked when she had herself back under control.

To keep her safe from Diego. To keep her away from George. To keep her from working herself to death. To figure her out. To love on. "All the reasons, Poppy. All the reasons."

"It's almost over," she said, giving his arm a reassuring pat that did nothing to soothe him. What was almost over? George's visit? The pregnancy? Their connection? He didn't fool himself that things wouldn't change once the baby was born. He and Poppy were too different. Theirs would not be an amicable exchange. He would want the baby as much as possible, and so would she. He would want the baby involved in sports, she would push it toward the arts. Right now they were in the glowing pregnancy phase, but once the baby arrived, real life would intrude. They would have to navigate the tricky world of co-parenting. The thought of not being present for every milestone made Sully unutterably sad. The thought of anything coming between him and Poppy made him want to unman himself and bawl.

"You worry too much," Poppy said, giving him a squeeze. She had an uncanny ability to read his mind, probably because, unlike hers, it was easy to read. "It will work itself out."

"Darlin', you're such a gypsy," he said. He hooked his arm around her shoulders, anchoring her beside him. It did nothing to help them walk on the rough terrain, but it did a little to soothe his soul.

"It's like being in an Austen novel," Sasha noted as the men selected their guns. Cal was a collector and some fine pieces were on the table. For Sully, who couldn't afford half the guns now spread before him, it was like Christmas. "The men shooting pheasants while the women look on, impressed. Poppy, swoon for us and make it official." Sasha snapped her fingers in Poppy's direction. Poppy tossed her a vague smile but was immersed in a conversation with Maggie about the bakery.

"Your girl gonna open a bakery?" Sully asked Cam as they inspected their weapons of choice.

"Nah, she's a connoisseur." He glanced around to make sure they weren't overheard and leaned in. "The woman makes the ugliest cakes I've ever seen. My brother-in-law, Ethan, and I have started keeping a log and ranking them. They taste good, though, and her pies are off the charts." He added the last with a flush of guilt over his disloyalty. "How's it going with Poppy? Congratulations on the baby, by the way."

"Thanks. It's…it's going…she makes me…have you ever wanted to shake a pregnant woman so hard her teeth rattle? And then kiss her until she can't remember her name?"

Cam's glance darted to his wife. "Yes."

Sully chuckled and swiped a hand over his face. "Any sage advice for me?" Cam had been the captain of their football team when Sully was a freshman and Cam a senior. Cal had always been in another stratosphere—older, taller, famous. Cam had felt more like a friend and, if Sully were being honest, the closest thing he'd ever had to a big brother.

Cam glanced at his wife again. "Be strong and steady. Persevere, and don't take no for an answer."

"Sounds like what you used to tell us before a big play," Sully noted.

"It's not so different, and this is the biggest play you'll ever make. If it's what you want, if it's really what you want and you're certain, then don't let anything or anyone stop you or get in your way. That includes her."

"Ah, man, this is the kind of talk that makes Poppy cringe," Sully said.

"I don't know about that. Think of who her dad is. She might say she doesn't want to be led, but I bet she does," Cam said.

Sully thought about that. The times when Poppy responded best were the times when he took charge, when he flat out told her she wasn't allowed to see Diego or date, when he forced her to bed. Perhaps his mistake was in listening to her words and not her actions. When she said she wanted to be solely in charge of her own life, perhaps what she really meant was that she wanted someone to come along and help carry the burden. Not a bully, but a full partner. *I have your back,* he'd told her. *I'm starting to believe it,* she'd replied.

He turned to look over his shoulder, his eyes seeking her, always seeking her. She felt his glance and looked up. Their eyes caught and held, and Sully gave her a smile, sending her secret messages with his mind. *You're mine, Poppy Dunbar. You might not realize it yet, but you are mine and no one else's.* Her lashes fluttered. He tossed her a wink and turned his attention to the range.

CHAPTER 29

The next day Sully and Poppy spent exploring with Sasha and George, showing them the sights of San Antonio. Poppy invited Jane and Blue, which seemed odd to Sully, and odder still when he saw Blue and Poppy exchanging secret hand signals. He would never understand the woman, never.

Jane planned the outing, despite the fact that it was practically Sully's second hometown. But after the day started he set aside his dismay and enjoyed the adventure. They went places he'd never seen, never even heard of.

"How did you find these places?" he asked Jane.

"Jane's a woman of many talents," Blue answered for her. They hadn't set a date for their wedding yet, but he looked at her with so much devotion Sully bet they'd be married within the year. Lucky stiffs.

When the sun set, they took a ghost tour, something else Sully had never considered. He didn't believe in ghosts, but it was still a hoot, and he enjoyed hearing all the stories and history. Poppy was squished beside him, shifting uncomfortably.

"How're you holding up?" he asked, his hand rubbing the secret spot on her back.

"Fine," she said, laying her head on his shoulder with a sleepy yawn.

"Are you having fun with your friends?"

"Yes. Do you like them?" She opened her eyes wider to survey him, as if his answer was important to her. He chose his words carefully.

"Yes. Sasha's an interesting character. I wouldn't want to face her in a poker game or boardroom, but as a friend she's fun." He brushed the stray hairs off her face and kissed her forehead.

"And George," she pressed.

"I think George seems like a fine specimen of humanity."

"But..." she prompted.

"But I like him better far away in New York." He gave her ponytail a light tug. "The better question is what do you think of your friends? You don't seem as happy to see them as I thought you'd be."

"No, I am, really. But we've both been working so hard, and I...I was looking forward to some family time, just the two of us." She reached up to brush the hair at his temple that was always mashed flat after he removed his hat.

"In a few days, we're going to go to your doctor's appointment, and then we're going to have a date."

"You promised me epic," she reminded him.

"I think finding out what's growing in here is kind of epic," he said, pressing his hand to her belly.

"Totally epic," she agreed, covering his hand with hers.

Sully drew in a breath, inhaling her scent, and that was when it hit him. He loved this woman. Beyond attraction, beyond duty, beyond frustration, beyond the baby, he was totally and completely in love with Poppy Dunbar. How did it happen? Where did it come from? He had spent his entire life searching for a lightning bolt of ever-after magic. It never once occurred to him it could steal over him like the whisper of a breeze.

"What?" Poppy asked, ornery smile always hovering on the periphery. "Did you actually see a ghost?" She turned to stare out the window.

"Poppy," he rasped.

She regarded him again, her amusement morphing to concern. "Sully? Everything okay?"

He couldn't tell her, not knowing where she stood, not with the man everyone considered to be her destiny hovering in the background. "You're my girl," he said instead.

Her smile returned in a flash, cheeks dimpling. "You think so?"

"Darlin', I know it," he said,

"We'll see," she said, resting her head on his shoulder again. He kissed the top of it. *We'll see,* wasn't exactly a ringing endorsement, but with Poppy every concession was monumental. And now that Sully realized the truth, he would never let her go, no matter what.

The next morning, George and Sasha left, but not before George asked to take Poppy for a walk. They were gone for a long, long time while Sully attempted to make idle small talk with Sasha, who was surly until at least noon and four cups of coffee. And then, if he was being honest, she only had about an hour of pleasant cheerfulness before she turned surly again. Even so, Sully liked her. No one ever had to wonder where he stood with her, as witnessed by her oh-so-glowing assessment of him: "You're a country bumpkin, rube, hick, yokel, but you're so darn sweet and hot I can't decide whether to adore or pity you." With flattery like that, how could she be anything but beloved?

When George and Poppy returned from their walk, they both looked resolved about something. Poppy wouldn't give in to Sully's glances so he could attempt to read her eyes, not that it would do him much good. The woman would likely always remain a puzzling mystery.

They said goodbye to their guests in ways that suited them both—Poppy with hugs and Sully with handshakes. They remained staring out the door until Sasha's rental car was far out of sight, and then Sully couldn't take it anymore.

"Poppy." He faced her, but she dodged his glance again, staring hard at his chest as she raveled her fingers in the string of his hoodie.

"Sully, I'm so exhausted. Could we maybe lie on the couch today and watch movies?"

He wanted to know what happened with George but, knowing Poppy, she would only tell him when she was ready. And then she would only tell him as much as she wanted him to know. "Are you asking to cuddle?"

She nodded, finally meeting his gaze. Her eyes looked fragile, wounded, and so weary. He cupped her face and leaned in to whisper. "Only if you find something ridiculously sappy I'll pretend to hate, something with singing, perhaps."

She beamed at him. "I promise not to tell the other Rangers when you sing along."

He kissed her cheek and let her go. She found a movie and they lay on the couch in what had become their normal position, Sully in the back, Poppy tucked against him in a cuddly embrace. His hand settled on her bump, thumb easing over a navel that was starting to protrude like a second nose. He was fascinated by every change in her body, enamored with it, practically obsessed with her feminine softness. He had no understanding of men who found pregnancy repulsive. To Sully it was the pinnacle of female desirability.

Poppy, prescient as ever, read his mind. "Are you still going to like me when I'm not pregnant anymore?"

"I'm always going to like you," he assured her, his voice a velvet whisper in her ear.

She snuggled closer and brought his hand to her mouth, kissing his palm. "We'll see."

He rolled his eyes, ready to do battle, but it was too late; she was already asleep.

Three days later, they sat in Poppy's doctor's office. Sully stepped out of the room while she changed into the little paper gown, but now he was back and gripping her hand, trying to calm both their nerves. This was it, go time. He was about to catch the first glimpse of their baby. From this moment on, there was no more pretending it wasn't real and happening. He was a father. He was ecstatic; he was terrified.

They were quiet, each lost in a world of future dreams and present nerves. After this Sully had an entire day of adventure planned, a new art museum, an up and coming restaurant. Cynically he wondered if any of it would matter. How could everything after this feel like anything but a letdown? They were going to find out the sex of their child. Nothing on earth was as amazing as that.

"Epic day," Poppy whispered.

"The epicest," Sully agreed, and she laughed.

"Boy or girl?" she asked.

"It will definitely be one of those," he agreed.

"You're so silly." She reached up to ruffle his hair, attempting to un-hat the mashed portions.

"And you're so…" he trailed off, unable to finish. *Unreachable,* was what he most wanted to say. They'd had a pleasant few days, after Sasha and George left. But Poppy's rental house was fixed, and she moved back home, leaving his house empty without her laughing, warm presence. They both returned to work, meaning they only saw each other for a few exhausted moments in the evening. Beyond that, something was different with her, and he didn't know what. She still wouldn't tell him what happened with George, but she'd been more aloof, less settled. Did she miss New York? Or, worse, did she miss George specifically? The unending confusion made his brain hurt.

He pressed his nose to her neck and inhaled. "You smell amazing."

"Vanilla oozes from my pores now," she said, now rifling her fingers through the back of his head.

He licked her. "Yep, I taste it."

She giggled and ducked away from him. "That tickles. What kind of weirdo licks a pregnant lady?"

The kind who can't get enough, he thought and some of his desperation must have shown in his eyes because she blinked once, solemn and surprised. Their gazes locked and the tension from the pie making night returned with force. It had been absent for days, but now it was back and seemed to have picked up where it left off.

"A bad time to be wearing a paper gown," she whispered.

"I'm about to have so many paper cuts," he whispered.

She snorted another laugh and the door opened. Sully sat back, now smoothing his own hand over his hair. He only hoped the doctor couldn't read minds the way Poppy could. Either way, he was certain his cheeks were flaming.

The doctor greeted Poppy, shook hands with Sully, and sat on a stool at the end of the exam table. She picked up the ultrasound wand. "Are we finding out the sex today?"

"Yes," Sully and Poppy agreed in unison.

"Here we go." She dumped a glop of jelly on Poppy's bare belly, and the ultrasound began. For a few seconds, she didn't speak, simply moved the wand and took pictures on the machine. Then the wand froze and the anticipation built to the breaking point.

"See those three lines?" she said. Poppy and Sully leaned forward, trying to see what she so clearly saw. "That's your little girl. Congratulations."

"You're sure?" Poppy breathed.

"Absolutely," the doctor said.

Poppy and Sully didn't speak or even look at each other while the doctor worked, though they did grip each other like a lifeline, almost afraid to take their eyes off the screen unless it became unreal.

The doctor printed a string of pictures and left them alone. "A girl," Poppy breathed.

"A girl," Sully said, his voice equally unsteady.

"Are you sad?" she asked, turning luminous eyes on him.

"Sad? Why would I be sad?" he asked.

"Sometimes men want boys," she said.

"No, Poppy, hey." He tipped her chin toward his. "I love girls."

"Obviously," she said, gesturing toward the bump. He rolled his eyes and she giggled, and that was it, he was broken. He pressed forward and kissed her with far, far too much intention.

At last she gave him a little shove. "I need to change out of the paper."

He nodded and reached for his hat. He dropped it, bent to retrieve it, and bashed his head on the side of the table.

"You doing okay there, Ranger?" she asked, fully amused now.

"No, I'm dying," he said. He stood, pressed the hat onto his head, kissed his finger, and touched it to her lips. "Hurry up so we can get on with our epic day."

"Yes, sir," she replied with feigned meekness.

He eased backwards out of the room, reluctant to be apart for even a minute. Once he was safely outside, he leaned on the door and sucked oxygen. Unknown to him, he was still holding the string of baby pictures. Unable to stand it any longer, he took a picture of one of them, the one marked "girl," and sent it to his mom. She replied a minute later with a series of emojis and symbols he could in no way discern or interpret.

"Did you text everyone?" Poppy asked when she finally emerged.

"Just my mom," he said. "I'll leave the rest to you."

She removed her phone. Her thumbs blurred as the text went out. A few minutes later, it began to chirp with all of the returns. "Maybe that was a mistake," she said, switching her phone to silent while she stood in line to pay the bill.

"I'm paying today," he declared.

"Sully," she intoned.

"Poppy," he returned.

"I've been saving for this," she said.

He gave her a look but otherwise didn't comment. When she sighed, he was fairly certain he won, but even so he had to hide his shock when it was their turn and the clerk told him the amount. A thousand dollars? How was that possible? He handed over his credit card, giving Poppy a side eye she studiously avoided. She had been careful not to tell him how much anything cost, so careful never to discuss her finances or health insurance, beyond stating she had everything covered.

"May I please see a breakdown of cost for the delivery?" he said, giving the clerk his most charming smile. It worked a little too well and she became flustered, shuffling papers until she finally remembered what she reached for. She handed it over.

"Of course that's merely our portion. There will also be the hospital admission, pediatrician, anesthesiologist, and any incidentals like a NICU stay, if one is needed."

"Thank you," Sully said, his eyes already scanning the paper. He gathered Poppy by the bicep and pulled her out of the office and to the car. She was silent and still, looking anywhere but at him.

He opened her car door, closed it, slid behind the wheel, put his key in the ignition, and turned to face her. "Three thousand dollars."

"That's pretty standard," she said.

"Three thousand dollars, and that's just your ObGyn. How much will the hospital cost?" he demanded.

She swallowed hard. "My portion after insurance will probably be about fifteen thousand dollars."

He blinked at her. "You don't have that kind of money."

"I do. I *will*," she stubbornly insisted, and some of her undying work ethic began to make sense. She was killing herself trying to amass enough money not to end up bankrupt. Sully had money, and she could have it, but even so it would barely be enough. It would drain his savings dry. He studied her, his breath rasping out in frustrated, panicky gasps. This was what she'd been dealing with, all these months, the knowledge that her insurance was worth almost nothing, that this baby would cost her everything and then some. And all this time she'd been carrying the burden on her own, blindly stumbling toward disaster, pushing herself beyond her limits.

"You can't know how much I want to turn you over my knee," he said.

"Weird," she replied, seemingly unconcerned.

"Poppy."

She put up a hand. "I'm taking care of it, Sully, okay? I have nearly ten thousand dollars in the bank and months left to earn the rest."

"Unless you get sick. Unless the baby gets sick. Unless you get in an accident. Unless *Huck's* burns down, unless..."

She held up a hand, cutting him off again. "Stop it, none of those things will happen. I'm handling it. I've got it under control."

"What you once again fail to consider is that you are not alone and this self-enforced punishment is completely unnecessary. Do you know how much it would cost a month to add you and the baby to my insurance?"

She shook her head, pressing her hands to her ears. He pulled them off. "A hundred dollars," he said loudly. "I have a thousand dollar deductible. A thousand dollars, Poppy. That's what it would cost you to have a baby on my insurance."

"So, what," she said, annoyed now. "You're asking me to marry you again for the insurance."

"No, I'm telling you. We are getting married, and you're going on my insurance. And my life insurance. And you're moving in with me and giving up your crummy, water-damaged rental. And we're getting you a car," he said, jutting his finger in her face.

"Anything else?" she asked, tone deathly quiet, lips pressed tightly together.

"Maybe a dog," he said, shrugging. In for a penny, in for a pound.

She gave him the death stare, her blinks slow and measured. He prepared himself for her blast of temper. He should have prepared more or better. "All right."

His head thumped against the door, his hat now tipped to the ceiling. "What?"

"Okay, I'll marry you."

"Oh, okay. We'll put something together as soon as possible."

She shook her head. "Today. Right now."

Was she trying to call his bluff? Waiting for him to bolt in panic? If so, she was about to be disappointed. "Fine." He started the car and headed toward downtown. "We have to get rings."

"I don't want a ring."

"You're getting a ring," he said, daring her to argue.

"My hands are in dough all day every day," she reminded him.

"Fine, we'll get somethin' cheap."

"Flatterer," she muttered.

His lips twitched as he pulled into the nearest Wal-Mart and parked the car. "Don't make me laugh when I'm trying to maintain my anger."

"Don't try to sound rational when you're clearly in the midst of some sort of breakdown," she returned.

"Deal." He came around, helped her out of the car, and led her to the ring section. "Look around, I'll be right back. I have to use the little Ranger's room."

"More info than I ever needed to know," she muttered, leaning close to peer at the ring selection. Sully darted out of sight and withdrew his phone, praying it would be answered. It was.

"'Sup"

"You answer the phone like a man," Sully accused.

"Shocking," Bailey replied. "Congratulations on the girl. Our turn next week. Bet you twenty bucks it's a boy."

"You're on, but the baby's not why I'm calling. It's Poppy."

"What about her?" she asked, all amusement gone now.

"We're getting married."

A pause. "Hurray? Why do you sound like that? I thought this was what you wanted."

"It was, *is*. But in true Poppy fashion she's demanding it happen now, right now. We're at Wal-Mart picking out rings."

"What? No, absolutely not. I want to be there, my parents want to be there, Jane will want to be there. Tell her she can't."

"Hi, have you met your sister?"

Bailey blew out a breath. "I could throttle her."

"Get in line. But if I don't do it now, she might pull a runner."

"You're right, she's fast and wily. Are you going to the courthouse?"

"Yes."

"Good. I'll get there, just stall her, okay?"

"I don't..."

"I said stall," Bailey snapped.

Sully came to attention, and he'd never even been a soldier. "Yes, Major. I'll do my best."

"Your best isn't good enough. I swear, Sullivan, I love you like a brother, but if my sister gets married without me, you'll regret it the rest of your life."

"Absolutely. It is all about you, after all," he said, full sarcasm now.

She let out a breath. "Sorry, but Poppy will regret it, too. I know she will. With me there, it will be real. Trust me, I know Poppy, even if I disagree with her flighty nonsense ninety nine percent of the time."

"Fine, I'll stall. But you'd better hurry."

"Hmm, it's cute how you think you can order me around. But I will hurry." She hung up without saying goodbye.

"Entire family is mental," Sully said, shoving his phone in his pocket and whirling to go back to Poppy. His fiancée.

CHAPTER 30

Bailey made it by flying Cal's plane. And not only did she stop and pick up Sully's mother and step-father along the way, she somehow convinced Cal to come along, Cal, who hated flying more than anything and had never taken a spin in his own plane before.

"Insane woman," Cal muttered, leaning against the wall of the courthouse for support. Everyone who passed by stopped to stare at him. Sully wasn't certain if it was because he was famous or because they'd never seen a six and a half foot tall man the color of wallpaper paste.

"How'd she get you to come along?" Sully asked.

"She threatened to come without me. Who flies a plane five months pregnant with high blood pressure? My insane wife, that's who." He sucked oxygen through his nose a few minutes, dabbing his cold and clammy forehead with the back of his sleeve.

"In any case, thanks for being here. I'm going to need a best man," Sully said.

Cal reached out and squeezed his shoulder. "Good luck, and I mean that. You're going to need it. Entire family's insane." He took another breath that ended on a snicker. "I swear," he muttered, pressing his hand over his eyes.

Bailey, thinking ahead to Poppy's comfort, had brought along makeup and a fancy dress, so the women were helping Poppy get ready. When it was their turn, they emerged and Sully stopped short. Working in food service meant she always wore her hair up. It was as wild and untamed as its owner, and almost always popping free of its confinement. But he had never seen it down before, as it was now. It tumbled down her shoulders in soft curls, landing in graduated layers below her collarbone. Sully had no idea if she wore more makeup than usual or her cheeks were naturally flushed, eyes big and dewy. All he knew was that no one on earth had ever looked more beautiful. He was rooted to the spot with awe, so much that Cal used his over-sized boot to kick him in the calf, giving him a nudge toward Poppy, his bride.

"Oh, wow," he whispered. It was all he could manage, short of breath as he was now and would likely always be.

"Last chance to back out and run away," Poppy offered.

He shook his head and crooked his finger, beckoning her forward, mostly because his legs lacked the ability to move. Poppy did so, coming to a halt directly in front of him. And then he was lost for words. What he wanted to blurt was how much he loved her, how much he had longed for this moment, how happy he was. But their family was very nearby and staring, weepy smiles on their faces. In lieu of words, he brushed his finger on her cheek.

She smiled harder. "Is this magical enough for you?" Her eyes slid around them, taking in the old and dank courthouse.

"The magicest," he said, leaning forward to brush a light kiss on her lips.

The ceremony was short and to the point, and then he kissed her again. They went to the restaurant of Poppy's choosing for lunch, along with his parents and Bailey and Cal. Poppy ordered all the desserts on the menu, and Cal insisted on picking up the tab. He seemed in good spirits until it was time to go back to the airport and then his fingers wouldn't let go of the door.

"I can't," he said, as close to keeling over as anyone had ever seen him.

"You don't have to," Bailey said. "I'll meet you at home." She pressed her palm to his cheek and took a step toward the plane. He grabbed her back.

"I don't want you to go without me," Cal said.

"Cal, you're being silly. Waverly and Joe will be with me." Bailey motioned to Sully's mother and step-father.

"I can do it," Cal said. He took a step away from the truck, but his hand still gripped the door and yanked himself back.

"This is nuts," Poppy interjected. "Sully will fly back with Bailey, Cal will ride with me."

"But…" Cal started to interrupt.

"I said you're riding with me," Poppy decreed, hands on hips.

"You know, I'm starting to see the resemblance between you and Bailey now," Cal said, but he looked relieved. Sully tossed him the keys to his truck.

Later, he mouthed to Poppy. She gave him a nod and smile, and they went their separate ways.

"Sorry," Cal apologized once they were safely in the truck. "Not exactly the start to your honeymoon you envisioned. Probably thought your brother-in-law wouldn't be involved at all."

"Nothing has ever been normal in our family," Poppy said, waving away his apology with flick of her fingers. "It was nice of you guys to come, nice of Bailey to Facetime my parents into the wedding."

"We wouldn't have missed it. Even me, with my idiotic fear of flying. You and Sully are important to us, and we're happy for you, so happy." She stared out the window with a vague smile. "You're happy, aren't you, Poppy?"

"How could I not be happy? Sully's the best," she replied, turning her gaze to the window again.

Cal stared thoughtfully through the window, a slight frown on his face. Understanding Bailey had given him zero insight into Poppy. The two sisters were as different as night and day. One thing he knew for certain, though, he hoped she did a better job of conveying her joy to Sully than she did to him.

It took no time at all to fly back to Cal's ranch and all the time in the world to drive his parents an hour home. Sully was impatient to see Poppy, not only because he missed her, but because he was afraid of what her brain might come up with in the interim. Panic? Regret? Denial?

When he walked into his house and didn't see her, his heart plummeted. She had gone to her house. He would have to go get her. But as he headed toward the door with a hefty amount of dread, she pushed it open, overloaded suitcase in hand. "Oh, hi, you're home," she said, using the back of her hand to push the hair off her face. She had changed clothes but left her hair down. Currently she wore one of the three hoodies she had stolen from him, this one from his days in training as a trooper. He wanted her more than he'd ever wanted anything in his life, but his body came to a grinding halt with the realization that they hadn't established exactly how that part of their marriage would play out. His glance darted up the stairs, back to her, and then away.

Poppy giggled. "Subtle, Ranger."

He let out a laugh, took off his hat, and rifled his fingers through his hair. "I didn't mean it like that."

"Sure you didn't."

"Would you listen to me a minute, you little imp. This isn't exactly a normal arrangement, and we didn't discuss anything beforehand. What I'm trying to say is that I'll not hold you to anything, not pressure you into anything you're not comfortable with."

She still stood in the doorway, and it was open. He could only hope his words hadn't been loud enough to carry and, if so, the neighbors wouldn't take his meaning. "Hmm," she said, studying him like a bug under a rock. At the moment he felt like one, exposed and squirmy. She closed the door with her foot, set her suitcase aside, marched forward, clasped his hand, and led him up the stairs to his bedroom.

Once there, she closed the door and pushed him down to a sitting position on the bed, standing in front of him, hands on hips. And then she stayed that way, seemingly waiting for him to speak.

"What's going on?" His voice was unmistakably ragged.

"You abandoned me the very second we got married and practically told me you'd be willing to have a marriage in name only. It seems to me, Sullivan, that I'm going to have to show you exactly how a wife should be treated." She pushed him back onto the bed and climbed up on his stomach, straddling it.

Sully, whose heart began to beat with a tremendous amount of hope, captured her hands in his and pulled her closer, pressing her chest to his. "Be gentle, would you? I'm a slow learner."

"No guarantees," she said, and kissed him.

Later, they were curled together in their go-to position, her back to his front, only this time they were in his bed. Sully was ridiculously glad not to have to camouflage his raging attraction to her anymore, not that he'd ever been able to, anyway. But at least now he didn't have to feel bad about it. She was his wife, for the foreseeable future until the baby was born, and forever after that, if he could help it.

She held his hand between both hers, inspecting it as she usually did. "What are you thinking when you do that?" he asked. He wanted to know all the things that went on in her mind.

"I'm thinking you have nice hands, big and calloused, but also gentle and tender. They're representative of you, I think."

He flipped her hand, making his own exploration. "Yours too, I'd say. They're small and soft and feminine but able to snap you with their strength." Her hands were freakishly strong from working dough all day. Her fingers maintained the toughest grip of any woman he'd ever known. He brushed his lips over her knuckles. "Poppy."

"Mm," she replied, sounding sleepy.

"What did George say to you before he left?"

She rolled onto her back and stared up at him. He could feel her mental debate, feel her waging war with herself about whether or not to tell him. Her right hand eased to her left middle finger, twiddling her new ring. "He said he's wanted to marry me for as long as he's known my name, that he used to sneak into Sasha's room and read my letters and picture me. And when he met me, I looked exactly like he imagined. Then we started being roommates, and it seemed like a sign, an omen. He said he was crushed when I moved away, and it strengthened his resolve even more for us to be together. And then he came here and saw the two of us together and…"

Sully felt like his life hung in the balance. "And what?" he prompted.

"And he realized I wasn't his. And he realized the person he always thought I was was merely a figment of his imagination, a projection of who he wanted me to be. What I said was true; he and I never spent any time together, never got to know each other. He apologized for putting so much on me, for making me feel bad for something that was out of my control, mostly his illusions and expectations of me. He wished us well and kissed my cheek goodbye."

Sully was quiet a few beats before he spoke. "Good guy, George," he said at last, snuggling her against him once more.

She laughed as she wriggled closer. "I've always thought so." They lay in peaceful silence a few more minutes, but neither was ready to go to sleep. "Sully."

"Mm."

"What were you thinking that night?" She rolled over to see his face again. "In the gazebo. Now that I know you, it seems so out of character."

His finger trailed over her face, his eyes tracing the path it made. "One night when I was a kid, a few months after my dad was killed, my mom let me stay up late to watch a meteor shower. It was so cloudy, I couldn't see a thing. And then, at the very end, when I was about to go inside and give up, the clouds broke, and I saw one perfect shooting star, a ball of fire, streaking toward earth. It looked so close, like I could catch it, if I tried hard enough. So I took off, my mom yelling behind me to come back, that I was barefoot, that I'd step on a rattler. I ignored her and sprinted harder because I was convinced if I could only catch that star when it fell, everything would be better again. My dad would come back, my mom would stop crying, the farm would stop going under. I ran and ran and ran, arms outstretched, reaching.

"And when I saw you sitting in that gazebo, all sparkle and sass and dimples, it felt a little like that night, like when the clouds broke and I saw the star. And then you kissed me. And when you pulled away, it felt like that night again, like I needed to chase after it with my arms outstretched, trying to catch a bit of magic before it went away."

"Looks like you caught it," she said, breathless.

"At last," he whispered, pressing her into the bed and kissing her again and again.

CHAPTER 31

Poppy and Sully settled into marriage as if it was what they'd intended to do all along. And the town let them. No one brought up their earlier denials or the fact that they'd lived apart the last five months, insisting they were only friends. If anyone suspected their arrangement was due to insurance, no one let on.

Sully and Poppy were content to play the same game, to never mention their future outside the baby's birth, to never mention their past apart, when they'd been adamant they weren't together. Neither of them knew exactly where the other stood, and both were too afraid to find out. And they were busy. If Sully thought Poppy would slow after the threat of impoverishment was over, he was mistaken. If anything, she seemed to be working harder. But suddenly the Cortez family was on the move and he was too distracted and swamped to comment.

"Honey, I'm home," Sully announced, letting himself in the front door. He paused to sort the mail, smiling when he saw the first piece of post with Poppy's name on it. He had wondered how he would handle the actuality of a sudden roommate, and so far he loved it. The house had never felt cozier or more alive.

"Darling," Poppy exclaimed, appearing in the doorway in time to toss her arms around him. It was their standard greeting, started as a joke the first day. Now, a few weeks later, both of them secretly loved it but kept up the pretense of a joke for the sake of pride.

"How's my little woman?" Sully asked, picking her up in a swallowing hug and burying his face in her neck. *Vanilla. Sugar. Butter. Pecans. Poppy.*

"Enthralled with my big, strong man." She kissed his cheek and hugged his neck. "You're sounding a bit breathless there, Ranger."

"It's because I'm filled to the brim with affection for you," he said.

She laughed and wriggled free. "Liar. It's because I'm the size and shape of a baby elephant now."

"A sexy baby elephant," he said, leaning forward to kiss her, hands on bump. It was a good thing his arms were long, otherwise he soon wouldn't be able to reach her. "How was your day?"

"You're not going to believe what happened," she said, gripping his hands.

"What?" he asked, gripping hers in return.

"I made pie, and then…"

"And then?" he asked with feigned suspense.

She leaned in to whisper. "And then I sold it."

He gasped. "Sounds like an adventure."

"Actually there was a bit of drama today. There was only one piece left right before I closed and Mrs. Black and Mrs. Marsh both reached for it at the same time."

"Please don't tell me my former Sunday school teacher and the town's oldest librarian came to fisticuffs over your pie."

"Sully, you know what I did?"

"What?" he asked, preemptively amused.

"I cut the piece in half and split it between them," she said.

"You're like Solomon."

"Your wife is wise," she agreed.

He blinked at her. "Hey, you're my wife."

"Please don't tell me you sustained another concussion today," she said, pressing her hand to his forehead.

"No, but sometimes the shock of discovery knocks me off kilter," he replied, twisting his face so he could settle a kiss on her palm. They sat down to eat supper, at the table now because Poppy insisted. *If we're going to make a go of this family thing, we're going to have proper manners.* Sully had balked at not being able to gorge ESPN while he feasted, but secretly he was pleased, both by the new rule and her implication they were a family on any sort of lasting basis.

"How was your work, you never said," she said, sliding a piece of chicken onto his plate. She liked to say she was a baker and not a chef, but her cooking was outstanding. Lately she'd been introducing Sully to all kinds of new cuisine. Tonight's chicken was courtesy of Morocco, cooked in a clay tagine with pearly couscous on the side.

"I'm multicultural now," he said, holding up a piece of chicken for inspection.

"Practically Nelson Mandela," she agreed. "Why are you stalling on answering my question?"

"Stop reading my mind, gypsy devil woman," he said, stuffing the bite of chicken in his mouth.

She waited him out, staring him down with her ridiculous stubborn sweetness.

"Want to make out?" he asked after he swallowed.

"Tempting," she said, leaning forward to wipe a blob of sauce from his lips. "Spill it, Langford. You're making me antsy."

"I can't always tell you things about my work," he said. Namely that things with the Cortez family were coming to a head, he could feel it.

"Believe it or not, I'm rather familiar with classified information. I spent half my life believing my father was a retired missionary, only to learn he's an active duty secret keeper. This doesn't feel like that. What aren't you telling me?"

"Some assignments are more dangerous than others," he replied.

She stared down at her plate, working out his cryptic statement. "Were you on one of those today?"

"Today and for the foreseeable future," he replied. The Cortez family was lethal. They were out for blood, and they played for keeps.

It was turning into an all out war, and Sully wasn't certain they had the fire power to win.

"Huh," Poppy said, pushing her couscous around her plate.

"What?"

"I always thought if I was with a soldier or cop, it would feel like it does when I know my dad is in danger."

"And it doesn't?" he guessed.

She shook her head. "Not the same at all."

"It's going to be okay, Poppy. Statistically…"

She yanked her hand away. "I'm not particularly interested in statistics."

He blinked at her, surprised by the flash of anger. She took a deep breath and let it out slowly. "I'm sorry," she said, her tone much softer. "I promise to be a good cop wife and smile pretty and not think about the danger." As proof, she gave him a cheesy grin.

"You can be a little concerned," he said.

"How much?" she asked.

"Enough for me to comfort and distract you away from it," he replied, sliding his hand under the hem of her skirt. She wore dresses every day she worked, and he adored it, along with everything else about her. How she was able to be so old-fashioned and girly, yet so steely and independent, was a never-ending riddle to his senses.

"Your chicken's getting cold," she said, returning the favor by easing her fingers under his shirt and onto his stomach.

"What chicken?" he said. No matter what else was between them, and half the time Sully didn't know, the physical thing worked well. Ridiculously well. Off the charts, really.

She shook free of his shirt, kissed his cheek, and motioned to his plate. "Eat."

"Tease," he said.

"You think so?" she asked, motioning to the bump.

"How long are you going to use that against me?" he asked.

"Until she's twenty five," she replied.

He winced. "Someday she's going to be twenty five. Stop it, you're making my heart hurt."

"Sullivan, you're adorable," Poppy said, happily chowing down on her chicken. Sully used the opportunity to stare at the top of her head. Sometimes everything was enough. He didn't need answers or declarations. He had faith they'd come in time, that someday soon Poppy would realize their marriage of convenience was more, was everything.

Feeling his eyes on her, she glanced up. "What?"

"Poppy, I..." he hadn't told her he loved her. He couldn't, not without some assurance she might one day feel the same. Every time he tried, he remembered all the many times she'd told him they were opposites, that he was too nice for her to ever love. He thought of Diego Cortez and his stomach wrenched. She had chosen him once, his opposite, his enemy. Only for a moment, but still. In the beginning he'd been bothered because Diego targeted her. But now, since their marriage, he became more bothered over the memory of Poppy choosing Diego.

"What did you do on your date with Diego?" he blurted.

She blinked at the rapid subject change. "What?"

"Your date with Cortez, what did you do?"

"I told you."

"Tell me again."

"We went to an art exhibit and talked about his work."

Sully tensed. "You talked about his work."

She shook her head. "Not that work. His hobby. He paints."

"He throws splatters at a canvas. I could do the same," Sully said.

"Maybe you should," Poppy suggested. "Might help with your rage."

He rolled his eyes, but some of the tension had seeped out of him. "What else?"

"We went to dinner and talked."

"What did you talk about?"

"Art again."

"Art," he said, using air quotes. "Guy probably believes spilled coffee should be framed and sold for a million dollars."

"Shouldn't it?" she said.

He opened his mouth to reply, realized she was purposely trying to provoke him, and got back on track. "What else?"

"We talked about his ex-wife and two children. I know you said he's a cold-blooded killer, and I believe you, but he sounded genuinely remorseful over the end of his marriage. Apparently she was his high school sweetheart. I got the feeling she didn't approve of his family. Maybe she knew or suspected what they were up to and urged him to get out. Reading between the lines, it sounded like she gave him an ultimatum and he chose the family. I can tell he still loves her. Kind of heartbreaking, really."

"What a sad, lonely sociopath," he said, but his mind wandered. What started out as jealousy had turned into something else. His team assumed the wife was another end to a means for Diego, but what if she wasn't? What if Poppy's words were true and she was a tender spot, had urged him to quit? What if they could exploit that to find a weakness? Diego was careful, so careful. But what if his decision to pursue Poppy turned out to be the cause of his own downfall?

"You're smiling like the Grinch after he stole everybody's presents. Kind of creepy," she said.

"A man can't hear that enough from the woman he's in…marriage with," he said, shoving a bite of chicken quickly between his lips.

So creepy, Poppy mouthed.

They finished the meal and he helped her carry their plates to the sink. "What are you doing now?" he asked.

"Washing dishes," she said, her back to him as she began to run the water. "Why?"

"I miss you," he stood behind her and massaged her back.

After a pause, she replied, "I miss you, too. We've been so busy since we got married."

"Let's quit our jobs. We'll get rid of our possessions, live in one of those tiny houses," he suggested in a whisper, his lips skimming her neck.

"Add a bunch of roommates, and I'm back in New York," she said, sounding wistful.

Sully stiffened. "You miss New York."

"Of course I do," she replied.

He withdrew slightly and straightened. "I thought you were happy here."

"Being happy here doesn't mean I can't miss it there," she said. She pouted up at him. "Why did you stop kissing me? Lips on neck, please."

"I suppose I could, since I got you knocked up. It's the least I can do."

"The very least," she said, tipping her neck as he resumed kissing her.

"You're a talented multitasker," he noted. "I'm doing some of my best work here, and you're still washing dishes."

"Dishes don't clean themselves," she replied.

"Be cool if they did, though," he said, switching to the other side of her neck.

"You are very good at the things," she said, a wet glass slipping out of her fingers.

"What things," he asked, his nose skimming her ear.

"The things, all the things," she said, tilting to lean against him and close her eyes.

"Why, Mrs. Langford, I do believe you're becoming incoherent."

"That's not, I…sh," she said. She turned and slid her arms around him, standing on her toes for a kiss.

"What about your dishes?" he asked.

"This is why paper plates were invented," she said. She skimmed her lips over his and pulled back. "Oh, I just remembered."

"How to kiss? Because up to now you've had me fooled pretty well," he said. He chased her lips with his, but she pulled farther back.

"No, this is serious for a minute. I got hired to do a wedding cake."

"Excellent," he said, settling his hands on her hips in what he dearly hoped was a suggestive arrangement.

She wriggled away. "No, wait. That wasn't the news. After I get paid for it, guess how much I'll have in my account."

"How much?" he asked, suddenly tense. Any mention of her

savings account had that affect on him. It felt like her emergency parachute, as if she were using it to plot a future escape.

"Twenty thousand dollars."

"Wow, great."

She settled onto the flats of her feet, deflating slightly. "I thought you'd be a bit more excited."

"No, I am, but, Poppy, you know my money is your money now. You don't have to keep plowing money into an account like the world is ending or something." He let her go to shove a hand through his hair.

"Of course I do," she said.

"What? Why?"

"Because…" she glanced away in frustration, apparently trying to choose her words. In the end, she chose the wrong ones. "I can't be dependent on you for everything."

"You're not dependent on me for anything," he said.

She spread her arms wide. "Are you joking? Look where I am, in your house, in your town, wearing your ring, sporting your name. There's hardly anything left of Poppy. All I have is my job and my account."

He took a step back. "I guess I was delusional enough to believe we're building something together here, a family."

"We are, but…" she rubbed a hand over her face. "If the situation were reversed, if you had to give up being a Ranger and move with me to New York, to give up on your dreams, your hopes, your friends, everything you've worked for your whole life, do you think it would be easy? That you'd settle in with aplomb and a plucky attitude? I mean, I'm trying my best here, Sully, but some days…" She trailed off and glanced helplessly out the window.

"Some days, what? You want to run away?"

"Some days. But…"

"Well, that's great, Poppy. A few more months and you'll be free." He motioned to the bump.

"That's a terrible thing to say," she replied.

"Is it as bad as telling your husband you can't wait to leave?" he asked.

"That's not what I said, not at all. It's like you're intentionally mishearing me."

"Or maybe I'm finally listening," he said.

They stared at each other, an ugly silence hovering between them. A part of Sully felt like he should confess everything—his feelings, his desire to stay together long after she stopped needing his insurance. But pride held him in check, pride and hurt.

She mustered a deep breath. "Sully…"

His phone beeped, doing nothing to lessen the tension and suspense. He reached for it, his frown deepening. "It's work. I have to go."

"Do you really?" she asked.

With a scowl, he turned the phone to show her the message from his lieutenant. *Need you. ASAP.*

She swallowed hard. "I'm sorry, Sully. I shouldn't have said that. This went somewhere I didn't intend, somewhere I didn't want it to go. I'm frustrated and upset and I wish you could stay so we could work it out."

"Me too," he agreed. It was a terrible time to leave. Sully felt like if he walked out the door this minute, she might not be there when he returned. He forced himself to step forward and cup her cheek. "I promise we'll fix it when I get back, okay?"

She nodded, sniffling a little.

"Don't cry, please. I can't leave if you cry."

"You should have thought of that before you married a pregnant basket case," she said, swiping impatiently at her eyes. She clutched his shirt and rested her forehead on his chest. He tipped her chin and kissed her, long and deep.

"Huh, what do you know. That makes it harder to leave, too." That earned a little smile. He kissed her cheek, grabbed his bag, and walked out of the house. Poppy stared at the open door, feeling empty and deflated. It was going to be a long and lonely night.

CHAPTER 32

When Poppy woke for work at three, Sully still wasn't home. Such was her faith in him that she didn't experience a flicker of doubt over his whereabouts, only a deep sense of regret that they'd argued before he went away. She'd said ugly things, harsh things that hurt him. Yesterday she received news from *Burton's* that they'd officially hired her replacement. Of course she knew they would, but it made everything tangible, everything real. All her culinary friends in New York were moving on and moving up. Poppy was stuck in an unknown Texas town, eking out a living by sheer force of will. Most days she was insanely proud of what she'd accomplished, humble as it now was. Yesterday she'd had a little pity party for what she lost. Why hadn't she told Sully that? Why hadn't she explained?

Pride held her back. She didn't want to admit, even to Sully, how hard she struggled to keep her head above water in the new venture, how close she'd come to losing everything. If Huck hadn't taken a chance on her, if she hadn't had that small cushion of savings to buy supplies… She shuddered to think of how close she'd come to failing, to sinking under the weight of another bad decision. Every dollar in her account was another sign of her success, a tangible way to say Hurricane Poppy was gone forever. She might have torpedoed her old career, but she was successfully making a new one, one metaphorical brick at a time.

Wearily, regretfully, she showered, dressed, and headed toward *Huck's*. Sully kept threatening to buy her a car, and Poppy kept putting him off. *Why do I need a car, with such a handsome chauffer?* She loved being able to walk to *Huck's*, or to the store, or anywhere else in town. It reminded her of growing up in Africa when she and her sisters walked everywhere. And of New York, which had seemed like a series of small towns, one after the other. Buying a car meant she was officially a country girl, but she supposed it was time. After the baby arrived, she couldn't depend on Sully to take her places. She needed it for emergencies, if nothing else.

She let herself into *Huck's* and flicked on the lights, pausing to make sure she heard no scurrying of little feet. After so many years in Manhattan, she'd never lost her fear of rats, nor the bacteria and mess they left behind. No feet. She breathed a sigh and stepped toward the kitchen, flicking that light awake, too. Her hand was on the refrigerator door, ready to give it a hard tug, when he spoke.

"Hello, Poppy."

She whirled and came face to face with Diego Cortez. At first her shock overrode her fear. Her hand flew to her throat, trying to push her heart back down. "Diego, my goodness, you startled me." She smoothed her hair because, even at three in the morning, he had the sort of buttoned down manicured look that made everyone else feel frumpy by comparison. And then, as he stood there staring at her, his black eyes wide and serious, her nerves began to prickle for different reasons other than surprise. "How did you get in here?"

"You're looking well," he said, as if they'd bumped into each other in the market instead of a closed restaurant in the middle of the night.

"Thank you. Why are you here?"

"You didn't return any of my many texts," he said, his bottom lip jutting in the semblance of a pout.

"I couldn't."

"Why not?"

Because you're a killer, and Sully forbid it. "There've been some recent developments in my life."

"Oh, like what?"

"I'm married now."

His smile widened, but in a way that sent shivers of dread down her arms. "How wonderful. Congratulations." His fingers flexed, drawing attention to the black leather gloves he was sporting. Still smiling the chilling smile, he stepped forward. Poppy stepped back, bumping hard against the refrigerator.

"Don't," she said, laying both hands protectively over her bump.

"It can't be helped," he said. One hand reached up to her neck. She opened her mouth, intending to draw a breath, but it was too late. His thumb pressed hard on her windpipe, cutting off her air. She pushed at him, hitting and flailing, caught between panic and a fierce need to protect her unborn child. He easily put his arm around her, pinning her to him as he continued to cut off her oxygen. Spots burst before her eyes, red, then, blue, then purple, and finally everything dropped to a hazy shade of black.

⚷

Sully wasn't sure which won at the moment—his exhaustion or his bitter disappointment. They'd received a tip about a heist about to take place, another live truck robbery, and they'd intercepted. Three of Cortez's men had been caught in the act. In the subsequent shootout, one was killed, one was badly injured, and the third was taken into custody.

Sully questioned him for hours, stepped away to take a call, and when he came back, the man was dead. Murdered in Ranger custody wasn't a headline anyone was looking forward to. For now they were saying it looked like natural causes, but everyone knew the truth. Cortez had gotten close enough to infiltrate, close enough to assassinate a potential informant onsite. And the worst part was that they had gotten nothing from him, not a word of connection to Diego Cortez.

And then Sully remembered Diego's wife. He sent one of his men to bring her in for a friendly chat. At the very least, it would be enough to rattle Cortez. And he wouldn't have the mother of his children murdered to keep her silent. It was highly likely she knew nothing about his business. She certainly couldn't know enough to bring down the operation. But maybe, just maybe it would be the spark they needed to make Diego stumble. Otherwise Sully would likely be dealing with him for the rest of his life as a cop.

To his further frustration, he'd spent so long grilling the now dead man, he had nothing left. He was spent, and his lieutenant sent him home. Later, he would go back and watch the tape of his lieutenant talking to Diego's ex-wife. It would probably all come to nothing, but he still wanted to see and hear the interview.

And there was still Poppy to contend with, already at work. He wanted to go straight there and demand a resolution to last night's drama, but of course he didn't. He respected her work, understood that her job was important to her. The best way to show her that was to support her and give her some space. Even so, the house seemed unnaturally still and silent without her there to greet him. He walked into the kitchen and sniffed, the hint of last night's Moroccan chicken still redolent. His phone rang, and he reached for it on autopilot, hoping it was good news. Maybe Cortez's wife cracked right away. Maybe they had him in custody. Maybe ponies became unicorns by wishing hard enough for horns.

"Sully."

"Yes," Sully said, confused by the unknown voice.

"It's Huck."

"Oh, hi." His surprise quickly evaporated into concern. "Is everything all right? Is Poppy okay?"

"I hoped you could tell me."

"What do you mean?"

"She's not here."

Sully's heart exploded out of his chest and skittered away. He dashed up the steps, three at a time, ripped open the closet, and saw her suitcase staring back at him. He spun in a circle and lifted her pillow. Her pajamas were folded neatly beneath. In the bathroom, all her makeup was present and accounted for. If she ran away, she took nothing with her. He ascertained all this in about five seconds, and then saw a piece of paper on his pillow. Picking it up, he saw her gentle, flowing script.

We'll talk tonight, handsome. Hope you got the guy. XO, P.

"What do you mean she's not there?" Sully finally found his tongue. Huck hadn't prompted him, seeming to understand he needed a moment to come to terms with the shocking proclamation.

"I came in this morning like usual. No baked goods, no Poppy. Weirdest thing, though, all the lights were on."

Sully gripped the phone so hard he thought it might crack. "Check the sink." The first thing Poppy did when she arrived at work, after turning on the lights, was to wash her hands.

"Huh," Huck muttered.

"What?" Sully asked, the dread of suspense already filling his chest.

"Her ring is here. And there's a note."

Sully swallowed bile. "What does it say?" he rasped.

"'You take mine, I take yours.' Weird. Does that mean anything to you?"

But Sully didn't reply. He couldn't, he had already shoved the phone in his pocket and sprinted to his truck.

CHAPTER 33

Poppy woke to a sound she recognized, the rhythmic click of a gun's safety mechanism. Her father had never succumbed to the nervous habit of sliding his gun's safety off and on, over and over, but one of his attachés in Africa had. She almost expected to hear her father's irritated growl, *Click that gun once more, Davies, and I'll wrap it around your neck.*

"For the record, and not that it matters, but I do like you, Poppy. If I'm being honest, you're the best first date I've ever had."

How did he know she was awake now? Poppy barely knew. Maybe he'd been talking the entire time, regardless of whether she was conscious for it. She tried to swallow and winced. The stabbing pain in her neck was nothing compared to her raging headache and—with a gasp of panic, her hand settled on her bump.

"Your baby's fine. I know exactly how long to press in order to make a person lose consciousness and how long to press to kill. Not my first time, as I'm certain you're aware."

Poppy felt a reassuring little jab against the hand pressing her belly. Her baby girl was fine, at least for the moment. Whether or not she stayed that way remained to be seen.

"Why?" Poppy asked. It was all she could say.

Diego let out a breath, staring hard into the middle distance. Poppy looked around, searching for escape. They were in a factory, that much she could discern. "Because this is war," he replied. "Your Rangers brought this on me, on themselves. I'm a businessman second, a family man first." He held up his wrist, reminding her of his tattoo. "They hounded and hounded and hounded, dogging my steps all day and all night. My kids asked me why the men with the white hats follow me all the time. And my wife..." he trailed off and swallowed hard. Poppy wanted to ask what happened with his wife, but her throat was too sore. Thankfully he didn't seem to need her prompting to continue.

"My wife told me she wants sole custody of the kids. She filed the motion today." He leaned forward, resting his arms on his legs with an earnest expression. "I already lost Avie, Poppy. I can't lose my kids, too."

"You still love her," she croaked. Why did she make the effort? To understand him? To try and connect? To divert and delay? She only knew it seemed imperative to keep him going.

"More than anything in the entire world. I still remember the first day I saw her. We were fourteen years old, first day of freshman year. I was so angry, such a punk kid. She was so sweet, so pure. Whenever I was with her, I felt like for one minute maybe I could be clean, you know? Like maybe I had a chance to turn over a new leaf, get rid of all the bad decisions. Start over. Be an upstanding guy."

"You could," she hissed.

He laughed. The sound was more sad than amused. "I tried, believe it or not. We were young, naïve, and in love. Seeing you reminded me of her. We were so happy, so ecstatic when she was pregnant with our first. For a few years I tried to keep on the upstanding side of the business. My dad thought it was a hoot, used to call my wife St. Avie. He was never faithful to my mom. There were always other women around. I never cheated on Avie, never even looked at another woman. All I wanted was her." He blew out a breath, his gun clicking faster. "Then my dad got sick. Decisions needed to be made."

"It's not too late," Poppy said. "Go back. Start over."

He gave her what was probably supposed to be a patronizing smile but too much evil leaked through. A shudder rippled through her and she rested both hands on the bump now, protective.

"Things start out small enough, you know? Fixing the books, a courier run. And then one day you reach the point of no return. I already reached that point when Avie gave me an ultimatum." He paused and glanced away, swallowing hard. "After the divorce, she started seeing someone. A lapsed priest, isn't that a kick? She must have a thing for men who can't stay away from sin."

"Are they married?" Poppy asked, wincing. Her throat felt like she'd swallowed broken crystals and some of them were still lodged inside.

"I killed him. Gutted him in the street and left him to bleed out like an unwanted fish. Not to sound cliché, Poppy, but if I can't have her, no one can."

Poppy wasn't immune to men who'd taken lives. Her father had killed men. How many, Poppy had no idea. But she did know it was either in self-defense or to protect other people. She had never heard anyone talk so factually about murdering another person in cold blood.

"See, that thing your eyes are doing, that's what Avie's did when she began to realize the awful truth of who I am. And now that she knows, it doesn't matter what I do. I could never do anything good enough to earn her love; she gave it freely. Now that I've lost it, it doesn't matter how low I sink because I'll never get it back again. She'll never look at me with the light of innocence and trust again, so what's the point? If you're going to hell in a hand basket, might as well take as many people with you as you can along the way, right?"

He was psychotic. Poppy realized then there was nothing she could say to help her cause. He had succumbed to darkness, had embraced the basest pieces of himself and given in to total depravity. The fact that he was able to pretend to be anything else must be due to the things he had learned from his wife. He could fake being a good person for a time, but it would never last.

"You're a cool one. Most people beg at this point," he said. "The former priest did. Begged like a little boy, cried and wept and prayed. I asked him if he'd be willing to trade Avie's life for his, if I let him live, gave him the option of sacrificing her to save himself. He said yes, didn't even have to think about it. What kind of man does that? I would die for her. I've already killed for her. I wonder if your little Ranger is willing to die for you."

Poppy flinched and gasped as the pain in her throat jostled through her. The baby in her belly woke up and began to kick furiously, as if somehow trying to help defend her mother. Maybe she carried Bailey's baby by mistake. Maybe Bailey would have a nurturing little screwup who baked too much and had a penchant for stumbling into trouble. Diego waved his hand. "Oh, don't for a minute think I believe he would trade you to keep his life. Those Rangers don't get the white hats for nothing. But being willing to step in and take a bullet for someone face to face is a whole different ballgame than a theoretical game of what if."

The factory came to a grinding halt. Diego tipped his head. "Huh, I thought we'd have more time. The Rangers usually aren't so quick to play catch up. I guess having one of their own in the game makes all the difference. Do you think Ranger Langford will come for you in person? I bet he will, he seems the type. Cool under pressure, in charge of his emotions." He leaned forward and slid the gun along her cheek. Poppy closed her eyes and tried to block his scent. She hadn't eaten in hours, and her nausea had made an unwelcome return.

"I'm going to make him watch while I kill you," he whispered.

"He'll kill you back," Poppy made herself whisper.

He laughed again, and this time the sound was amused. "A Ranger? Murder a man in cold blood? No. Here's how it will go down. I'll kill you, drop my gun, and put my hands up in surrender. He'll stand there and contemplate taking me out, and then he'll lower his gun in defeat, certain he's done the right thing, the honorable thing. He'll still need to look himself in the mirror as he grieves, you know? I'll go to prison where I'll keep doing my job, running my empire. And somewhere, someday, one of my men will slip into Ranger Langford's bedroom and slit his throat. Do you believe in the hereafter, Poppy? I do. Take heart you'll be together soon. Forever this time." He stood and hauled her up by the bicep, forcing her to walk beside him.

"Want to know what's going to happen next?" Diego whispered. By the glee in his tone, he seemed to be enjoying himself. "They're going to tell me to come out with my hands up. They have the place surrounded." He herded her to the center of the factory and up a narrow, rickety staircase. It looked like some sort of food production place, possibly candy. Poppy wondered if there was any significance in that. Did Diego take her to a sugar factory because she was a pastry chef? Dramatic displays appeared to be his calling card. In any case, the narrow overlook they were now ascending was just that: a place to look over the production line. It was so narrow they had to walk single file.

"Diego Cortez, this is Lieutenant Marshall of the Texas Rangers. We have the building surrounded and there is no escape. Come out with your hands up."

Diego held the gun to Poppy's head. "You ready for this, Poppy? This is where it gets good, this is where the players start to perform. Stay tuned, you're going to love this." He cleared his throat dramatically and called in a loud voice. "Send in Ranger Langford alone, and I'll surrender."

Poppy tried to yell, to tell Sully not to come, that it was a trap, but she couldn't get the words out. Not only was her injured throat too sore, but Diego was now pressing his free hand over her mouth.

They stood in perfect silence a minute until a door opened and Sully strode inside, gun at his side.

"If he's not alone, I'll know," Diego called.

"I'm alone," Sully said. "Drop your weapon in good faith."

"Come up here first, and I will."

Poppy tried to shake her head. Diego yanked hard on her hair, causing tears to leak out of her eyes. *It's not going to work. He's going to kill me anyway,* she wanted to say because Diego was right, and she knew Sully. He would never be able to kill a man in cold blood, and then he would spend the rest of his life in regret, tearing his hair out for not being able to save her, always questioning if he should have gone ahead and killed Diego anyway.

Sully climbed the ladder slowly, keeping a close eye on her and Diego. He stepped up onto the end of the walkway and raised his gun. Diego moved Poppy in front of him like a shield.

"So, Ranger Langford. I think we can agree you made a big mistake by involving my wife," Diego said, his tone conversational.

"You involved mine first," Sully said. "And now it's time to let her go."

"You know, I think you're right," Diego said. He tipped Poppy backwards over the railing, but she was ready for him. She clutched tightly, digging her feet into the metal floor beneath her. Thanks to the baby, she was no longer a tiny thing. While she didn't weigh as much as Diego, she wasn't a piece of fluff. Diego laughed. "Ah, Poppy, always have to make things hard. Fine, we'll do it the messy way." His gun raised to her temple.

"Poppy, close your eyes and don't open them," Sully said, his voice vibrating with a tension she didn't understand. It was more than fear, it sounded almost gleeful. Diego must not have understood it, either, because he paused, the barrel of the gun cutting hard into Poppy's flesh.

"Please don't tell me you think you're going to succeed in killing me first," Diego said. "There's no way you can shoot me without shooting her."

"You're right. You're so right," Sully agreed, the gleeful tone fully in place now. "I simply wanted to tell you something, something that might surprise you."

"What?" Diego asked, his tone wary for the first time since the ordeal began.

"I get it. The family thing. I would do anything to protect my family, my wife, my child. Anything."

Diego laughed bitterly. "Come now, Ranger. We both know you're not a killer. You shoot me after I get rid of her, and you'll spend the rest of your life in prison."

"Might be worth it," Sully said. "But I think you're right. Thirty of my colleagues are on standby outside. There's no way I could shoot you and get away with it. The only way it could work is if I snapped your neck and made it look like an accident."

Diego blinked at him. "There's no way you could do that."

"You're right," Sully said. "There's no way *I* could do that." He lowered his gun. As silently as he'd arrived, The Colonel reached forward, snapped Diego's neck, and tossed him over the railing, as easy as tossing away a twig, though the man must have weighed at least two hundred pounds.

Poppy inhaled sharply and stiffened. "Dad?"

The Colonel and Sully made eye contact. The Colonel shook his head and stepped backwards, disappearing without a sound. Sully stepped forward and gathered Poppy close. "No, darlin', just me. You can open your eyes now, but keep them on me, okay?"

She opened her eyes. Her pupils were wide with shock, and she trembled. Sully had his doubts he would ever get her safely down the rickety, steep staircase. They'd need to bring in the fire department and a ladder. Thankfully they had one on standby; they had everything on standby.

"Wh-what happened to Diego?" she asked, teeth chattering.

"There was an accident. He fell. You're safe now, it's over." His hand smoothed up and down her spine, bestowing comfort, shushing her. Meanwhile he spoke into his radio, called for an ambulance for Diego and one for Poppy, as well as the fire department to get her down.

His colleagues streamed into the building. The usual buzz of activity began to take place—pictures, a perimeter, interviews, statements. Sully would have to give an interview and statement, probably more than one. But his story would never change. *Diego was a wild man, flailing all around. He lost his footing and fell. I could hear the crunch of his spine as he landed, an obvious broken neck. A shame we didn't get to put him in custody, but these things happen sometimes.* He felt no remorse over the end of the man's life, none. He would have killed Poppy and their unborn daughter, he was certain. He did feel pity and regret for

Diego's ex-wife and children, but perhaps they had a chance for a fresh start, a life free of crime and family-related transgressions.

For now, Sully ignored everything and focused on Poppy, kissing her hair, her eyes, her temple, caressing her face, her spine, her bump. She leaned into him, trying so hard to be brave.

"B-Bailey would have roundhouse kicked him," she said after a long, ominous silence. Who was she kidding, though? Bailey never would have gotten kidnapped in the first place.

Sully didn't chastise her for comparing. Instead he continued to try and soothe her with his touch. He'd discovered her kryptonite—human contact—and used it with the potency of Lex Luther. "And what would Jane do?"

As she thought about that, her trembling started to subside. "Probably detail the history of the Chinese mafia. In Mandarin."

"That's why you're my favorite. You're a real girl," he whispered, pressing his lips to her ear.

"Flattery will get you everywhere, Ranger Langford."

"Apparently," he said, patting her bump, and somehow no one thought it was odd that they were laughing out loud while a dead man lay below, his neck at an unnatural angle.

In the heating duct halfway across the factory, The Colonel heard his daughter's laughter and smiled. *Thatta girl, Poppy. Way to make a comeback.* His daughters were as different as three girls could be, but all of them were strong and resilient. And all of them were happily settled with good men who loved them. Really, what more could a father ask for? Juniper would be so proud when he relayed for her the parts he could which, admittedly, wouldn't be many. And soon he was going to be a grandfather, twice over. When he thought back to how it all began, the unlikely pairing with Juniper Dunbar, *he* almost had to stifle a laugh. Life was funny sometimes.

CHAPTER 34

They didn't make Sully stay for the cleanup, nor would they have been able to if they tried. He rode with Poppy in the ambulance, cradling her the whole way. The EMT's didn't give him any guff over having to work around him, meaning one or both of them must have looked a wreck.

She and the baby were examined in the emergency room. The baby was given a clean bill of health. Despite everything, Sully smiled when he heard his little girl's strong and fast heartbeat. *A fighter,* Poppy mouthed. She had long since given up trying to talk.

Her trachea sustained some damage from the strangulation. Not enough to be an emergency, but enough to be of some slight risk for collapse. They decided to keep her overnight for observation. Sully would stay too, of course. At this point it would take the Jaws of Life to pry him away.

They sprayed her throat with numbing spray. Poppy refused pain reliever, not wanting to stress the baby, but they gave her an IV to get her fluids up quickly and allowed her to sip on whatever clear liquid she chose.

"I hate broth," she said, grimacing after she took a sip and set it aside.

"Save your voice," Sully instructed. The scratchy whisper hurt him just from listening. He couldn't imagine how much pain she must be in for her to sound that way.

"Better after the spray," she said, touching her fingers gingerly to her throat. "How'd you keep Bailey away?"

Sully blinked at her, deciding how best to explain. As soon as he left his house, he made two calls, one to The Colonel and one to Cal to tell him to bottle Bailey who, predictably, wanted to come take charge of the scene, momentarily forgetting her massively protruding baby belly. Only the news that her father was coming alleviated her desire to get in the plane and shoot someone. "Cal," Sully lied. "Must have hogtied her or something."

She shook her head. "No good. She can get out of ropes." She pressed her palm to his cheek. "Hey."

"Hey," he said, shaky and breathless with the nearness of losing her. He took a breath, mustered his courage, and tossed aside his pride. "Poppy, I love you so much. I've loved you so long, I don't remember when I started to love you. And I don't remember what it was like not to love you. I don't want this to end when you no longer need my insurance. Please stay, please keep being my wife forever and ever." Before she could respond, he decided to remind her of the one thing that definitively worked between them. He pressed his lips to hers and kissed her with far more gentle tenderness than he currently wanted to.

When the kiss was over, she rested her forehead on his cheek. "You do that well, in case I've never said."

He tapped her cheek, suddenly suspicious she had put him off. Eventually she looked up, eyes big and serious, and his heart plummeted. "You know what I thought when Diego talked? Before, I mean, when it was only me and him and he was giving me his psycho confessional."

He shook his head. Speech was gone for now. "I thought how much my taste in men has improved." She smiled and caressed his cheek with her palm. "Sully, you have no idea, *no idea,* how much I need and want you in my life."

"You do?" he asked, feeling suddenly shy, something he hadn't felt since he was a kid, if even then.

"I've done a lot of growing up this year, setting aside of self, focusing on our child. And along the way I realized part of that immaturity was holding on to the vision of some unknown someone. Actually it was George who helped crystallize everything in my mind. He saw everything between us I was too blind to see. He explained how easy it is to hold on to a phantom instead of the real thing. I didn't want to do that anymore."

"So…you're in love with me," he drawled.

"Excuse me, but I do believe I repeatedly said I would never marry a man for anything less than love, up to and including good insurance coverage. Also, there's this old African proverb: When a man comes home exhausted from a long day of work, helps you make pies, and tucks you into bed while washing your face, you marry him. Or something like that. I might have the translation wrong." She couldn't seem to stop caressing his face, his stupidly beautiful, beloved face. "I love you so much, Sully. I didn't dream big enough to imagine someone like you."

"But, and not to harp on a sore subject here, you seem so obsessed with the money in your account."

"I'm trying to save enough for a down payment on *Huck's*. He's not getting any younger, and I have plans. Big, expensive plans, Sullivan."

"You want to buy *Huck's*?"

"Yes. I've already spoken to him about it. We haven't signed papers, but it's definitely in the works."

He frowned, properly affronted now. "Were you ever planning to tell your husband the news you're expanding your empire?"

"Eventually, but I can see by your tone that's something I should have done sooner. I'll work on it. Having a partner doesn't come easily for me, but I'm trying, I promise I am."

"Miss Independent," he said, leaning forward to kiss her again. "New York was your dream," he added as he pulled away. It was probably unfair to make her talk when he knew she was exhausted and sore, but he couldn't seem to help himself. He had spent the last few months wanting to know what went on in her head and heart and dreading the answer. Now that the news was in his favor, he wanted all of it.

"It was, yes. But here's what I'm learning: we can have more than one dream in a lifetime. In fact, we can have a bunch. So here they are now." She reached up to caress his cheek again. "Have an amazing marriage to the best guy I've ever known. Rock this motherhood thing the way my mom did. And have the best little bakery/café this side of Texas. In that order."

"You're going to drag our tiny burg kicking and screaming into the spotlight and make it a tourist attraction, aren't you?" he asked.

"I guarantee it," she said.

"I adore you, you crazy insane career-obsessed gypsy." He leaned in to kiss her again.

When they parted this time, she checked the clock. "You haven't slept in two days. You should probably get going."

He snickered.

"What?" she asked.

"You said 'git.'"

"I did no such thing," she argued.

"You're becoming a Texas girl, through and through."

"Oh, have mercy," she replied, thumping her head on his shoulder.

"Maybe you always were, at heart. Maybe that's why I've always liked you so much," he mused.

"No, I'm citified, and I'm going to take our daughter on yearly pilgrimages to New York so she'll have some culture."

"Hey now, the hog calling contest is next week. That's culture."

"I know, I was asked to make pig-shaped cookies for it," she said.

"That's nice," he mused, yawning.

"Nice, nothing. I'm charging two dollars a pig."

He snorted a laugh in the middle of his yawn and kissed her. Life with Poppy would never be boring, and Sully would have it no other way.

EPILOGUE

"Ugh, Bailey's so lucky," Poppy said. She shifted her massive girth, trying and failing to get comfortable in the stiff hospital chair.

"I'm not certain getting her abdomen cut open counts as lucky," Sully said. Bailey's blood pressure had started to creep toward the danger zone the last few weeks. To be safe, her doctor ordered a C-section a week ahead of her due date.

"Still, she gets to be done. So lucky." Poppy said. She closed her eyes and inhaled, trying hard to push away the nausea. She had felt so good the last few weeks, and now in the home stretch she was bound to be miserable.

Sully began smoothing his hand over her leg, soothing her. The man had actual magic fingers. "Honey, what's this really about?"

"It's stupid."

He nudged her.

"Fine. I had this dream we'd have our babies on the same day," Poppy said.

"I'm sorry," he said, tipping closer to kiss her forehead.

This was why she loved the man, because no matter how silly and fanciful her daydreams, he never chastised her for it. She smiled and dipped her head to rest on his shoulder, but now his brow was furrowed.

"Your forehead is clammy."

"I don't feel so good," she replied.

"What's the matter?" he asked, his hand now pressing to her brow.

"My old friend nausea. It's like Moriarty and I'm Sherlock." She shuddered, fighting her gag reflex. Her mother, who had apparently been eavesdropping on them instead of reading the giant book of azalea varieties in her grasp, leaned forward and spoke.

"Honey, you know I was sick with all three of you girls when I was in labor. Felt like the flu."

"I don't think I'm in labor," Poppy said, wincing when her abdomen pinched painfully. Sully, who noticed everything, pressed his hand there now.

"Poppy, that's squeezing tighter than my amazing biceps," he said, which made her giggle, as he knew it would. But the giggle ended on a groan. All at once the pieces came together and she sat up straight.

"Hey, I think I'm in labor." Her family looked at her like, *Yes, we know.* She scowled at them. "Why am I the last to know everything?"

"You're not," Blue said, darting Sully an annoyed glance. He and Jane had used her father's billions and billions of unused frequent flyer miles to be there for the birth of Bailey's baby, but there had been a weird energy between Blue and Sully since their arrival. They'd had a few whispered conversations that ended whenever Poppy arrived. The only words she'd been able to catch from Blue were, "know how much I illegally hacked to find them that fast," and from Sully, "swore I'd never tell anyone." She had the sense it had something to do with her dad, but she couldn't imagine what. Blue was the one who worked for her father. What did Sully have to do with any of it? Maybe it was something about Jane. Poppy pushed it away as another wave of nausea rolled over her, coinciding with the tightening of her abdomen.

"It doesn't hurt, though," she said, looking to her mother for direction.

"It will," her mother said with a sympathetic smile.

"Come on, baby. Let's get you checked in," Sully said, attempting to lead her to the front desk. She shook him off.

"I can't until I hear how Bailey's turns out." Bailey and Cal had intended to find out the sex of their baby, but the baby stubbornly refused by keeping his or her back to them the entire time. *She really is carrying a mini-me,* Poppy thought and couldn't suppress her smile. It would serve her perfect sister right to be carrying a mini hurricane in the making.

An hour later, Sully became unbearably antsy and Poppy became unbearably uncomfortable when Cal appeared in scrubs, beaming.

"Girl. It's a girl."

"A girl!" Poppy exclaimed, delightedly clapping her hands. "Did you hear that, Sully? Two girls. They're going to be best friends, I know it."

"I'm sure you're right," Sully said distractedly. "Now can we please check in?"

"Fine," Poppy said, leaning on him heavily as she stood and waddled away. Juniper turned to her husband, tears of joy shimmering on her cheeks. "Did you hear that, Bear? Two more girls."

"Heaven help us," The Colonel replied, though he also smiled, or as close to it as he came.

"And Poppy thinks they're going to be best friends. Should we tell her they're likely going to try and kill each other most days?" Juniper mused.

"Let's save some surprises for the next generation," he said, and then because he could never resist when her face looked the way it looked right now, he kissed her. And then kissed her again.

Thank you for reading *The Ranger and the Hurricane,* book 7 in the Spies Like Us series. For more books, please check my website at www.vanessagraybartal.com

Vanessa Gray Bartal is a foodie who spends her time trolling bakeries and dreaming of new ways to use sourdough. When she is not baking (or eating), she loves to make music and spend time with her husband, three children, and sheepadoodle in rural Ohio. Her dream is to fill her books with enough coziness and warmth to brighten someone's day and make them smile. She would love to hear from you on Facebook or through email.